FLOAT

FLOAT

LAURA MARTIN

HARPER
An Imprint of HarperCollins*Publishers*

Float
Copyright © 2018 by Laura Martin
All rights reserved. Printed in the United States of America.
No part of this book may be used or reproduced in any manner
whatsoever without written permission except in the case of brief
quotations embodied in critical articles and reviews. For information
address HarperCollins Children's Books, a division of HarperCollins
Publishers, 195 Broadway, New York, NY 10007.
www.harpercollinschildrens.com

Library of Congress Control Number: 2017962477
ISBN 978-0-06-280376-4 (trade bdg.)

Typography by Ellice M. Lee
18 19 20 21 22   CG/LSCH   10 9 8 7 6 5 4 3 2 1
❖
First Edition

For my dad. Thank you for teaching me that the really great adventures happen outside your comfort zone.

"A ship in harbor is safe, but that is not what ships are built for."—John A. Shedd

CHAPTER ONE

A white SUV pulled into the parking lot, and I eyed it speculatively. It was definitely a contender. It had a big trunk, which was important since I didn't really like the idea of cramming myself into something as small as a Volkswagen Beetle, especially if I was going to be stuck inside it for more than a few hours. I wrinkled my nose at the thought, even though I knew full well that a bumpy ride in a stuffy trunk was preferable to what was ahead of me. I needed to find the right car, and soon.

"Stop staring," my mom snapped from behind me, pulling my focus away from the red minivan that was about to turn into the lot.

"I'm not staring," I mumbled without taking my eyes off the car. "I'm weighing my options."

"We've been over this," she sniffed, and I heard her shift her weight nervously as her high heels sank farther into the soft ground. "You don't have any options. You'll just have to make the best of it." I glanced over my shoulder at her as the minivan passed us, but my mom wasn't even looking at me. Instead she was looking around at the other families climbing out of their cars, staring in the exact way she'd just told me not to. I almost threw her own words back at her but swallowed them at the last second and scowled down at the ground instead. Someone had mowed the grass recently in this field turned temporary parking lot, and the toes of my stupid shoes were stained green. I scuffed at the dirt to try to wipe off some of the grass stain but only managed to get chunks of grass in the shoes' steel seams.

Giving up, I glanced back at my mom. She was eyeballing a black SUV that had just pulled into the parking lot, and I squinted at the official-looking logo painted across its side. There were so many different divisions of government involved in RISK services it was hard to keep track of them all, but I was fairly certain that I'd never heard of the TTBI. And from the *don't mess with me or I'll kill you* scowl on the guy's face behind the wheel, I decided that was a good thing. For the first time I was grateful that my mom had insisted on dropping me off herself. I was a level five, after all; she could have pushed me off onto my caseworker like that kid's parents obviously had. My mom was still staring, and I cleared my throat, eyebrows raised. She jumped guiltily, shoving her oversize sunglasses back up her nose and smiling the too-bright smile she gave police officers when they pulled her over for speeding. She wasn't fooling anyone.

Her nervous, fluttery hands found their way to my tie for the seventh time that morning, fiddling with it until it felt like a mini pinstriped hangman's noose. I'd tried to tell her that no one wore a tie to summer camp registration, but I'd been ignored. So now I was standing in the makeshift parking lot looking like a complete idiot as my mom's guilty smile melted off her face in the humidity. On second thought, maybe a ride from a government official wouldn't have been so bad.

A mosquito buzzed obnoxiously near my ear, and I slapped at it unsuccessfully. If the world were still survival of the fittest, I wouldn't last past breakfast. Which was why hitching a ride out of here in someone's trunk was one of my better ideas. My mom interrupted my pathetic plotting by handing me my large blue duffel bag and backpack, her over-hairsprayed hair barely budging in the muggy breeze. She gave my shoulder a squeeze and did her level best to look reassuring. She failed miserably, and I reluctantly gave up the car idea. The last thing I needed was to cause her to have a nervous breakdown. Again. I sighed. I probably wouldn't have had the guts to go through with it anyway.

Other kids, accompanied by an odd assortment of parents and uniformed officials, were filing past us with their own duffel bags and sleeping bags in tow. I squared my shoulders. If I was going to go through with this camp nightmare, maybe I could at least avoid looking like a complete goober and register myself.

"You know, Mom," I tried, making a mental note to ditch the tie if this worked. "I can take it from here. I wouldn't want you to hit rush-hour traffic on the drive home."

"Now, Emerson, don't be like that," she scolded. "I know this place is supposed to specialize in accommodating RISK kids, but I still won't sleep tonight unless I talk to your counselor myself."

My mother wobbled away on her apple-red heels toward the cabin proudly displaying a sign that read "Welcome to Camp Outlier." What a stupid name. Whoever named the camp probably did it to be funny or witty or something. It wasn't. I glared up at the sign as something hard and ugly tightened in my chest. The last thing I needed was to be reminded that I wasn't like everyone else. It might as well have said "Welcome to Camp Outsider."

"This place is the kid equivalent of sending Grandma to a nursing home," I grumbled.

"You think so?" quipped a voice at my elbow. "I thought it was a lot more like the kid equivalent of a zoo, except no one would pay money to watch us sleep." A blond kid with green eyes and a hooked nose stood staring up at the sign I'd just been scrutinizing. He had a thin, stretched look to him that reminded me of spaghetti and a wide-set mouth built for smirking. Which was exactly what he was doing. "Have you ever noticed that about the zoo?" he went on, unfazed by my lack of response. "All the animals are either hiding or sleeping in the one spot that you can't see them? We go every year, and I've seen the same lion's left butt cheek like ten times. But whatever, nursing home isn't a bad comparison as far as comparisons go. Although my nana got kicked out of hers for throwing a party where three people partied so hard they broke their hips. Think they kick you out for that here too?" He finally looked away from the sign and grinned at me, thrusting out a hand. "I'm Henry, but everyone calls me Hank." I stared at his offered hand stupidly. The last time I'd checked, twelve-year-olds didn't shake. After another second's hesitation, I reached for it anyway. But before I could grab his hand, it flickered. A second later it disappeared entirely. Yelping in surprise, I jumped backward.

"Inconvenient invisibility, a level four." Hank shrugged unapologetically. "Although you probably assumed that, seeing as you have to be at least a level-three RISK to end up here," he said, jerking his head toward the sign.

"Inconvenient invisibility?" I repeated, trying to remember if I'd ever met anyone with that particular RISK factor before.

Hank waved a hand dismissively. "Some days I'm completely invisible. Other days I'm not. Today I'm somewhere in the middle. Which is stinking lucky. Have you ever tried to introduce yourself to someone when they can't see your head?"

"No?" I said, not quite sure what to make of this kid.

He shook his head. "Don't. It involves a lot of screaming and fainting. Not the kind of first impression I like to make."

"I'm Emerson," I said, shaking a hand that wasn't there. It felt weird, so I pulled mine back quickly. Hank didn't seem to notice, as he was too busy looking me over.

"With those killer shoes and the weighted vest, I'm guessing you're a level three?" he asked. I shook my head and looked down at my feet, which were indeed encased in "killer shoes." The thick rubber-and-metal combo was covered in grass stains and mud, and I noticed one of the laces that wound its way up most of my shin had come loose. I bent to fix it, hoping my face hadn't turned red, but from the way my ears were burning, I knew it had. The stupid things had been modeled after normal shoes, but they weren't fooling anyone. The weighted vest I wore was also impossible to disguise, but it looked slightly less ridiculous than the shoes, so that was something.

"Hmmmm, let me guess," Hank mused as he circled me, his hand propped on his flickering chin. "A flyer? Level four?"

I shook my head again. That was always everyone's first guess. "Level-five floater." Hank whistled in appreciation at the level, and I shrugged. "I guess if you have to be a freak, being the freakiest of the freaks isn't a bad way to go."

"Seriously though," Hank asked, "how do you screw up floating so badly they assign you a level five? I thought they only handed that out to kids that, like, torch stuff or implode or something. No offense, but floating seems pretty straightforward." He didn't say it, but the implication was there. Floating seemed tame. Fluffy, even. Like if my RISK factor were an animal, it would be a bunny. It wasn't a bunny.

I shrugged. "Well, an inability to stop myself from floating straight to the moon is a good start. The level is because of danger to self, not dangers to others." I decided now wasn't the time to mention that I was also terrified of heights and puked if I got much farther than a couple feet off the ground. Being a floater was lame enough, thanks.

Hank hooted with laughter. I frowned, disappointed, even though I'd known it was coming. So this kid was a jerk too. Real nice. I was just turning to leave when Hank slapped his semi-invisible hand down on my shoulder.

"Sorry, man." He grinned. "It's just nice to meet someone more screwed up than me. Doesn't happen much, you know?"

I frowned at him for a second, but his laughing green eyes were earnest, and his ears chose that exact moment to disappear. I smiled in spite of myself. "I'm glad I could help." A loud wail came from the parking lot behind us, and we both turned to take in a glossy red sports car and the chaos surrounding it. A short boy with floppy gold hair had both of his palms pressed flat against the driver's-side door while a man,

8

presumably his father, had him around the waist and was attempting to peel him off. It wasn't going well.

"That kid seems thrilled to be here," Hank drawled.

"I kind of admire him," I admitted, thinking of my own abandoned plan to cram myself into some unsuspecting soccer mom's trunk. "I think we're all doing that on the inside, because we don't have the guts to do it on the outside."

"Speak for your own guts. Mine are made of steel, or rock, or whatever makes someone phenomenally gutsy." Hank paused, considering. "I think steel guts sound better, don't you? Rock guts make it sound like I have a problem. Anyhow, my point is, if I wanted to pitch a fit, I would. But I already decided this summer is going to be incredible."

"You do realize we're at Camp Outlier, right?" I asked. "The only reason kids come here is because the government required it. Although," I sighed, "I think my mom would have sent me even if that letter hadn't shown up. She's gotten so twitchy about me lately that her doctor made her take up yoga."

"I wasn't pumped at first," Hank admitted. "Shoot, I was so mad when my parents said I'd have to come that I went invisible on them for three whole days. It was a new record for me."

"Wow," I said, impressed. "What happened?"

9

"I flickered and became visible right as I was raiding the pantry." Hank winced at the memory. "Of course, I was naked, and my mom's book group got a good look at the Roberts family jewels."

I snorted. "You were naked?"

"As a streaker at a European football game."

"Do you normally walk around your house naked?"

"Well, my clothes don't disappear when I do," Hank explained as though this were obvious. "I would have been caught in two seconds if just my pants and shirt had been parading around. Anyway, I decided that since I can't avoid this place, I'm going to make it awesome. Just like I did when I became visible in front of the book club. Instead of slinking away, I did an Irish jig, took a bow, and made sure I grabbed the potato chips on my way out."

"I'm sure that went over well."

Hank shrugged. "Two of the ladies actually applauded. Personally, I think they must have gotten the best view. My mom is now officially banned from hosting book club. Dad was thrilled. He hates book club night more than doughnuts hate diets."

"That's it?" I asked skeptically. "You just decided it would be awesome, so now it will be?" There was a fine line between being nuts and brilliant, and Hank seemed to be straddling it.

"One word for you, my friend," Hank said, raising an eyebrow. "Girls. This camp is co-ed. I'm a glass-half-full guy, if you will. Carpe diem, YOLO, and all that." I still wasn't convinced, but before I could say anything, we were inside the cabin. The place smelled of coffee, sweat, and that stale-food smell that seemed to linger in cafeterias. A quick glance up revealed a large carved sign proclaiming this to be the dining hall. Today, though, it was registration central, the cavernous space busting at the seams with kids, parents, and caseworkers.

I'd barely taken in the general clamor before there was a squeal of excitement and two girls, probably fifteen or so, rushed past us to hug a petite blond girl who had just walked in with her parents and a rumpled-looking caseworker. Hank gave a loud wolf whistle and winked when the girls looked our way. They rolled their eyes at him, and he elbowed me in the ribs in a *see what I mean?* kind of way. The girls were pretty, all right, although one of them was wearing some sort of metal contraption over her right arm.

It seemed like a lot of the kids already knew one another, standing in loose groups laughing and joking while their parents riffled through thick piles of paperwork and talked to caseworkers wearing expressions of polite boredom. Speaking of parents, mine was making her way through the crowd like she was parting the Red Sea in stilettos, dragging a lanky guy in jeans and a red Camp Outlier T-shirt behind her. Her poor victim had the look of an all-American football star, with artfully tousled hair and dimples. It was because of guys like him that guys like me didn't have a chance of getting a girl. Ever.

"Emerson? Honey, this is Eli. He's going to be your camp counselor this summer." Eli grinned and graciously removed his arm from my mother's manicured clutches.

"Hey, man," he said. "Welcome to Camp O." I nodded as my mother thrust a large file into Eli's arms.

"I know I went over all of this when I registered him, but in case you forget, here is a full list of all his required accommodations as well as emergency procedures. There are also numbers in here for the head of the army's fighter pilots if he gets loose. Oh, and I put the number in for NASA if he gets that high and you need to retrieve his body, heaven forbid." My mom gave him a wide smile, but I recognized the slightly frantic look in her eyes. It was the same look she got every time I was evaluated for government classification, the look the fire department saw every time they'd come to peel me off a ceiling, and the look that usually required a sedative or two. It always made me feel heavy inside, like I wasn't the only one who'd been required to carry a weight around for the last twelve years. But instead of a fifty-pound vest and twenty-pound shoes, her weight was a brown-haired boy with a fear of heights.

She was hoping that this Eli guy would reassure her that body retrieval plans wouldn't be necessary. When he offered no such reassurance, she blinked hard and turned to me. "You are going to have a wonderful time, darling. Eli assured me that they've had children here before with your type of specialized RISK factor, and I just *know* you're going to make lots and lots of friends." Her voice was painfully overenthusiastic. Who was she trying to convince? Herself, or me? It was taking everything in me not to roll my eyes at her pep talk. She could wish for me to make all the friends in the world, but I would still be me. She brushed invisible dust off my shirt, then licked her thumb and wiped at something on my cheek.

"Mom!" I yelped in protest, stepping back out of spit-bath range.

"Sorry," she said, quickly pulling her hand back. She shook her head and plastered that atrocious smile back on. It made the wrinkles around her eyes more pronounced. She looked old. And tired. And maybe a little sad. "Be good," she said. "Double-knot your sleeping belts at night, and remember, a backup tether is nothing to be embarrassed about. There's extra cable, bungee cord, and carabiners in your bag, and make sure—"

"Mom, I got it," I groaned, cutting her off before she could really get going. "I've only been doing this for my entire life."

"Oh, I know, Boo-Boo, but I just get so nervous. You know that." I'd inherited the nickname after conking my head on one too many light fixtures as a kid. Before I could scrape what little ego I had back together again, she was hugging me in a flurry of blond curls and jangling silver bracelets. And then she was gone. Just like that.

Eli had a bemused expression on his face as we watched my mother floor our black van down the dirt driveway of the camp. I didn't think I'd ever seen her drive that way before. Like she'd just tasted freedom, and she liked it. It twisted my guts.

Eli thrust the thick file my mother had handed him back to me. "You're in Red Maple. It's the third cabin at the top of the hill on the left-hand side." Following his pointing finger, I looked through the window and saw two large hills, each with a grouping of small log cabins perched at the top. The hill on the right was littered with boys of all shapes and sizes trudging up and down carrying duffel bags. The hill on the left had an equal amount of girls doing the exact same thing. A forest sporting some of the biggest trees I'd ever seen leaned in on all sides, casting dappled shadows over the well-worn dirt paths of Camp O. I turned back to look at Eli and jumped. He'd shrunk about two feet, and I gaped down at him in surprise.

"I see you've already met Hank. Excellent. There are four other boys in the cabin," Eli explained as though nothing had changed. "Give that file to the camp nurse and then meet me outside in three minutes." I nodded numbly as he walked away. As I watched, he stretched back to his normal height and his wavy brown hair coiled into blond curls.

"Now that's not something you see, um, ever," Hank said. I jumped, having half forgotten that he was still there. We both watched Eli for another second, then Hank shook his head and turned to me. "I'll catch up with you in a bit. My parents are wandering around here somewhere, and I'd better get them on the road before they blurt out my embarrassing nickname. See you soon, Boo-Boo." He winked and disappeared into the crowd.

I glanced down at the thick file with my name across the top. Every paper crammed inside was familiar: doctors' evaluations, government evaluations, school evaluations, records of medications, records of incidents, records of required accommodations and safeguards, police files, and even two helicopter pilot reports from that time in the fourth grade when I'd taken my vest off on a dare. The sooner I could hand it off, the better.

I scanned the crowded space for the nurse's station. Large round tables had been pushed to the edges of the room, and the outdated fluorescent lighting made the sweaty mass of milling parents look a lot like ants swarming around someone's dropped sucker. By design, Camp O was a beacon for the extra weird and super screwed up, but I'd never seen so many of us in one place before. People like me, those whose RISK factors were so extreme we required an official evaluation and level assignment, were common enough to be a nuisance, but rare enough that we didn't run into one another very often. I was one of only two RISK kids at my school, which usually made me stand out in that awful *everyone is staring* kind of way that I hated. But now I saw kids wearing more complex contraptions than me, their parents or caseworkers in head-to-toe protective gear. Other RISK factors only revealed themselves in the occasional puff of smoke or flash of color.

Kids with "reoccurring incidents of the strange kind," or a RISK, as we were more commonly known, had started showing up almost thirty years ago. I guess in some ways I was lucky. If I'd been one of the first RISK kids, I probably would have ended up in a government testing facility or worse. For a long time kids like me were outcasts, not allowed to attend normal schools or be around the general public because of safety concerns, but by the time I was born and nearly floated out of the delivery room, the RISK Protection Laws had been passed. The labeling and testing systems that would eventually define my life had been set firmly in place, and the public was well informed that they were going to have to accommodate those of us with RISK factors so extreme that they caused a danger not only to ourselves, but to those around us.

Spotting the nurse's table, I stumbled toward it, dodging a kid with an extra pair of arms, a boy with little lightning bolts crackling around his head, and a girl who seemed to be magnetic.

A twisting line of flustered parents and caseworkers holding files similar to my own let me know that I'd found the right spot, and I took my place at the back of the line. A moment later a family walked up to stand behind me, and I glanced over my shoulder at them. The parents were sobbing as they took turns clutching a redheaded boy about my age in tight hugs. It seemed a bit overboard. The kid was going to camp, not war, after all. The boy was short, with a thin, birdlike frame that made him seem fragile, like if he sneezed too hard he'd break into pieces. He looked embarrassed and shot me an apologetic smile over his mother's shoulder. But the moment our eyes met he jumped as though he'd seen a ghost. I looked around, certain someone with a particularly bizarre RISK factor had come up behind me, but no one was there. When I turned back, the boy was talking to his parents again. It was then that I noticed the two officials standing on either side of the small family. Unlike the other RISK caseworkers identifiable only by the small RISK badges clipped to the front of their nondescript sweaters, these guys wore dark suits, with that mysterious TTBI logo embroidered in official-looking script across their lapels. This must have been the family that came in the black SUV, I realized, eyeballing the kid again out of the corner of my eye. What level of RISK warranted that kind of entourage? As the line continued to move forward, I couldn't help but glance over my shoulder at them a few more times. The boy had the strangest look on his face, like he'd just swallowed a live lizard, and he seemed to be purposefully avoiding looking in my direction. Weird.

When I finally reached the front of the line and spotted the smiling blond nurse, I forgot all about the boy and his crying parents. Her name tag read Nurse Betsy, and she was dressed neatly in a pair of blue scrubs with bubble-gum-pink polka dots. File folders, medical devices, and bottles of pills floated in the air while a disembodied pen wrote notes on Post-its and placed the items in filing cabinets and bins. I stared, trying to figure out if she was making the papers and pills float around her head like a deranged flock of birds, or if she had seven invisible people working for her.

When it was my turn, I thrust my file toward Nurse Betsy in the same way one hands off a poisonous snake. It was plucked from my grasp as if by magic and whisked away to the tub labeled Red Maple. Hank sidled up to me at that moment, a massive duffel bag over an invisible left shoulder.

"Do you think she'd lift me up and make me zoom around like that if I asked?" he mused.

"Would you really want her to?" I said as I watched a large blue pill bottle turn a somersault in midair before slam-dunking itself into a bin. Just watching it made me feel queasy.

"He's over there," Nurse Betsy's voice suddenly rang out, causing me to look away from the whirlwind of activity taking place five feet above her head. She was scowling at the two officials accompanying the redheaded boy and his family. When the men just glowered back at her, she huffed and pointed to where

Eli stood laughing with a group of other counselors on the far side of the cabin. Without a word, the men headed over to him. As soon as the men were gone the family visibly relaxed, and the mom actually made an attempt to wipe the tears from her eyes and smile at her son. Hers wasn't quite as forced as my mom's had been, but it rang just as false.

Hank readjusted the strap of his duffel bag and turned to me. "Ready to head up the hill?" he asked. Before I could respond, the cabin door flew open and the family we'd seen earlier trying to pull the kid off the red sports car exploded through. The short, boxy boy was being held in a full-nelson wrestling hold by his father, who looked furious. Eli excused himself from the two officials and hustled over to greet the irate group. A minute later the father let the kid go. I couldn't tell what the kid said to his dad, but from the way the dad's face was turning red, it wasn't good. None of this fazed the boy, though, who just made a rude gesture, grabbed his bag, and stomped over to where Hank and I stood watching.

When he reached us he flopped down on his bag, crossed his arms, and glared back at his dad, who was now in a heated discussion with Eli. Poor Eli, I thought. Why in the world would you ever want to be a counselor here? I hope he got paid a lot.

"I'm going to make them regret this," the boy growled, interrupting my thoughts.

"If you mean their decision to have children? I think you already accomplished that one," Hank said, grinning. The boy snorted. Shorter than me by about three inches or so, he had a soft doughy look to him completely at odds with his sharp, dark eyes. As we watched, the boy's father pointed at him, then tossed his hands in the air in frustration and stormed away. We didn't need to hear what he'd said to get his message— *I'm done. He's your problem now.*

The kid watched his father go and sniffed before turning to look us up and down. "You two don't look too freaky," he finally said grudgingly. Hank's neck chose that moment to blink out of sight, making his head hover weirdly above his bony shoulders. "I take that back," the kid said. "That's gross. Anyway, I'm in Red Maple with you, not that it matters. This place bites. I'm not staying." He pulled out a large black iPhone and squinted at the screen before holding it up to the ceiling. "Unbelievable," he muttered. "Not even a fart's whiff of a signal. How am I supposed to get an Uber with no signal?"

"This is Emerson," Hank said. "He floats but apparently not well. And I'm Hank. Inconveniently invisible."

"Gary," he said, his eyes never leaving his cell phone

as he continued to wave it at the ceiling. "I'm sticky. Level three."

"Sticky?" I asked.

"Yeah," he said, finally giving up on the phone and chucking it into a side pocket of his bag. "Like I stick to stuff." He pulled off one of the thick gloves he'd been wearing to reveal his hand. The palm was covered in a thin layer of flaky red paint. Seeing my glance, he snickered. "Dad's going to have to pay a pretty penny to have his precious car repaired. I think it cost him five hundred bucks the last time. Serves him right." When neither of us said anything, he rolled his eyes in exasperation. "I pulled the paint off the car," he explained. "Sticky. Remember? If I touched you with a bare hand you'd be attached to me for hours until my hand decided to unstick. And no offense, but I don't know you well enough for all the personal business that would entail." He crammed the glove unceremoniously back onto his stubby fingers. I eyed the gloves, wondering how the simple black material didn't stick to his hands.

"None taken," I said. Being stuck to Gary was not something I'd be volunteering for anytime soon. Or ever, for that matter.

Eli strode up to us, his nose shrunk down to half

its original size. "Well, that was about as fun as my last root canal," he said, grimacing. "Gary, welcome to Red Maple. I think this summer is going to surprise you. But if you try to pull any of the stunts that I just saw you pull with your parents, we are going to have issues." With that he stalked away to talk to the boy whose head appeared to be smoking.

Gary shrugged, unconcerned. "Whatever. What's he going to do to me that's worse than this joint?"

"I wouldn't test him," Hank said. "He's big enough to tie you in a bow and drop-kick your butt into that lake I saw on the way in. Plus, the police would never find him. He changes shape, like, every five seconds."

Just then Eli's voice boomed across the quickly emptying registration cabin. "Red Maple men," he thundered. "Rally at the cabin. The last one there has KP duty tonight!"

"What in the world is KP duty?" I asked.

"Do you really want to find out?" Hank asked as he threw his duffel over his shoulder and sprinted out of the building. I followed, substantially less speedily. Out of the corner of my eye I saw the weird redheaded kid attempting to pry himself out of his sobbing parents' arms while the two officials stood nearby. For the second time that morning I wondered what about him could possibly warrant that kind of supervision. He looked harmless, normal even. But of course, he wasn't. He couldn't be. Not if he was here. Turning my back on the boy and his depressing parents, I trudged after Hank.

"Let the summer begin," I grumbled.

CHAPTER TWO

The hill hadn't looked that big from the bottom, but it turned out to be a beast that chewed me up, spit me out, and somehow made every muscle in my butt feel like it was on fire. My mom had talked on and on about how much I'd love the taste of fresh air out here in the wilderness, but all I could taste was the Arby's I'd eaten for lunch trying to make its way back up my throat. By the time I stumbled up to the Red Maple cabin, my dress shirt was soaked under the armpits and around the collar, and I could feel blisters starting on my feet. The steel shoes were a pain to walk in under normal civilized circumstances; out here on the uneven terrain they were an absolute disaster.

I paused for a second in the doorway, breathing like a winded buffalo as I took in what would be my home for the next few months. This is it? I thought, wrinkling my nose. The only thing the cabin really had going for it was that it was large—a big box, really, with chipped concrete floors and a few sets of basic bunk beds pushed against the walls. Outsize windows sporting nothing but thin mesh screens covered every wall except the back one, and large industrial white lights marched in a row down the middle of the ceiling. Glancing around, I immediately noticed that the redheaded kid had managed to beat me up the hill despite my head start. His two burly officials stood near the bunk closest to the door, silently watching the poor guy unroll his sleeping bag. Were they going to be here all summer? I hoped not. They gave me the creeps. Hank interrupted my thoughts by chucking his duffel bag at my head.

"If you want a bottom bunk then you better hustle," he warned. "You took so long getting up the hill that the only one left is over there." He jerked his head toward the bunk closest to what I could only assume was the bathroom door.

I shook my head. "I prefer a top bunk." I thought about telling him about how I slept tethered above the bed but decided against it. He'd get to see all the obnoxious Emerson extras soon enough. No need to rush things. With a nod of thanks, I quickly nabbed the second-to-last top bunk, directly across from him. When Gary stumbled in a few minutes later, Eli was already rallying us to sit in the center of the cabin in a half circle for introductions.

"Lame," Gary muttered in my ear as he plopped down heavily next to me.

"Welcome to the best cabin on the hill." Eli smiled, his features all properly sized and in the right spot on his face. "You're going to be sleeping, eating, and adventuring together for the next two and a half months, so let's get the introductions out of the way. When it's your turn, say your name, where you're from, and what made you eligible for Camp O." Gary groaned audibly next to me, and Eli's eyes narrowed as he focused in on him.

"Gary! Thank you for volunteering to start us out." Eli smiled wickedly, and I wondered if Gary had met his match. Gary heaved himself to his feet and faced our small group.

"I'm Gary. A level three."

"Hi, Gary," Hank sang back. The group chuckled, and Eli shot Hank a look.

"This is not a group therapy session. For that you go second," Eli admonished.

Hank smirked.

"And Gary," Eli said, "no need for your level. Those don't matter here." I blinked in surprise at that statement. Levels always mattered.

"What was I supposed to say again?" Gary whined. "Chucklehead over there distracted me."

"Name. Where you're from. What made you eligible for camp. Go," Eli commanded.

"Oh, right. Gary. Chicago. I stick to things. I'm also a 'behavior problem.' Besides being a RISK kid, I also have ADHD and ODD but my dad just says I'm a pain in the—"

"We get the picture, Gary," Eli said, cutting him off. "Watch your language."

"Sorry," Gary muttered. "Anyway, I probably won't be here long, so don't get too attached to my sunny personality. Oh, and if you make fun of the gloves, I'll kick your—"

"That's enough," Eli interrupted. "Hank, you're next." Hank scrambled to his feet, all noodle legs and floppy hair.

"I'm Henry, but you can call me Hank. I've also been known to go by Humble Henry, Slick, or Fritz." At that moment his head decided to *fritz* out of sight, aptly demonstrating the name. He continued, unperturbed by his missing head. "I'm from Platte, South Dakota, and

I'm uncontrollably and inconveniently invisible. God decided that I was just too darn good-looking, so he made me invisible so the rest of you could have a shot at the ladies."

This brought on a round of laughter. I was next. How was I supposed to follow someone like Hank? I wasn't funny. I was lame. Following him was just going to accentuate the lameness. I slowly got to my feet, brushing invisible dust off my pants nervously and wishing desperately that I'd thought to ditch the tie that hung limply off my sweaty neck.

"I'm Emerson. Um, I have no nicknames? At least, no names I want to bring with me to this camp." No one laughed at my joke, just like I knew they wouldn't, and I tugged at my tie. Why had I just said that? I might as well have invited someone to pee in my shoes. "I'm from Phoenix, Arizona."

"What's with the vest and shoes?" a short black boy wearing glasses called out.

"Oh, um, right. I float. Just not well."

"Thanks, Emerson." Eli cut me off with a sympathetic smile. I think he realized that the longer I talked, the worse things were going to get. The other campers stood up and made their own introductions.

"Zeke, from Georgia," said the boy who'd asked about my vest. "I have sporadic X-ray vision." He pointed to his thick black glasses. "My regular vision is pretty bad too. Without these, I'm legally blind."

"Is there someone else you'd like to introduce everyone to?" Eli asked Zeke. "Seeing as he'll be rooming here this summer too."

"Right." Zeke grinned as he glanced around. "I forgot. He's here somewhere." I raised an eyebrow at Hank, but he just shrugged. Giving up his search, Zeke placed two fingers to his mouth and let out a shrill whistle. The sound of something grumbling and grunting came from the bunk directly behind me. I whirled in time to see a skunk, its black-and-white striped tail arching up over its head like an umbrella, come scampering out from under the bed. Someone screamed, high-pitched and girly, and I was already on my feet and headed for the door before I realized that it was me. Luckily, I wasn't the only one to flip. Gary let out a few impressive cuss words and the other boys were on their feet, some throwing themselves onto the top bunks of the beds while others, like myself, made a beeline for the door. Even the two officials flanking the redheaded boy had taken a few steps back, their hands going reflexively to their hips, where I noticed they sported empty gun holsters.

"RELAX!" Eli bellowed, and everyone froze, turning to look as the skunk in question waddled over to

Zeke and wound itself around his leg like a cat. Zeke bent down and scooped the creature up, cradling it in his arms.

"Uh," he said, with a worried look at Eli and then back at us, "this is Mr. Stink. He's excited to be here too?"

"You have a skunk?!" Gary said incredulously. "Who has a skunk?!"

"And you named it Mr. Stink?" I asked.

Zeke shrugged. "I was six when I got him. Six-year-olds aren't known for creative names."

"This is freaking awesome!" Hank said, climbing down off the top bunk he'd practically levitated onto a moment before to cautiously approach Zeke and the small black-and-white bundle that was currently ignoring us to investigate Zeke's front pocket. "Does it bite?" Hank asked, already extending his hand. "Actually," he said, pulling it back a second later, "rewind. Better question: If I touch it, am I going to get sprayed or whatever?"

Zeke shook his head. "His stink glands have been removed. He's my service animal. So you aren't really supposed to pet him when he's on duty, but I don't care if you do."

"I thought blind people were supposed to have dogs? Like Labs or golden retrievers or something?" Gary asked, not making any movement to come closer, even though everyone else was reaching tentative hands out toward the skunk, who snuffled his whiskered nose politely in our direction.

"Yes," Zeke agreed. "But I have X-ray-vision impairment. So I'll be able to see just fine one minute, and then without warning my eyesight shifts and instead of seeing what's in this room, I will only be able to see what's on the other side of that wall over there." He jerked his head at the solid wall in front of him. "I never know when it's about to happen, but Mr. Stink warns me right before an episode so I can sit down or get somewhere safe until it passes."

"Dogs do that too." Gary frowned.

"Not as well as Mr. Stink does," Zeke said defensively. "Plus, he's a lot more portable than a dog, and he'll live longer. There is an organization out in Ohio that trains RISK service animals. I could have had a monkey if I wanted, but Mr. Stink and I hit it off."

"You should have chosen the monkey," Gary grumbled, but no one paid him any attention. Now that the skunk crisis was over, everyone settled back down in the circle, even Gary, although he chose a spot as far away as possible from Mr. Stink.

A tall brown-haired boy with freckles and a turned-up nose stood up next. "I'm Anthony, and I'm from

Florida. Spontaneous combustion." When no one seemed to understand, he sighed and his entire left leg caught fire. I watched in amazement as the flames licked around his skinny calf. He slapped at the fire until it went out and sat down. I'd expected his clothes to crumble around him into ash, but they just smoked a little, letting off the not unpleasant smell of burned rubber. Were his clothes flame resistant? I made a mental note to ask him about it later. Usually it was considered rude to ask someone the specific details of their RISK, a fact my mother had hammered into my head whenever I'd been tempted to talk to another RISK kid at the doctor's office or evaluation services building. But here, maybe it would be okay.

My musings were cut off when the next boy stood up. It was the redhead. His clothes had the worn, too big look of hand-me-downs or thrift-store purchases, and his hair drooped shaggily over one eye so he had to continually flick his head to the side to see. He looked hopeful and terrified at the same time, as he scrambled to his feet and addressed his dirty flip-flops.

"Um, my name is Murphy. I'm from Lima, Ohio. I travel time."

"Time travel! That's so freaking cool!" Hank grinned at Murphy. "Isn't that an automatic level five? Or did they assign a brand-new level for time travelers, like a six, or a five and a half or something? I think I read that somewhere. So you can, like, jump around through the past or the future, right? Like Hermione does in the fourth Harry Potter book?" He paused, considering. "It might have been in book five, come to think of it. Also, how hot is Hermione?! Right? I mean, not in book one, but by book five? Total smoke show!"

"Not quite like Hermione," Murphy mumbled, scuffing his toe against the concrete floor of the cabin. "It was in book three, by the way, that she used that Time-Turner thingy, and then of course it shows up again in book seven." One of the officials behind him cleared his throat in an obvious *get on with it* kind of way, and Murphy cringed a little. "My time traveling is different, though. For one, I don't need that Time-Turner she used, and for another, I can't exactly control it. It really bites. Especially once people know about it. I've been asked who is going to win the Super Bowl more times than I can count."

"Who does win the Super Bowl?!" Gary asked. Hank rolled his eyes in exasperation and gave Gary a swift elbow to the ribs. Before Gary could retaliate, one of the burly officials stepped forward to address our small group. Murphy flinched backward, looking like he wanted to fold in on himself. And I don't know if it was that gesture or the kicked-puppy look in his eyes as he watched Burly and Brawny step in front of him, but I felt a surge of protectiveness for this strange kid. I scowled at the two men. What were they still doing here, anyway? Wasn't that the whole point of this place? To give us some freedom while still remaining under RISK-certified supervision?

"You may not ask Murphy those kinds of questions," the one I'd mentally nicknamed Brawny said. "Murphy is here on probation under special circumstances. Kids with time-travel impairments have never been allowed to attend an off-property facility like Camp Outlier. As such, the TTBI will be visiting occasionally to make sure that protocol is being strictly enforced."

"What's the TTBI?" Gary asked, not looking nearly as intimidated by these guys as everyone else did.

"The Time Travel Bureau of Investigation," Burly said.

"Never heard of it," Gary sniffed.

"You wouldn't have," Brawny said, and even Gary got the hint and dropped it.

Eli's pleasant smile never wavered, but his eyes narrowed. "Will that be all?" he asked the men.

"The supervision of a time traveler is not something to be taken lightly," Burly sneered. "If you value your job here, you'll let us do ours." He turned back to us, almost stepping on Murphy in the process. "Murphy

35

is not able to tell you anything about the past or the future. If he does, rest assured that there will be severe and immediate consequences for this entire cabin. Do I make myself clear?" We all nodded. Seeming satisfied, the two men turned their backs on us in order to speak quietly to Eli.

"Still think you're the freakiest freak?" Hank whispered, jerking his head at the two guys towering over Eli.

"I don't see what the big hairy deal is," Gary muttered. "We all know the Packers are going to win this year. I don't need a time traveler to tell me that. Talk about a bunch of grouches. What crawled up their butts?"

"Something prickly or poisonous or both." Hank frowned. "I'm glad they aren't my caseworkers. Mine is this nice old lady who's a dead ringer for Mrs. Butterworth."

"Huh?" I asked.

Hank took his eyes off the scene in the corner to cock an eyebrow at me. "You know," he prompted, "the lady on the syrup bottle? Mrs. Butterworth? What kind of lame childhood did you have? Anyway, my caseworker looks just like that. Gives me a sucker after every visit."

Gary was looking at Hank like he was something

he'd found stuck to the bottom of his shoe. "You're weird, aren't you?" he finally said.

"Extremely," Hank agreed. "Don't worry. You'll grow to love me." Gary didn't look at all convinced.

Murphy was still standing awkwardly behind the two men, who seemed to have forgotten him completely. He shifted uncomfortably for a second, seeming unsure of what to do with himself. After a moment he sat back down on the floor, his red hair flopping back over his forehead. I wondered briefly if I could ask him if I end up floating away someday, but a quick glance at the two men still talking to Eli reminded me just how bad of an idea that would be. My butt was starting to go numb from sitting on the unforgiving concrete, and I fidgeted impatiently.

Burly and Brawny finally left five minutes later, and it was as though the tension in the room went with them. Murphy didn't look up, seeming intent on studying his flip-flops, one of which had been patched with some well-placed duct tape. Not that I blamed him—now that those guys were gone, every eye was on him. Better him than me, I thought selfishly.

"Well, I think that's it," Eli said briskly, clapping his hands and drawing our attention back to him. "You have ten minutes to get unpacked and settled in before the battle begins."

"Battle?" Hank asked. Eli wiggled his eyebrows at us mysteriously and disappeared behind the curtain that separated his bed from the rest of the cabin. The unpacking didn't take long. I shoved my clothes into my designated dresser, threw my sleeping straps onto the top bunk, and clambered up to secure them to the bed. I refused to wear the vest and shoes to sleep, but without them, I found myself bobbing along the ceiling, praying no one opened a window. The sleeping straps were my own design, made from my dad's old leather belts, suspenders, and bungee cords. It was about the only useful thing he'd ever done for me, leaving those belts behind when he walked out on Mom and me. I wondered momentarily if anyone else had parents who'd divorced because one of them just couldn't handle having a kid with so many problems. I'd read somewhere that parents of RISK kids were 85 percent more likely to get a divorce than those with normal kids. I guess I couldn't blame my parents for being a statistic.

Eli reemerged from behind his curtain wearing camouflage pants and a tight black tank top. His face had been painted with smears of black and green, and he had a black bandanna wrapped around his head. A coil of rope snaked around his waist and a red piece of fabric hung from his pocket. Just then Gary came out of the bathroom and saw Eli.

"Who invited G.I. Joe?" he asked.

"All right, men." Eli grinned, ignoring Gary. "Capture the flag begins in exactly five minutes. The Red Maple men have *never* won a CTF championship, but that all changes this summer. I'll explain the rules while you gear up." He dumped a large bag of matching camouflage pants, black tank tops, and black bandannas on the floor. We all stood there looking at that pile of clothes like maybe if we just stared long enough they'd go away. Everyone, that is, except Hank, who immediately started digging through the stack.

"What?" he asked when he noticed us looking at him. "I need the biggest size possible so my muscles don't rip the seams." He flexed spaghetti-thin arms completely devoid of muscle, and the ice was broken. I wasted no time yanking off my sweaty dress shirt and tie and chucking them unceremoniously under the bed. By the time Eli had helped us smear the green and black paint across our faces, I'd managed to bob to the ceiling, forcing Hank to pull me back down. Anthony had accidentally lit Zeke's tank top on fire, pounding on him so hard to put it out that he knocked him on his butt with a resounding whump that sent his glasses clattering across the floor. Thankfully, Eli didn't look put out by his uncoordinated and admittedly pathetic team.

He pulled the red piece of fabric from the rope on his belt and showed us the red maple leaf emblazoned across it. "Okay, men, each cabin is given a flag. Tonight we have to hide ours somewhere on camp property. Over the next few weeks each cabin will attempt to capture other cabins' flags. The cabin with the most flags on the last day of camp wins. We have to hide our flag west of the registration cabin, and it can't be attached to anything living. Last year the White Oak boys attached their flag to a skunk. Half of the male campers got sprayed and had to eat outside for the entire summer. Not cool." He glanced over to where Mr. Stink sat next to Zeke like a tiny black-and-white striped shadow. Someone had tied a bandanna around his neck, and he was watching Eli through his black button eyes as though he understood what he was saying. Eli grinned. "No offense, Mr. Stink."

Zeke shrugged. "None taken."

"How do we capture another team's flag?" Anthony asked, seeming completely unaware that his left ear had caught fire.

"You just run up and grab it." Gary rolled his eyes. "The name kind of explains itself."

"Close," Eli said. "You have to steal their flag and bring it back to our territory without getting caught.

If you're caught, you're jailed for the rest of the game unless your teammates can bust you out by sneaking onto enemy territory and tagging you."

We followed Eli outside. There were four other cabins on our hill, and in front of each was a group of boys. I was happy to see that all the other campers were dressed equally ridiculously. Eli strode to the center of the dirt clearing, where the other counselors were waiting around a gigantic fire pit. All of them were in their early twenties, and like Eli, seemed to have their own unique RISK factors. To our left were the cabins with the thirteen-year-olds and fourteen-year-olds, and to our right were the fifteen-year-olds and sixteen-year-olds. I'd known we were the youngest cabin, but somehow seeing the thirteen-year-olds and fourteen-year-olds standing there with the beginning of facial hair and muscles, I felt about two instead of twelve. Compared to us they looked like NFL football players, and I understood why Red Maple had never won before.

"Okay, men," Eli said, trotting up to us. "Rules are set, and the territories have been divided. We got the east sector of camp, so we're going to have to get creative, since most of that section is taken up by the lake." Just then one of the other counselors rang a bell.

41

"GO! GO! GO!" Eli yelled, heading into the woods at a dead sprint. This time I didn't hesitate and took off. Well, I did my version of taking off, which looked more like the shuffling run of an eighty-year-old with bad hips. Stupid weighted shoes. Despite my best efforts, I fell behind everyone in a matter of minutes. Hank noticed and dropped back to walk with me while the rest of the guys poked along the edge of the lake for potential hiding places.

"It's not easy to run in those things, is it?" he asked.

"You could say that," I grumbled, giving them a dirty look. The shoes were awful, ten times worse than the vest, but a level five was required to have at least two layers of protection. The vest was layer one. The shoes were layer two.

Hank made a face. "Dude, ditch 'em."

I snorted. "No one says *dude* anymore. That word went out in the nineties. It's like *groovy* and throwing a peace sign."

"I say it, dude. I'm bringing it back. And I say ditch the cinder-block shoes."

I shook my head. "If I don't wear them, and my vest comes off, I'll be waving good-bye from the moon."

"So don't take the vest off. Easy-peasy. Problem solved. Carpe the ever-loving diem. Remember?"

"It's too dangerous," I explained, my mother's years

of warnings buzzing in my head like angry bees.

"And if you don't take them off, you don't get to really *live*," Hank countered.

"I'd rather not float out of our atmosphere and have my bones crushed and my lungs freeze," I muttered as I watched the forms of Eli and the Red Maple men shrink farther into the distance.

Hank shrugged. "Your call. But if it was me? I'd rather really *live* for a year than watch my entire life from the sidelines."

I bit my lip. Hank had a point.

Before I could think better of it, talk myself out if it, or puke, I quickly unlaced the shoes.

"Attaboy!" Hank crowed, thumping me on the back in excitement. I hefted both shoes off the ground and turned to tell Hank that we'd have to put them somewhere safe until I could come back for them, when Hank yanked one from my hand and heaved it into the lake. I stood frozen as it hit the water with a resounding whump and sank.

"What did you do that for?!" I spluttered, not even caring that my voice had done that embarrassing squeaky crack thing it did sometimes. Those shoes had been specially made for me and had cost my mom a small fortune.

"You don't need them," Hank huffed as he reached

for my other shoe. I tried to yank it backward out of his grasp, but Hank's noodle arms were deceptively strong.

"Knock it off," boomed a voice behind us. We both froze. Our cabin had circled back, and now five sets of eyes watched me fight over what might be the stupidest looking shoe ever manufactured.

"What's going on here?" Eli said.

"Emerson doesn't need this, sir," Hank said, finally succeeding in pulling it out of my hands. "So I thought it should sleep with the fishes, take a long walk off a short pier, visit Davy Jones's locker."

"I get the picture," Eli said, his green eyes twinkling. "That gives me a brilliant idea. Hand it over." He quickly tied our flag to my shoe, and without asking me if it was okay, chucked it into the middle of the lake. "Good luck finding that!" he crowed. The entire cabin cheered.

"My mother is going to murder me," I muttered as pathetic little bubbles gurgled on the surface of the lake.

"Then I suggest you enjoy the last two and a half months of your life," Hank said, clapping me hard on the shoulder. "You can thank me later."

"Don't hold your breath," I muttered, and stalked off after Eli, uncomfortably aware of my newfound weightlessness. I walked around at home sometimes without my shoes, so the feeling wasn't completely foreign, but I'd never done it outside before.

"Time to do some reconnaissance," Eli announced, interrupting my thoughts. "That's the fastest I've ever hidden a flag, and now I want to know where everyone else is hiding theirs." He rubbed his hands together like a supervillain. "Emerson, go with Murphy and Zeke and head west." He pointed up the hill, where a stand of pine trees stood like soldiers. "That's Redwood territory. Their counselor likes to hide their flag high, so keep your eyes peeled. Meet back at our cabin in twenty minutes. Remember, if you're caught, they can put you in their jail, and you'll have to start there when the real game begins. So don't get caught." I could hear him rounding up the other boys, sending them each in varying directions with their own set of instructions, as I headed up the hill after Murphy and Zeke. For the first time in my life, keeping pace with other kids my own age wasn't a struggle. I double-checked the straps on my vest, suddenly very aware that it was the only thing keeping me grounded.

"We need to move quietly. Like wolves, or sneaky ninjas or something," Zeke whispered once we were in the trees. He was carrying Mr. Stink in a messenger bag that he wore over his shoulder. At first the little animal had ridden with his head poking out, but I think he'd fallen asleep. "I got a good look at the Redwood guys," Zeke went on, "and I'm pretty sure they all eat their Wheaties with a side of steroids in the morning."

"What RISK factors do you think Team Chest Hair has?" I asked.

Zeke shrugged. "No clue. I noticed a kid with orange skin and another with a few extra fingers and toes, but who really knows, you know? We're all snowflakes."

"Snowflakes?"

"You know . . . . different? No two alike? It's what my mom always says."

"Right," I agreed, "because that doesn't make us sound like walking Hallmark cards. Seriously, dude. Snowflakes?"

Zeke wrinkled his forehead and shoved his over-size black glasses up his nose. "Did you really just say *dude*? No one says *dude* anymore."

"I heard it's coming back." I shrugged. Murphy hadn't said a thing yet, and I glanced at him out of the corner of my eye. "You okay?" I asked.

He jumped a little, as though I'd somehow surprised him. He blinked, then nodded quickly, jamming his hands into his pockets. "Sure."

"We're allowed to talk to you as long as it's not about time-travel stuff, right?" I asked.

Murphy nodded. "You don't have to, though. I'd understand."

"So those two guys," Zeke said, "your caseworkers or whatever, they seem like a real blast. Betcha have lots of laughs with them."

Murphy cracked a reluctant smile. "Yeah, something like that."

"So where do you think they would hide their flag?" I asked him.

He looked around the woods, his brow furrowed in thought. "I'm with Eli," he finally said. "If I were in Redwood I'd hide my flag high too. I mean, if you're huge, you should totally use that. Right?"

No sooner had he said it than the sound of deep male voices floated through the woods, and we froze.

"Where can we hide?" I whispered, looking around frantically.

"Over there," Murphy said, pointing to a massive fallen tree covered in a tangle of moss and weeds. The voices were sounding louder every moment, and I hurried after Murphy and Zeke toward the tree. My plan was to just hide behind it, but Zeke tucked his messenger bag with Mr. Stink under his arm and climbed

47

right inside its large hollow end. Before I could think it through I was diving in after him, trying not to think about the bugs and spiders that probably lived inside. Murphy climbed in a moment later, successfully sandwiching me in the middle. The log smelled like my grandmother's basement, and my hands squished in the rotten wood. To make matters worse was the fact that in order to fit Murphy inside the tree too, my head was practically up Zeke's butt and Murphy's head was jammed into the back of my thighs. I knew dogs made friends this way, but I didn't see the appeal. The voices stopped a few feet from our hiding spot, and I tried not to breathe.

"How soon do we eat? I feel like we've been stomping around out here for hours," a gravelly male voice said.

"That's because we have. We're never going to find a spot as good as last year. I still think that hiding it underneath the girls' toilets would be killer," responded another guy.

"Out of bounds, remember? I'm not getting DQ'd," said a third. All the voices sounded like they belonged to big dudes. Really big dudes.

"What about that log?" asked the first voice. My heart stopped, and I felt Zeke's butt clench against the top of my head. If they found us in here, we would have put our team at a major disadvantage before the game even really began. And worse than that, we'd be the guys who'd gotten caught hiding inside a stupid log.

"No, not the log. It looks like it's got poison ivy all over it."

I instantly felt itchy. It reminded me of second grade when a kid in my class got head lice, and even after I'd been checked by the nurse, I'd felt nonexistent bugs crawling around on my head for days.

"I say we just stick it in the tallest tree we can find and break off all the climbable branches at the bottom. If they can't climb it, they can't get it." This was from the first voice again. He seemed to be the leader.

"Fair enough," agreed the other guy. "We can always move it later. Plus, I'm starving. If I don't get some food in me soon, I might just eat the flag."

"That would keep it safe for at least a day," chuckled one of the boys. "As an added bonus, I don't think anyone would try to capture it even when it did make an appearance."

"Hey," one of them said, his tone suddenly on edge. "What's that?" My heart skittered nervously in my chest. We'd been spotted. There was a scratchy scraping noise coming from in front of me, and I wondered if Zeke was about to make a run for it.

"Skunk!" cried the first voice, and there was the sound of frantic scuffling as the boys took off into the woods. A minute later we pried ourselves out of our log to find Mr. Stink pawing the dirt with his long claws, a fat earthworm clutched in his jaws, completely unaware of the crisis he'd just helped us avoid.

CHAPTER THREE

We made it back to our cabin in one very itchy piece. When Eli heard about the potential poison ivy, he handed us all bars of a milky pink soap and sent us to the bathrooms, which were a fresh horror I hadn't even considered. To say the bathrooms were primitive would have been being nice. When Eli had warned us that we'd better get to know one another, he hadn't been kidding. The first thing I spotted when I walked in was the pea-green toilets. They were hard to miss, as they sat in one solemn row down the middle of the bathroom. Just the toilets. No stalls. Apparently privacy was not a consideration at Camp O. And then there were the showers. I walked in with my towel wrapped around my waist and my weighted vest on to discover twenty showerheads sticking out of the wall of a concrete box with a drain that Mr. Stink was currently investigating while Zeke peered at the shower faucet in the corner.

"Real nice," I muttered as I threw the pink soap on one of the ledges as far from Zeke as I could get. I didn't have anything against the kid, but I'd never showered in a room with anyone else before, and giving everyone some space seemed like a good idea. Murphy came in a minute later, surveyed the scene, apparently came to the same conclusion I had, and chose a shower in the opposite corner from Zeke.

"My school's a lot like this," Zeke said, finally managing to turn on his shower. "If you've seen one guy's bare butt you've seen them all."

I'd already strapped a bungee cord around my ankle, and now I just needed something to tether myself to. This was always a challenge at school, and one time I'd had to resort to tying it to the showerhead and floating on the ceiling with the water spraying straight up. It wasn't an experiment I wanted to re-create. To my surprise I spotted a convenient metal ring in the floor. Eli hadn't been lying when he told my mom that they'd had kids like me here before. I looped the bungee through and double-checked my knots. Satisfied,

I shrugged out of my weighted vest, shucked off my towel, and turned on the shower. My feet were floating a comfortable two inches off the ground thanks to the bungee, and the water felt wonderfully cool.

Remembering the poison ivy, I grabbed the pink soap and scrubbed. It had a weirdly antiseptic smell that quickly filled the steaming room. The shower across from me suddenly came on, and I glanced up from the putrid pink suds that now liberally coated my arms. Water was splashing off and cascading around an invisible body. Well, an almost invisible body. One of Hank's hands was still there as it worked at washing nonexistent hair.

"Did you get into poison ivy too?" I asked.

"No. I just smell like a billy goat's butt, or Mr. Stink's backside before he lost his stink or whatever, so I figured I should rinse off before we head to dinner. Meals are co-ed, you know. This is our only chance at a first impression with the ladies. Nice leash by the way."

"Nice hand," I shot back.

"Dang it." He held up the offending hand. "I thought I'd gotten it all."

"If you beauty queens don't hurry up, you're going to make us all late to dinner, and you won't like what that entails," Eli called, his voice echoing off the concrete walls. Within thirty seconds the showers were off and all of us were running, my weighted vest slung over my still dripping shoulders. Eli had us at a full sprint toward the dining hall before I could really register what was happening, and we slipped through the doors moments before a cabin of girls. The dining hall was the same cabin that had been used for registration that morning, but the large wooden tables were now scattered around the room instead of being pushed up against the wall, and the heady smell of roasted garlic made my stomach snarl hungrily. Eli led us to a table in the middle and gave us the zip-it signal. It wasn't until we sat down that I realized I'd actually kept up with everyone else. For the first time in my life I wasn't the last guy in, and as I watched the girls' cabin we'd just beaten reluctantly shuffle up to the front of the room, I felt a rush of gratitude that my shoes were resting comfortably on the bottom of the lake.

Hank leaned over, and the overpowering combo of deodorant and too much cologne made my eyes burn a little. "What do you think they have to do?" he whispered, jerking his head toward the girls.

I shook my head. "No clue, but I'm glad it's them and not us."

"You can say that again," Murphy said.

"What do they look like?" Zeke was squinting at the line of girls, his nose scrunched in concentration.

"They're all Victoria's Secret models," Gary drawled sarcastically, jumping a little as Mr. Stink poked his head out of Zeke's messenger bag. Gary frowned as Mr. Stink's nose busily sniffed the tabletop. "That can't be hygienic. Couldn't you leave the rat at home?"

"One of the girls seems to have stretchy limbs," I told Zeke, distracting him before he could get into it with Gary. "Two seem to be a bit blurry, so they're either invisible or superfast or something. The girl on the very end just turned into a cocker spaniel, and the other two seem completely normal but everyone seems to be giving them space, so who knows." The dining room hushed as though on cue, and the girls shifted uncomfortably as all eyes turned to them.

"Welcome to Camp Outlier!" boomed a voice. My head swiveled to find the speaker, and I spotted a grizzly-bear-sized man making his way to the front of the hall.

"That guy's blue, right?" Zeke whispered.

"He's blue," Hank confirmed.

"It's like the Hulk and a Smurf had a kid," Anthony murmured in awe, and I glanced over at him. He was the only guy I hadn't really had a chance to talk to yet, and I noticed that he sat a little apart from the rest of us, his right eyebrow quietly on fire. There was an ear-splitting squeal of protest from the speaker nearest me, and I turned my attention back to the blue man, who had just grabbed a microphone. He messed with it a second, tapped it with his fingers to make sure it was on, and then smiled broadly at us.

"My name is Mr. Herbert Nelson Hendrickson the fourth, and I'm the head counselor here at Camp O. For simplicity's sake, you may all call me Mr. Blue." He grinned and winked at us conspiratorially. "It's easy to remember. I'd like to take a moment to welcome back our alumni. It is wonderful to see so many familiar faces, but I want to extend a special welcome and message tonight to our new campers." Everyone hooted and clapped until Mr. Blue motioned for silence. "This year is a special year for a few reasons. The first being that this is the first year that Camp Outlier, or Camp O as I know many of you like to call it, qualified as an off-site RISK facility. I assure you that getting that certification was no small task, and every counselor here has undergone extensive training to make that possible. With the new observation laws now in effect, our upper-level RISK campers would have been unable to attend camp without this new qualification, and that wasn't something we were going to allow to happen."

All around me kids were nodding their heads, and I mentally kicked myself for not paying more attention to the news. Of course I knew that there were new observation laws requiring RISK kids of a certain level to be monitored during the summer, but I hadn't really paid much attention to the specifics.

Back when it became obvious that RISK kids were here to stay, a whole new branch of government had been developed to handle this new "crisis." Because that's what we'd been for a long time, a crisis that no one really knew what to do with. Not that much had changed on that front. With each RISK kid presenting their own unique set of issues, it was a constant scramble to figure out new regulations to keep us safe and everyone else safe from us. One thing was pretty consistent, though—as long as we were segregated by levels, with regulations and requirements encumbering our every move, the general public slept better at night.

"Tonight marks an important moment in your history as well," Mr. Blue went on. "I know you've all grown up a bit sheltered and overprotected, and rightly so, but not here. While you're here, you're just a camper. While you are here, you are among equals, you are free to be you, whatever that might mean." Mr. Blue looked each of us in the eye. His gaze was unwavering, drill-sergeant-like, and I wasn't sure if he scared me or impressed me. Probably a bit of both. "Your RISK factors will be dealt with, supported, and managed, but your time here is going to be spent just being a normal kid." Gary snorted next to me. Mr. Blue's speech was nice, but Gary wasn't buying it. I saw a few campers with similar looks of skepticism, but unlike Gary, all the other kids had an almost painfully hopeful look in their eyes.

"When I founded this camp twenty-five years ago, I had a hard time thinking up a name that fit. I didn't want it to be named Camp RISK, since that was a name that was placed on us without our permission. So I named it Camp Outlier, because to be an outlier means to be set apart from the main system. And it was my hope that this place would be a way to separate yourself from a system that does not define you. We are different, but we are more than the sum total of our RISK factors."

"That's what outlier means?" Gary said, just loud enough for our table to hear.

"What did you think it meant?" I asked.

He shrugged. "I dunno. Maybe something about lying outside?"

Hank snorted. "I can beat that! I thought it was some kind of pun, you know, like a camp out? Camp Outlier?" I started feeling slightly better about not paying attention to the new observation laws. At least I'd had the foresight to google what the heck an outlier was before showing up at camp.

"Shhhh," Eli said, and we turned our attention back to the front of the dining hall.

"We have a little ritual here at Camp O," Mr. Blue went on, "and since the young ladies from the Monarch cabin have so graciously decided to arrive late, they will be helping serve your table, along with one KP helper from each of the cabins."

"You're our KP man tonight, Gary," Eli said, gesturing toward a long, narrow partition that had just opened on the far wall of the cabin. Huge platters of spaghetti and garlic bread were being placed on the shelf as the girls of the Monarch cabin dutifully went to each of the round tables carrying large pitchers of water and lemonade.

Gary looked like Eli had just smacked him with a rotten fish instead of asking him to grab our food. "Wait a minute. KP duty means I have to play waitress to everyone?"

Eli chuckled. "If you want to be a waitress, no one will stop you, but I think you meant waiter. KP is short for kitchen patrol. Each boy at this table will have to take a turn this week, but you were lucky enough to be the last one to the cabin today, so you get the honor of going first."

59

Gary crossed his arms, and I remembered the scene he'd made that morning at his parents' car. "And if I refuse?" he asked.

"We sit here and starve," Eli said, sitting back as though he had all the time in the world.

"Do you think he'd really make us starve?" Hank whispered to me loudly enough for the whole table to hear. "That spaghetti smells amazing, and I might just eat Mr. Stink if he doesn't get a move on."

Zeke rolled his eyes and pretended to cover Mr. Stink's tiny ears as we laughed.

I was momentarily distracted from the battle of wills taking place by the girl who'd turned into a cocker spaniel earlier. She had turned back into a girl, a very pretty girl with the biggest brown eyes I'd ever seen. She plunked a sweating pitcher of lemonade down in front of me, and I was about to take the pitcher of water from her hand when Hank's elbow connected with my head. Hard.

"Sorry, man," he apologized, never taking his eyes off the girl as he fumbled, all flailing arms and spindly legs, to extricate himself from our table. I rubbed my head and watched as he performed one of those sweeping bows that Prince Charmings are known for, but no one ever actually does in real life.

"Milady," Hank drawled as he took the pitcher from

her hands and set it down on our table without looking, causing half its contents to slosh across the battered wood. "I'm Hank, semi-invisible gentleman of the Red Maple cabin." He plucked her hand from her side, raised it to his mouth, and actually kissed it. By now half of the surrounding tables were watching his antics and hooting in appreciation.

The girl's face was blushing a rosy pink that made her even prettier than before as she looked up at Hank through thick lashes. "Molly, I'm Molly," she murmured. Her voice had a slight southern lilt to it, and I felt my stomach do an odd flop. Hank dropped to one knee, and somehow I just knew that he was going to begin professing his love or undying admiration for her or whatever. But before he could start, she shifted back into a cocker spaniel and bounded back to her own table. The giggles and hoots coming from the neighboring tables would have made me want to die of humiliation, and I almost felt a little sorry for Hank. But I shouldn't have. Completely unfazed, he simply brushed himself off, gave another one of those ridiculous bows, and sat back down.

"I'm in love," he professed, as a disgruntled Gary slammed a plate of soggy garlic bread down in front of us. Apparently Eli had won, but not soon enough for us to get a plate of the eatable bread.

"I saw her first," I grumbled. "If you hadn't decided to bash me in the head with that noodle arm of yours, maybe she would have told us more than her name before you scared her off." Hank just shrugged and grinned, his ears comically invisible, and I had to laugh.

Anthony reached for the plate of bread just as his hand caught fire and our garlic bread went from under-cooked to black in two seconds.

"Sorry," Anthony apologized as he smacked at the flames with his hand.

"No problem." Eli grinned, grabbing a piece of bread that was still on fire and smothering it in his bowl of spaghetti. "I like mine burned." The entire table quickly agreed, bravely dousing their own smoldering bread in spaghetti sauce.

I had never had a meal quite like this one. The food was good, and I was surprised to discover that I actually did like my toast burned. At home, since it was just me and my mom, most meals were spent in front of the television, our plates balanced on our laps. Here the conversation buzzed and flew across the table as we took turns sharing our stories of capture-the-flag scouting in hushed whispers. Zeke, Murphy, and I all conspicuously left out that we'd hidden *inside* the rotten log, not behind it. Afterward Eli explained that the plans for the following day involved swimming, archery, and basic survival training. He had a wicked gleam in his eye, though, that made me wonder what he knew that we didn't.

Out of the corner of my eye I noticed that Molly was no longer a dog. She glanced over at our table a few times as the girls from her cabin giggled and squealed in that high-pitched way girls our age always did. Those giggles had always bugged me back home, probably because they were so often aimed at me. I couldn't picture Molly giggling like that, though. I bet she had a laugh like warm honey.

Dessert was a gigantic tub of vanilla ice cream with a pitcher of hot fudge. Gary even managed to get the ice cream to the table before it melted. His face twitched a little as he set it down to whoops of delight, as though he wanted to smile but wouldn't let himself.

After scooping a huge bowl of ice cream, I turned to ask Murphy to pass me a spoon only to discover that there wasn't just one Murphy sitting beside me, there were two. I jumped in surprise, almost upending my bowl of ice cream into my lap. One of the Murphys was wearing the ratty T-shirt and shorts from earlier, but the other was wearing flannel pants and a red hooded sweatshirt, which seemed odd considering how hot it was outside. They were huddled together conspiratorially, and I noticed that the new Murphy looked a little wide-eyed and frightened as he whispered into our Murphy's ear. I grabbed an extra bowl of ice cream and pushed it toward the scared-looking Murphy's hand. He seemed startled, but he took it. But before he could take a bite he was gone, the spoon that had been halfway to his mouth clattering to the tabletop. Just like that. Glancing around in surprise, I realized that I was the only one who'd noticed the exchange. Everyone else was too busy watching Hank sing "The Star-Spangled Banner" through a mouthful of ice cream. Murphy's eyes silently pleaded with me not to tell, and I nodded.

That night, we had a campfire outside our cabin. Anthony was kind enough to light it, and Zeke entertained us with stories about Mr. Stink. I found myself sitting next to Murphy. The night had turned chilly, and I hunched my shoulders inside my T-shirt and scooted closer to the roaring heat of the fire. Murphy looked just as cold as me, and I noticed that his T-shirt had a few small holes around the hem and at the edges of the sleeves, like the fabric had started to disintegrate from too many times through the wash. While I'd forgotten to grab a jacket from the cabin, I wondered if he even owned one. He caught me staring and frowned.

"Don't ask, okay?" he hissed.

"Ask what?" I asked, surprised and embarrassed

that he'd caught me gawking at his threadbare clothes.

"Don't play dumb," Murphy muttered, and I remembered the second Murphy that had joined us at dinner.

"Oh," I said, relieved, "that. I wasn't going to ask."

"Yeah, right," he laughed, sounding a little bitter.
"Everyone asks. They can't help themselves. It's so stupid too. People are always convinced that I'll be able to
tell them if they're rich in the future, or good-looking,
or if they have a hot girlfriend." He directed this last
comment with a sidelong glance at Hank, who was
busy demonstrating how to balance a marshmallow on
his invisible nose.

"I won't ask," I insisted. And it was true, I really
wouldn't. I knew what it was like to have people pry
into things you didn't want to talk about. Plus, those
two guys this morning had seemed pretty serious about
the whole *severe and immediate consequences for this
entire cabin* bit.

"Good," Murphy sniffed. "Because you know what?
The future? It sucks."

"I try not to think about the future," I admitted.

This comment seemed to catch Murphy off guard,
because he stopped scowling at the fire and looked at
me. "Why's that?" he asked.

I shrugged, feeling a little embarrassed. "Isn't it
obvious?" When Murphy didn't say anything, I shifted

a bit on the knobby log I was sitting on and looked into the fire instead of at him. "Because I'm not sure if I get one." Kids like me, level-five RISKs, weren't known for living to a ripe old age. It's not like we couldn't, it's just that one mistake, one careless moment of forgetfulness, could be it for us.

"Well," Murphy said after a moment. "I'll tell you this. Not knowing if you have a future is a lot better than knowing."

"What do you mean?" I asked, glancing over at him.

Murphy leaned back, running his hands absentmindedly over goose-bump-covered arms. "Nothing," he said. "Forget it."

"Well," I finally said, to break the now awkward silence, "today's turned out a lot better than I thought it would." It was the truth too. When I'd found out that I'd be coming here instead of spending my summer at home, I'd been furious. I'd taken my anger out on my mom, even though it really wasn't her fault that the government had imposed new regulations. Somehow, it had all *seemed* like her fault. Murphy noticed me watching him and stopped rubbing his arms, tugging subconsciously at the hem of his frayed T-shirt.

"Right," he said, forcing a smile onto his face, "camp is going to be great." I wanted to ask if he knew that for a fact, but remembered my promise just in time. I bit back the question and refocused on the story Anthony was telling about accidently lighting his history teacher's pants on fire. If Murphy didn't want to talk about what was bothering him, I wasn't going to be the one to pester him about it.

"I almost forgot," Eli's voice broke in a few minutes later. "Wait here." Bounding to his feet, he jogged back to our cabin, emerging a minute later with a big cardboard box. "Red Maple men," he said, setting down the box, "time to represent." Pulling back the flaps of the box, he pulled out bright-red hooded sweatshirts with the words "Red Maple" emblazoned across the leaf symbol of our cabin. Without any further explanation, he began tossing one at each of us. He paused for a second when he got to Anthony, digging around in the box until he found a sweatshirt encased in a special plastic bag. He pulled it out and threw it to him.

"Flame-retardant fabric," he said, grinning. "Enjoy." Anthony beamed, and I knew I had a similar smile on my face as I pulled the sweatshirt over my head and leaned back from the fire, no longer needing its warmth. Murphy hadn't put his on yet, and he shot Eli a questioning look.

"How much are they?" he asked quietly.

"No cost." Eli smiled. "Just a perk of being a Red Maple man." Looking relieved, Murphy shrugged into his own sweatshirt, and his morose mood of moments before vanished as he sat up a little straighter.

The rest of the night passed in a blur of crackling logs and sticky marshmallow-covered fingers. But despite the lighthearted atmosphere, I couldn't help but notice that although Murphy was definitely more cheerful, he still seemed preoccupied with something. Apparently, guarding the secrets of the future wasn't all it was cracked up to be.

"I told you camp would be phenomenal," Hank yawned from across the darkened cabin later that night after Eli had called for lights-out. I double-checked the belts around my ankle and waist that were keeping me tethered to the space six inches above my bed and smiled.

"I call dibs on Molly," I replied, more to bug him than because I really thought I had a chance.

"Dude, you can't call dibs on a girl," Hank said. "Although, did you hear Eli talking to the Monarchs' counselor earlier? Apparently they are joining us for swimming tomorrow. I'm going to sweep her off her pretty little feet."

"You mean paws," Anthony called.

"Shut up, fire butt," Hank shot back.

"I probably won't be here tomorrow," Gary grumbled. "If I can't figure out how to get an Uber, I'll walk home." I glanced across the room to see him scowling down at a piece of paper he'd just finished writing something on.

"Okay, Ace," Hank called. "You have fun hiking across the gloriously gigantic state of Michigan."

"I'm serious," Gary snapped as he shoved the piece of paper into an envelope.

"I wouldn't worry too much about tomorrow," Murphy muttered. "You should all stop talking and get some sleep now. We won't get much tonight." I was confused for a second, wondering if Murphy had been to camp before or something, when I remembered his visitor at dinner. I narrowed my eyes at him, but all I could make out in the moonlit gloom of our cabin was a tuft of red hair poking out of a threadbare sleeping bag.

"What does that mean?" Zeke asked from the bunk beneath mine, where I could just make out the faint waffling sound of a snoring skunk. I shook my head. Who'd have thought I'd be bunkmates with a skunk?

"Fat chance of sleeping," Gary grumbled. "This mattress feels like it's stuffed with gravel, and it smells like my dad's feet."

69

"I'm actually quite comfortable," I said, grinning in the dark. "I would highly recommend sleeping on air."

"I'll trade you floating for invisibility," Hank said. "But just for tonight."

"Lights are out! That means the talking stops!" Eli's voice boomed across the cabin, and I rolled over, my limbs gloriously weightless, and fell asleep.

Mom,

This place bites and you need to come back and get me. Now! All the kids in my cabin are Grade-A freaks. One kid even lights on fire. Do you want your baby boy burned alive while he sleeps? Because he shares a stinking bunk with me! My counselor, Eli, said they don't have Internet access out here, so I have to write this stupid letter instead of emailing this like a civilized person. It's the dumb dark ages or something around here. I wouldn't be surprised if they had someone show up on horseback to deliver it to you. Absolutely ridiculous.

I'm serious. Come get me, or I'll find my own way home. Or maybe I won't even go home, since you've made it clear

that you don't want me there. All Dad
had to do to get me out of that stupid
government regulation was make one
phone call, and you know it. Don't make
excuses for him, either. Come get me.
Now.

Gary

PS I'm not sorry about Dad's car. I told
you what would happen if you forced
me to come here. I hope it costs him a
fortune to fix.

CHAPTER FOUR

I was ripped from sleep by someone trying to yank me out of bed. I tried to yell, only to discover that a sock had been jammed into my mouth—a dirty sock, from the taste of it. The person tugging at my arm obviously hadn't planned on me being strapped to my bunk. Despite some pretty impressive flailing on my part in an attempt to escape, I found myself being held down by multiple hands while my safety belts were unstrapped. Then I really freaked. I thought I'd been doing my best to get away before, but now I had adrenaline and pure panic on my side, and I bucked and twisted with everything I had. I didn't have my vest on, and if those belts came off I was in danger of floating out the open window.

"Easy, kid," came a low voice in my ear. "We aren't going to hurt you." Through the gloom I saw that the rest of my fellow campers were already gathered in the middle of the cabin, blindfolded, gagged, and in the custody of some of the muscle-bound sixteen-year-olds from the Redwood cabin.

"This kid's a flyer or something," whispered the voice that was busy undoing my ankle straps.

"Tie him to the skinny guy and the short, grumpy-looking one. They should be enough to keep him grounded." I couldn't tell who the speaker was, but the three boys surrounding me each grabbed the end of a belt and floated me over to the group like a balloon they'd just bought at the fair. If I hadn't been so terrified, I would have felt ridiculous. Moments later I found myself tied by the wrists to Hank and Gary as we were forcefully pushed out the open door of our cabin into the cool night air. As I was shoved past Eli's bed, separated from the bunks by no more than a thin curtain, I was shocked to see him still sleeping peacefully. Maybe a little too peacefully, considering our captors weren't being especially quiet. I glanced around for Mr. Stink, but he was nowhere in sight, apparently having opted to stay in Zeke's bed over whatever this was. Smart skunk.

The boys kidnapping us were dressed in head-to-toe black, complete with stocking hats and badly applied face paint. One of them saw me looking and jumped guiltily. "Why doesn't the flyer have a blindfold on?" he asked.

"Come on, George. Wasn't that your job?! Who has an extra bandanna?" And then I was blindfolded. The ropes around my wrist pinched and twisted my skin, but the pain was actually reassuring. Man, I hoped they'd double-knotted them. I tried to keep track of how many steps we went in each direction, but my feet weren't touching the ground, and counting other people's footsteps was freakishly hard. All I could tell was that we were heading downhill. An engine roared to life, and we were instructed to climb into the back of what I assumed was a truck. I floated after Hank and Gary, banging my shins painfully on the tailgate before it was slammed shut, and we were moving.

I'd never ridden in the back of a truck. I'd seen kids do it before, but my mom had never allowed it. For a second I worried that I was about to end up flying out behind the truck like some kind of bizarre, kid-sized flag, but it turned out that Hank's and Gary's combined weight was enough to keep me securely grounded—a fact I stopped being thankful for quickly as every dip and bump of the gravel road vibrated up through the metal of the truck bed and straight into my butt bones. With nothing better to do, I began counting seconds in my head, trying to gauge how far we'd gone. Did sixty seconds equal a mile or less than that? I'd reached four thousand, five hundred and twenty-four seconds after losing count twice when the truck stopped. The sock was yanked from my mouth and I spit, trying to get rid of the taste of feet. The voices of my fellow campers immediately started as they lost their own gags.

"Whose socks were those? Man, that was some serious funk."

"Disgusting! You couldn't have used a clean sock? What kind of monsters are you?!"

"Where are we? Why did you take us?"

"I knew I should have run away. If I get out of this, my dad is totally going to sue you guys."

"Please tell me you kidnapped the Monarch cabin too! No offense to Emerson, but I would much rather be tied to one of them."

"Shut up, squirts. And relax." The voice was manly in a way that I hoped my voice would be if it ever dropped like my health teacher promised. We were hauled bodily out of the back of the truck and then forced to our knees, shoulder to shoulder. When our blindfolds were finally removed we found ourselves blinking up at the guys of the Redwood cabin. They were even bigger than I remembered. A blue pickup truck, just as rusty and decrepit as I'd imagined it would be, sat behind them, its headlights cutting two wide swaths of light through the darkness of the surrounding forest. The night air was crisp, and the crickets buzzed so loudly I could barely hear myself think.

"Welcome to Camp O initiation." This came from a big, burly, blond kid who seemed to be the one in charge. "Four years ago, we were where you are now, and I think Max almost crapped his pants. Didn't you, Max?"

"Screw you, Chad," Max said.

"Initiation?" Zeke asked.

"A rite of passage, if you will," said another guy.

"Are you going to pee on us or give us wedgies or something?" Gary asked. I shook my head in exasperation. Rookie mistake. The last thing you did in situations like this was give your captors creative torture ideas.

"You've been watching too many *Dateline* specials about cheerleader initiations," snorted Chad. "But the answer is no. The news has given initiation rituals a bad rap, but this isn't anything like that. We aren't here to pick on you. That's not the point. In fact, you will look back at tonight as one of your favorite Camp O memories. I know we do."

"Fat chance," Gary muttered beside me. He shifted,

making the ropes connecting our hands pull painfully. He shot them and then me a dirty look, as though this was somehow my fault.

"This is a long-standing tradition here at Camp O," Chad went on. "And when you guys are in Redwood someday, we expect you to do the same thing to the newest crop of Red Maples." I tried to imagine what I'd look like if I survived long enough to become a Redwood guy and failed. Probably because at that very moment, I was one faulty rope knot away from dying.

"Did you double-knot these ropes?" I asked, my voice high-pitched and squeaky in that way it always got when I was nervous. I cleared my throat to try again, but Chad was already turning to the kid on his left.

"Did the girls get the dresses?"

"Girls?" Hank perked up beside me. I glared at him. Here I was having a near-death experience, and all he could think about was girls? If my hands weren't tied, I'd have hit him. Probably.

"They're late," said another boy.

"They're always late."

"They had to drop off the Monarch girls, remember?"

"Did you just say the Monarch girls?" Hank called. "Because if they are part of this whole thing, I'm all in." The Redwood guys ignored Hank.

"They'll be here in a minute," said a short boy with white hair and washed-out features. "Caroline just contacted me and said they're running late." He placed his fingers to his nose and stared into the distance. "She said to tell you not to flip your lid."

"Holy crap! He's telekinetic or telepathic or whatever," Anthony hissed. "That's so much cooler than spontaneous combustion!" As if to prove a point, his knee chose that moment to catch fire, and he pounded it awkwardly in the dirt in an attempt to extinguish the flames. To the Redwood guys' credit, no one laughed. And it was that, the not laughing, that reminded me that they were just as screwed up as us. I wondered if, with enough practice, I'd look that comfortable in my own skin.

"Not me, just my nose, and it isn't reliable," the pale boy replied when Anthony stopped doing his odd little knee shuffle. My brain was still trying to figure out how your nose could be telepathic when I heard the sound of a vehicle approaching through the trees. The rusty red twin to our pickup pulled up, and the girls who piled out of the back made me immediately start to sweat. They were dressed in head-to-toe black, like the guys, but they looked a lot better in it than the guys did. Their flashlights beamed across our faces, momentarily blinding us in the glare.

"Way to be on time, ladies," Chad said with a smirk.

"I messaged Sam to tell him we were running late, so don't have kittens," the pretty brunette said, giving Chad a quick peck on the lips before joining the other girls in pulling large shopping bags out of the back of the truck.

"Red Maple squirts, say hello to the ladies of the Buckeye cabin," Chad said.

We all mumbled *hello* and *hi* and *what's up*. Trying to sound cool while in your pajamas tied up to a bunch of other guys in their pajamas was impossible. My shoulders hunched up around my ears involuntarily, and I felt my face flush. Hank took the opposite approach.

"You didn't tell me this was going to involve supermodels!" he called out, causing a few of the girls to laugh.

"That's enough out of you," Chad chuckled.

"He has a point," said the pale boy. "This is so much better than when we got initiated." He turned to us. "Our first summer we each got our very own pink Speedo to wear back to camp. We decided to spice it up a bit this year. Put our own spin on things."

"I don't like the sound of that," I muttered to Hank, trying to imagine what could possibly be worse than a pink Speedo.

"Do you think she'd go out with me?" Hank was staring at the pretty brunette who I assumed was Caroline.

"Not if you were a cancer kid, and she was your Make-A-Wish," Gary said, tugging hard at the rope holding us. My wrist bones popped in protest. Murphy was looking at Gary with the same strange expression on his face that he'd worn that morning at registration. When he noticed me staring at him, he quickly looked away again. I don't know why, but something about his expression made it seem like he was hiding something, and I wondered what it could be.

"Like you have any better chance," Hank shot back at Gary.

"Quiet!" Chad yelled. "Ladies, I believe you said that the marvelous Miss Mary would be able to handle this?"

"No problem," said a small, mousy girl with glasses. "We just need to decide who goes in what dress. Oh, and we have to do their makeup." She held up a pink cosmetics bag and shook it so we could hear the metallic clink of compacts and lipsticks.

"Dresses?" I squeaked. "Makeup?"

"If it's all the same to you," Hank called out, "I'll take the Speedo. I look fabulous in pink, and honestly my butt is one of my best features."

"You are a butt," Gary grumbled, and I snorted despite myself.

"Sorry, kid," Chad chuckled. "Not an option. I'll see what I can do about the pink, though."

The girls ignored us, grabbing handfuls of taffeta, silk, bows, and ruffles out of the shopping bags. They shook out the crumpled fabric to reveal eighties-style prom dresses. I'd seen pictures of my mom wearing a dress like that, her hair all flipped to the side and teased to within an inch of its life. The girls began holding them up to each of us, debating if the coloring went with our hair or if we were a size four or a size six. Finally they made their decisions and a dress was laid out in front of each of us. Mine was a washed-out hunter green with lace trim, puffed sleeves the size of basketballs, and a gigantic bow across the butt, size four. Hank got his wish, and was given a short pink number with floppy ribbons at the shoulder, size zero, and Gary's was a neon purple with ruffled tiers and only one sleeve, size fourteen. I couldn't help a slight twinge of relief that I hadn't ended up with Gary's monstrosity. It was hard to see what dresses the girls picked out for Murphy, Anthony, and Zeke from my spot between Hank and Gary, but at least one of them had polka dots. To make things even worse, the girls started brushing neon blue powder across our eyelids, smearing bright-red lipstick on our lips, and using these fluffy paintbrush things to apply what I assumed was blush liberally across our cheeks. I'd watched my mom put on makeup at stoplights enough times to know that this wasn't how it was done. A glance to my right affirmed that Hank's makeup was more rodeo clown than cover girl. I shouldn't have turned my head. The girl doing mine almost jammed the wand of her electric green mascara directly into my left eyeball. I missed joining Zeke in the vision-impaired department by about a half second. I kept my eyes forward after that. When they were finished, they stood back, giggling over the effect. The dresses were still laid out in front of us, and I suddenly realized something truly awful. Since we were tied up, the girls were going to have to put those dresses on us, which meant . . . I gulped and my stomach flopped uncomfortably at the thought of being naked in front of these girls.

Mary stepped forward, rubbing her hands together. "You may feel a slight tingle," she warned. The tingling began, and I squeezed my eyes shut. My pajamas vibrated for a second, and then the sensation stopped just as abruptly as it had begun. I snapped my eyes open to discover Mary holding a neat stack of our pajamas. The cool night breeze blew across my bare legs, causing mountain-sized goose bumps to ripple up the back of my calves. Glancing down, I was relieved to discover that I wasn't in fact naked; instead I found myself clad in the hideous green dress, butt bow and all. Why in the world would a girl ever wear something like this? It made me feel uncomfortably vulnerable, and I prayed the wind wouldn't blow the whole stupid thing up around my ears, exposing my underwear for all to see. My knobby knees and hairy chicken legs were bad enough. A quick glance to my left and right revealed that everyone else was in the same boat. The Redwood guys and Buckeye girls burst into laughter, and my face flamed red. To my surprise, Hank was laughing just as hard as the rest of them, his peals of laughter echoing out into the dark forest.

"What's so funny, princess?" Gary snapped at him. "You look like an idiot."

"I know!" Hank howled, doubling over. "So do you! We look freaking hilarious. This is priceless. Oh man, I wish I had a camera."

"Your wish is my command," Chad said. There was a blinding flash as he snapped a picture.

"So this is it?" Zeke asked. "You drag us to the woods, hocus-pocus us into dresses, take a few humiliating pictures, and drive us back to camp?"

"Oh, you're not being *driven* back to camp." Caroline grinned, revealing dimples.

"Is she hot or what?" Hank muttered. Under any other circumstances, I would have agreed. All that hair, and the lips and stuff, but right now, I kind of hated her.

"You ready, Ace?" Chad asked a dark-haired boy with sharp features. Just then I heard a slight rustle behind me and felt someone take my hand and jam it into Gary's.

"Hey," Gary yelped, "what are you doing, Emerson?" I twisted around to see who had put our hands together and caught a flash of red hair as it ducked back behind a tree. Had Murphy escaped somehow? But a quick glance to my left showed him still tied to the end of the row, his brown polka-dot dress pooling around his bare knees. I tried to pull my hand away from Gary, because really, the last thing I needed was to be wearing a dress and holding hands with a guy, but it didn't budge. It was as though his skin had melted onto mine, suctioning our hands together.

Ace turned his startlingly light-blue eyes to us. "Ready," he said. A second later my limbs froze. I had no idea what level RISK you had to be to freeze other people, but I had to imagine it was impressive. My brain felt like it was no longer in communication with the rest of me, and I could do nothing but watch helplessly as a guy whose hair seemed to be made completely of porcupine spikes and another guy who glowed faintly in the dark quickly began moving between us, unfastening the ropes that tied our hands together. My stomach dropped. They were moving from opposite ends of the line, and they were going to get to me at the same time and untie me.

My worst nightmare was about to play out before my eyes—actually, scratch that. This was worse. Even in my *worst* nightmares I hadn't died with a gigantic bow on my butt. I was frozen, immobile, unable to even cry out, to warn them that their harmless initiation was about to kill me. Why hadn't I said something sooner? I should have started screaming bloody murder as soon as that gag came out. But I hadn't. I'd let girls and prom dresses and the shock of being in the middle of the woods at night distract me from the one thing I was never supposed to forget about. And now I would become just one more RISK statistic, another sob story on the five o'clock news.

Chad had turned his back to us to make out with Caroline, his hands shoved into her dark-brown hair. The whole process looked kind of messy, to tell you the truth. The rest of the boys were huddled around a map someone had spread across the truck's tailgate, not paying attention. The belt on my left wrist came undone at the same moment the one on my right did, and my heart threw itself against my rib cage in a vain attempt to escape my body before it left terra firma forever. Not that I blamed it. I waited to jerk upward, but apparently Ace's ability to keep my muscles frozen extended to my floating as well. As soon as he stopped doing whatever he was doing, I was dead. Was this how criminals felt having their last meal, like they might wet themselves? Or vomit? Or both simultaneously?

Chad untangled his tongue from Caroline's and turned to us, an arm flung casually across her shoulders. "Okay, boys, here's the deal." He grinned. "It is four a.m., which means you have four hours to make it back to camp by breakfast. Head straight east. We're going to hide a compass for you, but we're not telling you where. We also hid a flashlight and Oreos. Just in case. Good luck."

"Hold up, Chad. Shouldn't we put their blindfolds back on so they don't see where you hide that stuff?" one of the girls asked.

"Oh yeah, I almost forgot." He smacked his head in mock horror and winked at her. I wondered if I would ever be able to wink at a girl like that, all cool and stuff. The answer was probably no. Actually, it was definitely no, as my life expectancy had just shortened to the next few seconds. I would die a winking rookie.

The girl named Mary, who'd put us in the dresses, huffed, stepped forward, and snapped her fingers. I choked as the blindfold was suddenly tied around my mouth like a gag. I heard startled grunts next to me, and Mary swore.

"Smooth," Chad drawled sarcastically. "But I think we were hoping you'd blindfold their eyes, not their mouths."

"Shut it, Chad," Mary snapped. "I'm better than I used to be. Just be glad I didn't mess up and put *you* in a dress instead of one of them." This sent everyone into peals of laughter. Mary snapped her fingers again, and the world disappeared as I was blindfolded again. Things just kept getting better and better.

"Good luck!"

"Don't break a nail!"

"Careful for the bears. They're hungry this time of year."

"Don't scare them, Chad. There aren't any bears around here."

"Is it weird that I'm jealous of them right now?"

"No, I was just thinking the same thing."

"I still can't believe this is our last year at Camp O. It seems like yesterday we were in Speedos running through the woods."

"I still have mine. You know, as a memento."

"You probably still fit in it."

A truck door slammed, and the sound of the engine faded into the distance. I began to hyperventilate. So this was how I was going to die.

CHAPTER FIVE

I didn't want to die like this. As soon as that Ace kid got too far away to keep us frozen, I was going to go shooting skyward. My mother would have nothing to bury. My tombstone would read, "Died with a Gigantic Bow on His Butt. Also, Big Loser." Not exactly ideal.

Four heartbeats later, my body lurched upward, and I screamed. But just as suddenly I was jerked to a halt. My blindfold fell off, and I found myself hanging upside down, my hand still gripped by Gary.

"What the!" Hank yelped, yanking off his blindfold. Both his arms were invisible, as were his neck and shoulders, which made his dress look like it was acting independently, but despite that he managed to grab onto my flailing free hand and haul me back to earth. Zeke helped him wrestle me down, but I kept bobbing skyward again. The skirt of my dress had flopped down around my ears, successfully blinding me, and I wasn't much help. So I just yelled and screamed. A lot. It took two whole painful minutes and someone throwing out some fairly impressive cuss words, but the guys finally managed to shove me back onto the blessedly solid ground. Hank plopped himself down on my chest to act like a human paperweight, and I shut my eyes for a second as I swallowed the screams that still wanted to rip out of me. When I opened them again everyone was crowded around to look down at me, and it was all too much. Despite my best efforts to prevent it, I started to cry. Hard.

"It's cool, man. You're okay. Take deep breaths or whatever," Zeke coached encouragingly. I nodded, but the hot fat tears just kept coming, slipping sideways off my face to pool uncomfortably in my ears.

"Should we smack him?" Anthony asked. "That's what they always do in the movies. Someone starts freaking out and someone else smacks them, and then they're fine." He paused for a second, considering. "Although I probably shouldn't be the one to do it. I could accidentally catch him on fire, which would totally defeat the point of the exercise."

"I volunteer," Zeke offered.

"He's fine," Murphy snapped. "Just give the kid a second, okay, Dumb and Dumber?"

"Just don't get up, Hank," I sputtered. "Holy crap. I'm still alive. I thought I was dead. Why didn't I tell them that I float?"

"Girls are dangerous," Hank said. "Pretty girls especially. They turn your brain to mashed potatoes."

"Man, mashed potatoes sound really good right now," Anthony sighed. There was the thump of someone hitting him, and he yelped. "Sorry," he grumbled. "I bet I'm not the only one who's hungry, though."

"Gary, you saved him. That was pretty cool," Zeke said.

"Whatever." Gary shrugged. "He's the one who grabbed my hand."

"No I didn't," I protested.

"Well, someone did," Hank said, looking from Gary to me and back again.

"It was me," said Murphy, the white polka dots of his dress seeming to glow in the dark gloom of the forest. "I did it."

"No you didn't," Zeke said. "You were tied to me." Just then *another* Murphy emerged from behind a tree, dressed in flannel pants and a black T-shirt. We all gaped in surprise, our heads swiveling from the Murphy

91

in a dress to the Murphy in a T-shirt.

"You're a twin?" Anthony asked.

"Not a twin." The T-shirted Murphy shrugged. "Just from the future."

"I thought the rules of time travel were that you couldn't ever run into yourself or, or, um, something bad happened?" Zeke finished lamely.

The Murphy in the dress rolled his eyes. "That's all just junk television guys made up to make the plots of their science-fiction movies more interesting."

T-shirt Murphy nodded. "The truth is that I can run into myself all I want. I just can't tell other people that I'm from the future."

"Aren't you telling us?" Zeke asked, looking confused.

T-shirt Murphy nodded. "What I'm doing right now, meddling with things, is ten kinds of illegal. So what just happened, the way I saved Emerson, it has to stay a secret."

"Wait a second," Gary interrupted. "Isn't this exactly what those big guys warned us about today? I'm not going to jail for this."

Murphy in the dress looked nervous as he glanced from us to his future self. "Are you sure they can keep this secret?" he asked his future self. "What if the TTBI finds out?"

T-shirt Murphy waved a dismissive hand. "They don't." He glanced over at Gary. "You don't go to jail either. Although, for the record, the TTBI doesn't *do* jail. What they do is worse."

"Gee, thanks," Gary said. "I feel so much better now."

"This is so weird," Anthony said, shaking his head. "And cool. But mostly weird."

"It's not cool," dress Murphy snapped as he glared at the future version of himself. "What I just did was reckless, and I shouldn't have done it."

I looked up at him, this entire situation feeling a little surreal. From my position on my back, the guys looked weirdly tall as they stood around me in a loose semicircle, their faces barely visible in the moonlight. What Murphy had just said finally sank in, and I frowned up at him, feeling a little indignant. "So you should have just let me die?" I asked.

"Yes," Murphy in the dress said with a scowl at his future self and then sighed. "And no," he conceded.

I wondered if it was possible to be mad at yourself for something you knew you'd eventually do, and what that would feel like.

"You really need to chill out," the future Murphy said with a shake of his head. "Man, I forgot how twitchy I was at the beginning of camp."

"I'm not twitchy!" dress Murphy shouted.

"You are," Hank said. "It's cool, though. I would be too if Big and Bigger had dropped me off at camp this morning."

I snorted.

Hank looked down at me, eyebrow raised. "What's so funny?" he asked.

"I nicknamed them Brawny and Burly," I admitted.

"Hulk and Bulk," Zeke chimed in.

"Well, their real names are Jones and Johnston," Murphy said, a reluctant smile tugging at his mouth. "Although even those are probably just names the bureau gave them. They aren't guys you mess with."

"They made that real clear," Zeke sniffed.

"Don't worry," future Murphy said. "They won't be back for a while."

"What does that mean?" Hank asked.

Future Murphy crossed his arms. "Sorry," he said. "Can't tell you that."

"It's about time you shut up," Murphy in the dress muttered, plopping down onto the ground. "Now do you see why time traveling is seriously *the* worst?" he asked.

"Relax," future Murphy said in a nonchalant tone I'd yet to hear current Murphy ever use. Anthony was right. This was really weird. It was then that I noticed

Gary was still holding my hand, and I tried to tug it away. No luck.

"Told you I was sticky," Gary grumbled. "There goes my plan of running away tomorrow. I might be stuck to you for the next week."

"I don't even care," I said as I wiped away the tears still clinging to my cheeks with my free hand. "It beats dying."

"Debatable," he grumbled.

"I helped save your life too, you know," Hank piped up proudly. "Another thing to check off the old life list."

Zeke had taken his glasses off and was attempting to clean them on the hem of his dress, but he looked up at Hank's comment. "Don't you mean a bucket list?" he asked.

"Nope." Hank shook his head. "My list isn't a bucket list. It's a life list. I don't want to do things before I'm dead; I want to do things that make me feel alive."

"Sounds stupid," Gary said.

"Like what?" Murphy in the dress asked.

"Like a midnight bonfire with hot chicks," Hank explained, scrunching his nose in concentration as though trying to recall something. "Let's see. I also have jumping off a bridge, skinny-dipping with hot chicks, skydiving, eating an entire pie, French-kissing a hot chick—"

"I'm sensing a theme," Anthony interrupted with a smirk.

"I get it." Zeke nodded. "Like, life's not about the finish line, it's about the race?" I raised an eyebrow at him. First the snowflake analogy this morning, now this? Seeing my look, Zeke shrugged. "My mom put a poster that says that up in my room. Her answer to having a RISK kid is motivational quotes."

"My mom's answer is anxiety meds," I blurted out without thinking. A second later I wished that I could snatch it back out of the air. That was too personal.

Anthony looked down to where I was still lying on the ground underneath a dress-wearing Hank. "Sounds about right. After what just happened I could use some anxiety meds myself."

I smirked. "Your mom too?"

He shook his head. "Nope. My dad. My mom's a freaking rock. She takes all the crap that comes her way and says 'thank you, sir, may I have another?'" I eyed Anthony, thinking that that explained a lot. He carried himself like he wasn't ashamed to take up space, like he wasn't a burden. It reminded me a lot of how professional football players acted in their post-game interviews, cocky, confident, and cool. If I'd had a mom like Anthony's, would I carry myself like that too? I wasn't sure. Anthony turned to Hank. "Anyway, enough about my mom. Finish about the life-listing thing. I'm interested."

"Well," Hank said, shrugging, "Zeke had an exceptionally fluffy way of putting it, but our vision-impaired friend was right on the money. Life really isn't about the finish line; it's about all the cool stuff you get to do on the way there."

"A life list." Zeke nodded, savoring the taste of the words. "I think you're right. That's better than a bucket list."

"According to my life list I'm ninety-eight," Hank said proudly.

"What do you mean, you're ninety-eight?" I asked. "You're twelve, just like the rest of us."

"Nope," Hank said, shaking his head. "I'm ninety-eight. I was ninety-seven until I saved your life."

I glanced up for support at the circle of guys surrounding me. "Am I the only one who doesn't know what he's talking about?"

"It's like this," Hank explained. "We've all grown up with government-assigned levels, right?" Everyone nodded, all too aware of the labels that dictated which schools we were allowed to attend, what accommodations our schools had to make for us, and what kind of government monitoring we were required to be under. I raised an eyebrow at Hank, not exactly sure where he was going with all this.

"Well," Hank said, shrugging, "I don't know about you guys, but I always hated it. I mean, really, just because I'm a level four, it doesn't change who I am."

Gary whistled. "You're a level four? Why? Danger to yourself or danger to others?"

"Neither," Hank said. "Criminal risk. Apparently the ability to be invisible in any form makes me a liability for breaking into people's houses, banks, government buildings, you get the idea."

"Do they know that you'd have to break in naked?" I asked, remembering his book club story.

Hank laughed. "Yes, but they don't seem to care. Anyway. The whole level system got me thinking about age. If someone could just assign me a level without asking my permission, then I should be able to just assign myself an age."

"Assign yourself an age?" I repeated, thinking it sounded a lot like his pronouncement when we first met, that he'd just decided camp would be great and so it would be. Like if he willed it and wanted it bad enough, he could make it happen.

"It's like this," Hank said, shifting on my chest so he could look down at me. "I don't think that people should age just because they managed to survive one more year. That's dumb. I could sit on my couch for an entire year, but that doesn't mean that I *lived* another year. You know?"

"So we create this life list," I clarified, "and we get older every time we do something on the list?"

"Exactly. So what would be on your life list, E-dawg?" Hank asked, peering down at me from his perch on my chest. Before I could think of something, or tell him not to call me E-dawg, because, seriously, E-dawg? Anthony's hair ignited, lighting up our gathering, and allowing me to take my first really good look at Hank. His dress was bunched up around his hips, and his skinny legs poked out comically. Lipstick was smeared across his cheek, probably from the scuffle to get me back to the ground, and the rest of the guys weren't much better in their blue eye shadow and frills. I burst out laughing.

"Aw, man, he's gone crazy," Zeke said. "I've heard of this. Too much stress or whatever."

"Let me smack him," Gary said, "please. Even if my other hand gets stuck to his face, it will be worth it."

"No, no, I'm fine," I choked out. "It's just that Hank was right—we look freaking hilarious." The other boys began examining one another too, and soon the woods were reverberating with peals of laughter. It got worse when Zeke started curtsying to everyone, and Hank kept asking if his mascara was running. I was laughing so hard I couldn't breathe, although having Hank on my chest didn't help matters. Crisp pine-scented night air was pumping in and out of my lungs, and I was alive. It felt good.

"Did you have running through the woods in a dress on your life list?" Zeke finally gasped.

Hank shook his head as he fought to get himself under control. "No way, dude. I mean, it looks like an eighties prom barfed all over us." That set us off again, and it took another few minutes before we were able to breathe.

"Okay, well, I hate to break up this party," Anthony said, slapping at his head to extinguish his hair. "But according to my watch, we have three hours and forty-five minutes left to get our dress-covered butts back to camp. Which is a problem, because I have no flying clue which way camp is."

"Also," I added, "I would rather not float away and die a horrible death."

"Right, no horrible death for E-dawg," Hank agreed, readjusting his position on my chest.

"Is there anything heavy we can hang around his neck?" Zeke asked.

"We could tie him to a string and bring him home like a balloon," Anthony offered.

"No. No string. No floating," I protested. "My cousin

from Colorado did that to me when I was five, pretended I was his own personal screaming balloon. Of course, it's no fun when your screaming balloon pukes on you, so he let go. I ended up bobbing along the ceiling of the local mall while the fire department tried to figure out how to get me down. My mom fainted. We made the news. It was a mess."

"Easy, killer. No string. No Emerson balloon. We get it." Hank patted me none too gently on the forehead.

"We could ask future boy," Gary said, turning to look for T-shirt Murphy, but the only Murphy left was the one wearing the dress.

"I'm gone." Murphy shrugged. "I won't know what I missed out on, or what I came back to, until it happens."

We all stared at him a moment.

"Yeah, it bites," he said. We all kind of shook ourselves and refocused.

"Did they leave any of the rope behind that they tied us up with?" I asked hopefully. "If you tie me to Hank and Gary again, like they had us in the truck, I should be fine."

"I found some," Anthony called from our left, but no sooner had he said it than the rope went up in flames, along with his right arm.

"Sorry," he said as he beat at the fire crackling along his arm. A moment later the polyester fabric of his dress ignited, and he was forced to drop to the ground and roll around to put it out.

"Murphy, can you go look?" Zeke asked. "I can't see squat out here without my glasses, Hank's holding Emerson down, Gary's stuck, and Anthony keeps lighting stuff on fire."

Murphy nodded and came back moments later with two sections of rope. Zeke snatched it and crouched to tie me to Hank.

"Double-knot it," I instructed, craning my head to watch. "Are you double-knotting it? I changed my mind. Triple-knot it. Quadruple-knot it. What comes after quadruple?"

"It's called *quintuple*," Gary grumbled.

I nodded. "Good. Do that. Or better yet, just keep putting in knots until you run out of rope." I sounded whiny, but I didn't care. "Make it tighter."

"Don't make it tighter," Hank grunted. "I'm already losing circulation in that hand."

"Well, it doesn't help that the darn thing is invisible," Zeke grumbled.

"Can someone please explain to me why the blind kid is tying the knots?" Gary asked.

Zeke paused in his knot tying to scowl at Gary. "I'm not blind. I'm legally blind. It's totally different."

"Because our other option involved being set on fire.

That's why," Hank reminded him. "Hey," he paused, looking around. "Where's Mr. Stink?"

"Sleeping under my bed," Zeke said, giving the knot tying Gary and me an unnecessarily hard yank that made the joints of my wrist pop. Gary shot him a dirty look, which he ignored. "I figured it was better that he not come along on this particular adventure."

"Good call," Hank said, nodding in approval. Just then Gary's hand came unstuck from mine with a soft pop. Gary promptly balled it into a fist.

I flexed my fingers. "Thanks again, man."

"No problem. Not like I had a choice. Just be glad we're unstuck. I had my hand stuck to my mom's shoulder once for three whole days." He shuddered at the memory. Hank climbed off my chest, and I bounced upright. The ropes held. My feet still hovered uncomfortably an inch or two off the earth, but a little adjustment had them back on solid ground again a moment later. I let out a sigh of relief.

"Three and a half hours left," Anthony said.

"It would help if we knew which direction they drove away, but those stupid blindfolds screwed that over," I said.

"They drove that way," Zeke said, pointing to our left. We all stared at him. "X-ray vision, remember? I had an episode while we were blindfolded. I know exactly which way they went. Unfortunately, there were about a dozen twists and turns on the way here, and I have no clue how to get back to camp."

"Well, we need to find that compass then, and I wouldn't mind finding the Oreos, either," Hank mused.

"The compass is right there," Zeke said, and pointed upward. We all craned our heads, and I thought I could make out a small circular object dangling forty feet in the air from the branch of a tree. How had the Redwood guys managed it?

"How in the world are we going to get that down?" I asked. No one responded, and for the first time I noticed the unusual silence surrounding me. Looking away from the compass, I discovered five pairs of eyes staring back at me. My stomach sank. I knew what was coming.

I shook my head. "No way. Don't even ask. I'm not doing it."

"How else are we supposed to get it down?" Zeke asked.

"I don't know. Think of something else. Anything else. No." They kept looking at me, and my heart sank.

"Don't worry. You don't die," Murphy murmured, picking at a piece of lace that had come loose from his dress.

"See! You don't die. Everyone wins!" Hank slapped my shoulder awkwardly with the hand not strapped to mine. I sighed, recognizing a lost battle when I saw one. Either I could do this willingly or I was going to be forced to do it. And after Hank and Gary had just saved my life, it felt a little ungrateful not to help out.

Ten minutes later, I was giving myself a silent pep talk as I floated upward. The ropes around both my ankles were triple-knotted, and Hank and Gary had the other ends looped around their waists. I squeezed my eyes shut as the branches of the tree brushed my face and the rough bark scratched at my bare arms. If I couldn't see how far off the ground I was, then I wouldn't freak and barf. No barfing. No freaking. No point, I reminded myself. Murphy said I survived this, and he would know. Wouldn't he?

"You're only a foot or two away," Hank called encouragingly. "Stick out your right hand." I followed his direction and groped for the compass.

"More to the left!"

"Not your left! Our left!"

"Higher. A few more inches."

"Hey! I found the Oreos under that bush over there."

I suddenly felt my right leg shoot up a few feet, and I yelped.

"Sorry, man. I wanted an Oreo." Hank's apology sounded too far away, and I was tempted to open my eyes. I didn't.

As Hank reeled his rope in, successfully evening out my legs, I felt my hand brush against something smooth and metallic. A moment later my fingers closed around the compass, and I yanked it free.

"Get me down! I got it! Down! Now!" I demanded. The ropes tightened, and seconds later I found my feet back on solid ground.

Murphy immediately got to work tethering me to Gary and Hank again. I suppressed the urge to drop to my knees and kiss the ground like a sailor who has just survived a shipwreck and glared at Murphy instead. "I thought you didn't tell anyone their future," I said accusingly.

"I don't." Murphy grinned at me in the dark. "I was lying. I just knew you wouldn't do it if you were worried about dying."

I scowled. "Not cool."

Murphy finished checking the knots and handed me a stack of Oreos. They were double-stuffed, which was the only kind worth eating. "Well, you didn't die, did you?" He shrugged apologetically. "So, no harm, no foul."

I wasn't sure if I agreed with that philosophy, but I popped an Oreo into my mouth and chewed.

"It's too stinking dark." Gary wrinkled his nose and pressed it closer to the compass.

"Didn't Chad say something about a flashlight?" I asked. As soon as I said it, I wished I hadn't. What if it was in another dumb tree?

"We don't need the flashlight," Anthony said, shutting his eyes and balling his hands into fists. A moment later his left foot burst into flame. Gary quickly crouched to read the compass in the glow.

Anthony sighed sheepishly. "I was trying to get my hair to light again."

"Yeah," Gary grumbled from his spot on the ground. "That would have been nice." He stood up a moment later and pointed into the darkness of the forest. "We need to head that way." Anthony quickly extinguished his foot.

"Less than three hours," Zeke called as he and Murphy ran ahead of us, their dresses bobbing away into the shadows of the trees.

So we ran. And we ran. And I hurled. But not from floating. Apparently you couldn't go from not running more than a few lead-heavy steps in your life to a marathon without some consequences. Hank took it well, but I accidently got puke on Gary's feet, which he was less than pleased about. As we ran we talked over life lists. Well, the guys talked about life lists. I was too busy trying to get enough air into my lungs. It turned out that almost everyone had made bucket lists at some point except for me. The thought had honestly never occurred to me. On the contrary, I'd spent a huge amount of time and energy avoiding the things that pushed me out of my comfort zone. As we ran, I listened to the other boys come up with things for their lists, and I began mentally composing my own list. Hypothetical, of course.

The sun was just coming up when we finally spotted the camp almost three hours later. We were sweat-soaked, scratched, mosquito-bitten, muddy, and for some of us, splattered with a little bit of vomit, and I'd never seen anything more beautiful in my entire life.

"Two minutes till breakfast," Zeke wheezed. "If we are the last ones there, we have to serve everyone in these things."

Anthony grimaced down at his tattered dress. "We could skip breakfast," he suggested.

"If we skip, I'm eating you for breakfast," Hank warned.

"You need to get a new joke," Zeke said. "You totally used that one last night."

"Who's joking?" Hank asked.

Gary suddenly put his hand to his forehead, shading his eyes as he looked across camp at the woods opposite. "Are you seeing what I'm seeing?" he asked.

"Unless it's food, I couldn't really care less," Hank said.

"Seriously," Gary said stubbornly. "Look!" So we looked where he was pointing, and I saw what he meant. The woods were rustling, and every now and then a bright puff of something colorful would kind of poof into the air. Before I could say anything, a pack of girls erupted from the woods.

"Are those feathers?" Anthony asked.

"Those are feathers, all right," Hank confirmed. The girls were jogging, although in a much more organized and less pathetic fashion than we were. Plumes of blue, purple, and yellow feathers molted off them as they ran, sending rainbow-colored clouds of the stuff into the air.

"Move!" Gary yelled in my ear, and there was a sharp tug on my wrist as he sprinted forward. "We can't let them beat us," he called. "I hate KP duty!"

Everyone caught on a moment after that and soon we were in a full-on sprint toward the dining hall. The girls spotted us and broke into a run, leaving a jet stream of feathers in their wake. We skidded to a stop on the doorstep of the dining hall just as they came up the stairs. Now that they were closer, I could see that the feathers hadn't been stuck to them with glue or honey like I'd originally suspected. They grew directly from their skin, fell out, and grew back a second later. The girls were looking us over too and grinning. I became acutely aware of the ropes tying me to Hank and Gary, which gave the impression that I was a gigantic puppy they'd decided to take on a walk. Perfect.

"Victory!" Anthony yelled, his hands thrust in the air. Unfortunately the motion sent a tiny ball of fire zinging toward the ceiling, where it left a large black burn mark on the wood. The motion ripped a hole in the shoulder of his dress and one of his bows fell off with a plop.

A tall blonde with bright-green eyes crossed her arms, purple feathers falling off her like fluffy rain. "Get on with it, then," she said. "You won fair and square."

"What he means is, after you, gorgeous," Hank purred, dropping to his knees as he attempted one of his sweeping bows. Unfortunately, he'd forgotten that he was attached to me, so like boy-sized dominos I was yanked into my own awkward bow, followed by a furious Gary. Glancing up, my eyes caught Molly's laughing brown ones, and my face flushed red. In that moment, nothing would have made me happier than throttling Hank.

"Thanks," crooned the blonde as she walked past us and into the bustling dining hall, followed by the rest of the Monarch cabin.

"Are you kidding me?" Zeke cried as the door swung shut behind them.

"Remind me to kill you for that," Gary said, regaining his footing and brushing at the feathers that clung to his knees. If the smell of bacon, waffles, and maple syrup hadn't wafted out of the door as soon as they opened it, I think we might have walked away. But our hunger won out over pride, and we filed in after the girls. The dining hall became momentarily quiet as everyone took in the sight of us. There was humiliation, and then there was whatever this was. Hank, never one to miss an opportunity, grinned, threw his arms in the air, and spun like a ballerina in the *Nutcracker*. However, ballerinas usually didn't have other people attached to their wrists, and Gary and I were forced to spin with him. The entire hall burst into raucous laughter, and even as I felt my face turn as red as Anthony's dress, I laughed too. The Redwood guys were on their feet, clapping and stomping, and soon the entire hall was applauding as we limped toward our table and a grinning Eli, with a very disgruntled Mr. Stink perched on our table beside him.

"I must say the eighties is a good look on you boys," he chuckled. "I'm glad to see you. You know the rules; last cabin in gets KP duty. So get busy. I can't eat until you do, and I don't know about you, but I've worked up quite the appetite. Zeke, you have some explaining to do to Mr. Stink. The guy hasn't stopped scolding me and grumbling since he woke up."

Zeke grinned as he scooped up a skunk that was indeed grumbling and giving him a very disapproving look. Eli turned to me, my weighted vest in hand, and I had to keep tears of pure joy from my eyes at the sight of it. He quickly slipped it over my shoulders, then untied me from Gary and Hank, who immediately moved off to grab the waiting pitchers. As Hank hurried over to pour water for the Monarch cabin, I noticed that his dress had gotten a huge tear across the back so that his polka-dot boxers were peeping through. Serves him right, I thought, still remembering my awkward bow and spin.

"I was a little worried when I saw your vest here this morning," Eli confided as I tightened the straps across my chest.

"I survived." I shrugged, slightly surprised by my own nonchalance.

Eli winked and sat down at our empty table as I headed to the Redwood table with a pitcher of orange juice. The guys all clapped me on the back, congratulating me on my initiation into Camp O, and I realized that they hadn't been lying last night when they'd said they were jealous of us. Would I ever look back at this morning in a ridiculous dress and think it was one of the best mornings of my life too? A breeze from an open window chose that moment to blow my dress up around my waist, Marilyn Monroe style, sending the table of girls behind me into fits of giggles.

I doubted it.

Hi Mom! Hi Dad!

Miss me yet? Camp is turning out better than I thought it would. Tell Dad he can stop worrying about me setting the place on fire. I've already done it, twice, and it turned out okay. No one even got mad. Well, actually, that's a lie. This kid Gary in my cabin was furious. Which was dumb because the fire didn't even get that close to his bunk. So what if it melted a little bit of his cell phone? He hasn't been able to get it to work since we got here, so I don't know what the big deal is. He talked this kid Murphy into switching bunks with him, but I don't mind. Murphy is really cool. He sucks at time travel, but he is freaking awesome on these survival hikes that

Eli takes us on. He ate two worms and a cricket yesterday when everyone else was too chicken to try anything but the sassafras leaf tea. (Which was nasty, in case you were wondering.) I'm not sure how he did it. The worms just looked so slimy, even if they are a decent source of protein. I accidentally torched my worm so badly it kind of disintegrated, so there's that.

I can't believe that we've been here for a week already! I could use a few more T-shirts and socks if you get a chance to send a package. One of the kids in my cabin has a skunk as a service animal. (Can you believe it?! A skunk!) Mr. Stink (that's the skunk) got into my dresser and stole a bunch of my stuff to make a nest under one of the bunks. And from the way he looks at me when I get close, I don't think I'll be getting them back anytime soon. Besides, who wants to wear underwear with skunk drool on it? Anyway, give Baxter an extra treat for me. Has his hair grown back yet?

We really need to flame-retard him more often. Poor dog is going to start thinking his name is Baldy.

Anthony

PS If you send T-shirts and socks, send some chocolate too.

CHAPTER SIX

The next morning was a blur. All I wanted to do after our nighttime run through the woods was shower and go to bed, but it turned out that wasn't an option. Eli jam-packed our days with everything from archery lessons to survival hikes, and it was three days before I realized there wasn't even a TV on the property, let alone Wi-Fi.

Eli wasn't the only one with plans, and before I really realized what was happening Hank had us all writing out life lists. I was reluctant to join in Hank's particular brand of crazy, but after a lifetime on the sidelines, I wanted to be in the game. So I doggedly dived in with everyone else. It felt weird to start off at age zero, but it didn't take all of us long to add a few years. Some of the things on our life lists were pretty easy to check off, like dive to the bottom of the lake or learn how to say the alphabet backward. Others, like French kissing a girl, well, those were going to be harder. But by the end of the first week I was officially four by Hank's bizarre brand of logic. Zeke was six, Gary was five, and Anthony was nine.

Murphy in particular became a life list junkie. He approached everything like he had nothing to lose and took every opportunity to check something off his list. Because of that he was already a whopping fifteen. Even Hank was impressed. After the first few days of camp he loosened up and lost the twitchiness that his future self had commented on in the woods on initiation night. His lopsided grin became almost as common a sight as Hank bowing. I fell into bed every evening exhausted, sunburned, and happy.

I found myself on Friday night gearing up for the second big capture-the-flag battle. As I shrugged into my camouflage shirt, I glanced anxiously out the window. The sky had been continually darkening throughout the day, and the air had that tangy smell that meant a storm was coming. It would be a real bummer if the battle got canceled because of rain.

"Okay, men," Eli said as we all crouched in our

camouflage and war paint in the middle of our cabin. His shape had been shifting more than usual today, probably because he was excited about the battle. He barely resembled the guy my mom had handed me off to, with his black buzz cut, short beefy stature, and wide-set eyes. "Tonight we are allowed to start actually capturing flags. Remember, each of the cabins has its own territory. If anyone comes near the lake, catch them and put them in our jail."

"Where is our jail again?" Zeke asked.

Gary rolled his eyes at Zeke. "The canoe dock, remember?"

"Right," Eli agreed. "If someone gets put in jail, the only way they can get out is if another player makes it to the jail, tags the player, and hauls butt out of there."

"Wait, you mean there are no free walk backs to our own territory after we tag someone?" Hank asked.

"Not at Camp O. We are going to go after the Silver Birches and the White Oaks tonight. The Redwood boys will probably be sniffing around our camp, but we don't want to go after them yet, especially as we have a rough idea that their flag is near that log you three hid behind. Emerson, you take Hank and go after the Silver Birches. Zeke, Anthony, and Gary, you three are in charge of the White Oaks. Murphy and I will be patrolling our territory to catch anyone who comes snooping around." A ripple of excitement went through me at my assignment. The Silver Birch cabin was the cabin of fourteen-year-olds. We'd hung out with them at the archery field the day before. They were nice guys, although their RISK factors were a bit more bizarre than most. All I could say was that I was glad I wasn't magnetic. It looked like a real pain.

Everyone was nodding eagerly, and I bit back a grin. Murphy looked excited, and I figured that was a good thing. I'd started using him as a gauge of sorts. If he looked upset or sad, something bad was probably going to happen, like Zeke breaking his glasses or Anthony setting a cabin wall on fire. If he looked happy, we were okay. I figured that he was also pretty excited about the possibility of checking off another goal. Everyone had added *Capture another team's flag* onto their list. Turning my attention back to Eli, I blinked in surprise as he began expanding back to his usual six-foot height. Some things at Camp O were harder to get used to than others.

A bell started clanging outside our cabin, and we scrambled to our feet, jostling and pushing to make it out the door. All six cabins were grouped around the stone fire pit where Mr. Blue was standing, his arms crossed over his chest and a huge grin on his face.

"Welcome, men!" he boomed. "Take a knee." We

did, and he began pacing back and forth in front of us, meeting each of our gazes in turn. "Tonight the real battle begins, but we have rules here at Camp O. Rule one: stay on the boys' side of the hill. The girls are having their own flag competition tonight, and we don't want you messing up each other's games or canoodling in the woods unchaperoned, right, Hank?" Mr. Blue shot Hank a look, and everyone chuckled. Hank's flamboyant attempts to woo the Monarch girls were well known by this point.

"Rule two is that you play clean. Any team caught pushing, shoving, or fighting is immediately DQ'd. Understand?" Everyone nodded. "Rule three is to stay on camp property." Just then the sky unzipped and the rain that had been threatening all day came pounding down, making our shirts stick to us and our face paint run in drippy smears of green and brown. I sighed. I'd been really excited about playing. Before I could get up to head back into our cabin, Mr. Blue blasted his whistle, and everyone took off.

"Wait, what?" I asked as Hank grabbed my arm and hauled me to my feet.

"What do you mean, what? We have to try to find the Silver Birches' flag. Weren't you paying attention?" Hank let go of my arm, and I ran after him.

"I heard, but it's raining," I protested. The water

was running off me in sheets as the sky got darker and darker overhead, and I shivered as the icy streams sent goose bumps rippling down my back. I'd never been out in the rain for more than a few seconds, usually sheltered under my mother's umbrella while she squealed about her hair. This was definitely different. The jury was out about whether it was a good different.

"No kidding. What was your first clue?" Hank huffed as we ducked under a branch and kept running. After a lifetime of *not* running, I'd spent most of my first week of this summer making up for lost time. We passed out of neutral ground and into Silver Birch's territory.

"Where should we look?" I asked while whipping my head from left to right, trying to spot the silver flag we'd come here for. Suddenly Hank slid to a stop. My feet skidded, and I hit him going full speed. We both landed face-first in the mud. I spit out a mouthful of muck, barely registering that Hank was hauling me up by the neck of my shirt.

"What did you do that for?" I snapped, trying in vain to wipe my muddy face off on my even muddier shirt.

"Shhhhhh," Hank hissed. "I heard something." The next thing I knew I was being dragged toward a pine tree. "Quick, up," Hank commanded. Without waiting for a response, he leaped, grabbed a branch a few feet in the air, and swung himself up. I tried to make the same leap and failed. I wish I could blame it on the weighted vest, but really it was a general lack of practice. So I contented myself with scrabbling up the lower branches.

We huddled in soggy silence as the rain pounded down on our heads. The knobby stick we perched on dug painfully into my tailbone, and I shifted impatiently. Nothing happened. "I don't think you really heard anything," I muttered, and was about to jump down when the muffled squelch of feet on soggy leaves met my ears. Moments later two Silver Birch boys came out of the trees.

"Are you sure they came this way?" asked a boy whose skin had a rather sickly greenish hue to it. His name was Eric, but I couldn't for the life of me remember his friend's name.

"Positive. It was the skinny kid who's always bowing and the one who wears that huge vest." This kid had an extra set of arms positioned just below his regular set. I turned to give Hank a terrified *what do we do now* look, but Hank was gone. Next to me sat a pile of soggy camouflage pants, polka-dot boxer shorts, and a mud-covered tank top. I blinked in surprise.

"Hank," I whispered. "Dude, are you naked right now? Not cool!" I shouldn't have whispered.

"There he is!" Eric yelled. Without stopping to think, I dropped from the tree and hit the mud running. They were after me in a heartbeat. We slipped and slid across the soggy forest floor, over the nearby stream, and back toward Red Maple territory. We were almost in sight of the lake when I felt four sets of hands grab onto my shoulders. I was caught. We went down in a tangle of too many arms. The too-many-armed kid and Eric hauled me to my feet and dragged me back up the hill.

The Silver Birch jail was in the middle of the creek. Not on an island in the creek, or a rock in the creek . . . *in* the actual creek. So I waited to be rescued in knee-deep water as mud ran in rivers over my shoulders, down my neck, and into my underwear. And somewhere, running around the woods naked, was my invisible best friend. Things weren't looking so good.

Eric was left to guard me. He was handsome, in a chiseled-jaw-and-big-shoulders way girls seemed to like, and I wondered if being green hurt his chances with girls. He ignored me and busied himself by pacing twenty feet in every direction, alert for anyone attempting a rescue mission. It was a waste of his time. No one would come for me. I wasn't Hank, who any of the Red Maple guys would bend over backward to save, or Zeke, with his quick wit, or Murphy, with his lopsided grin. I was just a very muddy Emerson, and even I wouldn't jump in this stream for muddy Emerson. Once I'd resigned myself to that fact, I did what Eli had told us to. I looked for their flag. And I looked, and I looked. But I didn't see anything. What I did see was the kid with too many arms leading an equally wet and bedraggled Anthony toward the stream.

"Hey, man." He nodded as he came sloshing through the water to stand next to me.

"Weren't you supposed to be going after the White Oaks?" I asked.

Anthony shrugged sheepishly. "I got lost. Zeke knows I got caught, though. He might try to free us." Thirty minutes later, no one had tried to free us. In the meantime the Silver Birch guys managed to catch a guy from Redwood and another from White Oak. The creek was getting pretty crowded, and the rain was coming down even harder than before. I tried to play it off like standing in the freezing rain in the middle of a downpour was something I did every day. Really, I was kind of miserable, and this whole capture-the-flag thing was losing its fun factor fast.

I noticed Hank then. Okay, so not really Hank, just his left big toe. At first I thought I was seeing some kind of bizarre white frog hopping across the mud, but then I noticed that the frog was leaving Hank-sized footprints in its wake. I elbowed Anthony in the ribs to get his attention and flicked my eyes toward Hank's approaching toe. Eric was about ten yards away when all of a sudden Hank went from invisible (except for his toe) to completely visible and completely naked as he splashed into the stream.

"What the . . . ?!" the other boys in jail yelled as naked Hank tagged us, and we launched ourselves out of the creek.

"Jailbreak!" Eric bellowed, and the sound of pounding feet thundered behind us. We flew through the rain-drenched forest, Hank's white butt leading the way as we jumped over puddles and ducked under dripping branches. The sky lit with the crack of lightning and the roll of thunder, and I let out a whoop just for the joy of it. The Silver Birch guys were gaining on us, and I dug deep, forcing myself to keep up with Anthony and naked Hank. If we could just make it to the lake, we'd be home free. Hank flickered and went completely invisible again as we slipped and slid down the hill. Luckily the mud was flying so thick that it soon coated him so that I could see his muddy outline just ahead of me. We flew past the boathouse, and I heard our pursuers stop short as we entered our own territory. Safe. We slid to a stop, panting.

"Nice one, man," I huffed, slapping Hank on what I

really hoped was his shoulder.

"Thanks," he puffed.

Anthony shook his head as he attempted to scrape the mud off his arms and legs. "Naked? Seriously? That's commitment."

Hank became visible again, a wide grin spread across his face. "Wave to the nice Silver Birch boys," he called, wiggling his fingers at the fuming guys standing in the woods. Just then Zeke came flying out of the trees on the other side of the lake, a white bandanna hoisted over his head in triumph, Mr. Stink perched precariously on his shoulder, his claws digging into the wet fabric of Zeke's T-shirt for all he was worth.

"No way! He's got a flag!" Hank whooped. We charged around the lake. Zeke was standing just inside our territory, his hands on his hips as he performed a strange victory dance that involved a lot of butt wiggling, elbow thrusting, and spinning. Mr. Stink saw us coming and jumped off his shoulder moments before we tackled Zeke midspin, hooting and laughing.

Eli came rushing out of the trees, and we all cheered as we ran back to our jail, where Murphy was guarding a guy from White Oak and another kid from the Pines. A gigantic lightning bolt slashed across the sky, and we heard the bell signaling that the game was over for the night.

"Time to head in," Eli yelled over the rain. Just then he noticed Hank's semi-invisible form and did a double take. "Hank?" he asked. "Where are your clothes?"

"I left them up a tree. It was either that or get caught." Hank shrugged.

"Well, we might want to get some clothes on you before parading you back into camp."

"Good call," Hank said, grinning. "If the ladies all mobbed me at once we'd have a problem on our hands."

I would have missed what happened next if I hadn't been looking right at Murphy. One second he was laughing along with the rest of us, and in the next he was gone. I yelped, and everyone turned to look. I saw my own surprise mirrored on their faces.

"Freeze," Mr. Blue boomed. I jumped. In the shock of seeing my friend disappear, I hadn't noticed him approaching.

"Eli, do you have the red rocks?" Mr. Blue asked, not taking his eyes off the spot where Murphy had disappeared.

"Yes, sir," Eli said. He reached his hand in his pocket and pulled out a small pouch I'd never seen before. No one moved as Mr. Blue took six smooth red stones out of the bag and placed them in a circle around the small puddle of water that marked the spot Murphy had been just moments before.

"That should do it," he said, stepping back. "Eli, please post a watch on that spot. Notify me on my radio when he returns."

"I volunteer," Zeke said. "There was a traveler kid at my old school. I know the drill. Besides, Mr. Stink loves grubbing for worms in the rain." Mr. Stink waddled up, sniffing tentatively in the direction of the red rocks.

Eli nodded. "Thanks. The rest of you need to head back to the cabin and change." Then he remembered naked Hank and sighed. "Emerson, go with Hank to get his clothes, please." I wanted to protest, to ask what had just happened and what the rocks meant. But I didn't. I just followed naked Hank into the woods.

CHAPTER SEVEN

When we got back to the cabin, fully clothed, we found Eli holding a garden hose. "Arms out," he commanded. We obliged and he hosed the majority of the mud off us before sending us inside for showers. Afterward, as we were all getting dressed, Anthony asked the question I'd been wondering since the moment Murphy disappeared.

"Why do we have to watch the red rocks?" he asked Eli.

"Time travelers always return to the same spot," Eli explained. When we still looked confused, he sighed. "Like, the *exact* same spot. If something else is in that spot when he tries to come back, well." Eli made an exploding motion with his hands, and the blood drained from my face.

"He dies?" Hank gasped.

"He might," Eli said. "Or he might explode whatever is in the spot. Either way it's not pretty. It's safer to keep the area clear."

"Agreed." Hank nodded. "I've never seen a squirrel explode, and I can't say that I want to."

"Emerson," Eli said, startling me from my thoughts. "Can you go take over the watch for Zeke so he can shower? We need to meet down in the dining hall in a half hour, and he can't do that covered in mud." I nodded. The rain had stopped, and my feet squished loudly in the soggy grass as I headed toward the lake, the image of Murphy disappearing replaying over and over again in my head.

Zeke was happy to turn over his circle-watching duties to me, although I think Mr. Stink would have preferred to stay and paw through the mud. I settled in to stare at the rocks. The first ten minutes I spent hunched over, channeling all my focus on the circle. When nothing happened, I relaxed a little. The rain had stopped, leaving the air with a freshness that any laundry detergent would envy. The frogs and crickets started a low hum as the sun sank behind the row of pine trees that bordered the lake. This place really is beautiful, I thought as I took in the view.

Suddenly there was a loud pop, like a firecracker going off, and I jumped guiltily, my eyes flying to the circle of red rocks. Murphy was back. I stumbled to my feet, taking in his tear-streaked cheeks and red swollen eyes.

"You okay, man?" I asked.

He nodded, wiping his face off with his sleeve. I shifted nervously from foot to foot. What was the protocol after someone had a bad time-traveling trip? Was I supposed to hug him? Tell him it was okay? Asking him where he'd been or what he'd seen wasn't allowed, but he just looked so miserable, standing there in the dusky evening light, that I had to say something. "Are you sure?" I asked. "You look terrible."

Murphy seemed like he was about to nod again, but then he slumped and shook his head. He sat down, absentmindedly picking up the small red rocks and pocketing them. "I usually don't get this rattled when I jump time." He shook his head. "Gosh, I've been doing it long enough. But now," he said, swallowing hard, "now it's different."

"Different?" I prompted.

Murphy rolled two of the rocks around in his hand, studying them as he rubbed at his running nose. "It's just that now, every time I go, I wonder if this is the time I don't come back."

"What do you mean?" I asked.

Murphy glanced up at me. "Can you keep a secret, Emerson?"

"Of course," I said automatically.

"Swear?" he prompted. "Because telling you any of this could get me and you in serious trouble."

My stomach clenched as I remembered the menace in Brawny and Burly that first day of camp, but I nodded.

Murphy studied me a moment longer before sighing. "I don't survive this summer."

"What?" I asked, certain I hadn't heard him correctly.

"That's why I'm at Camp O." He shrugged. "It's pretty obvious that my family couldn't afford to send me here."

I glanced automatically at his ratty shorts and worn-out tennis shoes and then hated myself for it. "What do you mean, send you here?" I asked. "We *had* to come here. Remember? The government sent out those requirement letters. They passed that new regulation law or whatever."

Murphy laughed, but the sound was hollow and sharp. "Did you actually read that letter, Emerson?"

That caught me off guard, and I thought back to the day the letter had arrived in the mail, complete with its official seal and fancy letterhead. My mom had read it twice, and then immediately disappeared into her office to make phone calls. It wasn't until later that week that she told me that since I was a level five, the government required that I be under regulated supervision for the summer months in order to ensure the safety of the public. I'd been furious. The only reason I was a level five was because of danger to myself, not anyone else. My mom had explained that it didn't matter why I'd received the level, just that I had. I'd been about to argue with her further, but I'd stopped myself. As my mom stood there, that letter clasped in her hand like it was the last lifeboat on the Titanic, I could see that she was relieved. It hurt, even though I *knew* that she dreaded summers full of extra equipment, caseworker check-ins, and the added stress of documentation. That letter was her ticket to freedom, and all it was going to cost her was one son.

"Well, did you read it or not?" Murphy prompted, snapping me back to the present. I shook my head, feeling like an idiot.

"I thought as much," Murphy said, sitting back. "The letter didn't require us high levelers to go to camp," he said with a jerk of his head toward the cabins on the hill.

"It required that we be supervised and accommodated for by a government-approved organization or facility. This camp costs money. A lot of money, actually. The free options included children's hospitals, juvenile detention centers, and summer school programs."

"Oh," I said stupidly. I hadn't realized that Mom had paid for me to come here, that she'd *chosen* this camp for me. It made me feel a little guilty about all the awful things I'd thought about her.

"So, what do you mean, that's why you're here?" I asked, still trying to understand what Murphy was telling me.

Murphy shrugged. "This camp was my Make-A-Wish."

My jaw dropped in horror. "You have cancer?" I gasped.

"Nope." Murphy grimaced. "But Make-A-Wish is for kids with stuff other than cancer too. It would have been easier to get my wish if I *did* have cancer though. My poor parents had to do mounds of paperwork for me to qualify, since I don't have a terminal illness or anything. I'm the first RISK kid to get approved for a wish. Make-A-Wish did a whole bunch of publicity about how they were making the wish come true for a RISK kid, or I don't think the TTBI would have let me come."

"Is that why those guys, the TTBI officials, came to drop you off?" I asked, some of the mystery tangled around Murphy finally starting to unravel.

Murphy nodded. "It was one of the TTBI's requirements."

I felt numb, as though this conversation wasn't really happening. "I'm still confused," I admitted.

Murphy slid the two red rocks he'd been fidgeting with into his pocket and looked at me. "Sometime in the next few weeks, I'm going to time travel, and I'm not going to come back."

"Like come back to camp?" I knew I was being purposefully dense, but I didn't want to understand what he was telling me.

"Like come back, *ever.*" Murphy frowned, kicking his heels in the puddle of water at his feet. "I've traveled to the future, and I'm not there. My parents have a grave for me and everything." He shuddered and made a face. "A really ugly grave actually, and they planted yellow tulips around it."

"But why did you choose camp?" I asked, thinking of about ten places I'd ask to go instead if it were me, none of which involved toilets without stalls.

Murphy nodded. "When I first qualified for it, I wanted to take my whole family to Rome. My mom's always wanted to go, and since the whole Make-A-Wish thing was her idea in the first place, I thought it would be nice. But then you told me about camp, and—"

"Wait a second," I said, holding up my hands. "I never told you about camp."

Murphy nodded. "You did. At my funeral. I time traveled and got to attend about five minutes of it. Everyone was there, Gary, Hank, Zeke, Anthony, you . . . even Eli. Of course, when I traveled I had no idea who you guys were, but it was obvious by the way you talked about me that you were my friends. Which was weird, ya know, since I've never really had friends. Anyway, when you stood up to speak, you mentioned camp. Thanks in advance, by the way. You say some really nice stuff."

I shook my head, trying to take it all in. "That's beyond creepy."

"You can't even imagine," Murphy sighed. "As I sat in the back row of that church listening to you talk about this summer, I knew that it was what I wanted. Friends. Camp. One last summer to really live it up."

Suddenly I flashed back to the scene his parents had made on registration day. It made sense now.

"How soon will it happen?" I asked.

"No clue. All I know is that I don't make it home from camp. I had to beg my parents to let me come here. They wanted to spend every last second with me, but I couldn't stand it. My mom couldn't even look at me without bursting into tears."

I tried to imagine how my own mom would have handled something like that and winced at the mental picture. "Wow, that's rough," I said.

"Well, they won't really be living without me completely. I've traveled to the future and seen them. Today's trip makes the eighth time, I think. It's one of the reasons my mom let me come. She knows she'll get to see me at least a few more times."

"What's that like?" I asked, realizing now why this particular time travel had rattled him more than usual. He'd been hanging out with his parents, his future parents who'd lost a child.

Murphy shook his head sadly. "Intense. Lots of tears. Lots of hugs. More tears. The first time it happened I'd jumped into the future when I would have been sixteen, I think. I let myself into my house, just like I always do when I time travel to my own neighborhood, and my parents about had a meltdown. That was when I knew I'd died. We just stood there, bawling. It was awful."

"I'm sorry," I said, hating myself for saying those words. Saying I'm sorry was a lot like offering to empty someone's pool with a teaspoon. Nice, but not helpful.

"Well, we can't let that happen!" cried a voice behind

us. We both whirled, but there wasn't anyone there.

Murphy sighed. "Hi, Hank."

Hank flickered back into view. Naked. "If you think we're just going to sit around and wait for you to die, you're crazy!"

Murphy raised an eyebrow at him. "Hank, I appreciate your sentiment and all, but one, you can't change the future. Not only is it impossible, but it's against the law. And two, why are you still naked?"

"I'm not *still* naked." Hank rolled his eyes. "I'm naked again because I was trying to sneak up on you." Just then we heard the sound of the dining hall bell summoning us all for our nightly snack.

"This conversation isn't over," Hank said, pointing at each of us. "But you need to get changed, and I need to get my clothes back on." Hank turned and bounded up the hill, quickly disappearing until nothing but his head was visible bobbing away into the distance.

Murphy sighed. "Well, so much for a secret." When we got back to the cabin, Murphy quickly threw on the Red Maple sweatshirt Eli had asked us all to wear, and within moments the three of us were jogging toward the dining hall. Hank frowned, his normal buoyant good mood conspicuously absent.

"Hank, it's okay," Murphy said. "I've come to terms with it."

"It's not okay," he cried. "It's not even close to being okay. Emerson and I will come up with something."

"You can't," Murphy said. "My parents spent almost every penny they had on time-travel specialists, medications, doctors, books, and special equipment. None of it worked. The Time Traveler Bureau of Investigation even put us under, well, investigation, since it's pretty common for time travelers to break the law if they find out they're going to die."

"But—" Hank began, but Murphy held up a hand to cut him off.

"Listen to me. If there were a way to save me, my parents would have found it. Got it? I shouldn't have mentioned it to Emerson, but today's trip rattled me more than usual. It was a stupid moment of weakness. Can we just forget about it, please?"

Hank frowned. "Are your parents time travelers?"

Murphy shook his head. "No. My grandpa was. He died at age twenty-nine. Same deal. Time traveled one day and never came back."

"Wait a minute," I interrupted. "So you might not actually die. You *might* just get stuck somewhere?"

Murphy nodded. "Honestly, I'm not sure which would be worse. Some of the places I've traveled would be pretty awful to get stuck in."

"I need to noodle on this," Hank said as we climbed the dining hall steps.

"Noodle on it?" I asked.

"Think, contemplate the possibilities, meditate, muse, ponder, ruminate, consider."

"We get the point," Murphy said with an eye roll. Hank was quiet as we walked into the dining hall, even ignoring the table of Monarch girls, who all whistled at him. The hall smelled like warm chocolate, and my stomach snarled despite my preoccupation with Murphy. As we wove our way around the large, round wooden tables full of laughing and shouting campers, I could almost see the wheels in Hank's head turning. It made me feel better. Hank wasn't going to go down without a fight. Which was good, because I wasn't either.

CHAPTER EIGHT

We slid into our seats at the Red Maple table, and all the guys welcomed Murphy back. Murphy returned their greetings with a smile, shooting Hank and me a warning look that very clearly told us to keep our mouths shut. I frowned, and Hank avoided Murphy's gaze as he bit into a cookie, chewing thoughtfully. Mr. Blue stood up to give an update on who was in first place for capture the flag, but I wasn't really listening. I felt like I'd stepped away from the happy bustle of our table, away from the congratulatory cheers when Zeke's flag capture was announced. I barely tasted the gooey chocolate chips in my cookie as my mind puzzled over

Murphy and everything he'd told us. It was a lot to process.

"All right, men," Eli said, banging his hand on our table to get our attention a few minutes later. "Finish up those cookies. Those of you who need to take medications, please stop by Nurse Betsy's office. Lights-out in an hour."

I crammed one last cookie into my mouth and clambered to my feet with Murphy and Anthony. Hank, Gary, and Zeke didn't need meds, so they raced back up the hill to be the first in line to play tetherball. Murphy and Anthony joked and messed around as we hopped over mud puddles on our way to the nurse's small cabin that perched at the edge of the woods. I normally joined in, but today I hung back and watched instead, my mind still preoccupied. Anthony did a spot-on impersonation of Hank as he pretended to bow and flirt shamelessly with a tree, and I burst out laughing despite myself. This walk to the nurse's cabin was one of my favorite parts of the day. Which was utterly bizarre, since back at school, having to report to the nurse every day was not only a pain in the butt, but also ridiculously embarrassing. I'd hated standing in that little glass office like a goldfish in a bowl, waiting for the nurse to hand me my pills while my entire class filed past on their way to lunch. It wasn't like that here. Over half of us had to take some kind of medication, or have a treatment done. Plus, Nurse Betsy kind of rocked, and watching her in action was better than some circuses I'd been to.

We got to her cabin and had to wait in line behind a few girls from the Swallowtail cabin and four of the Monarch girls. My built-in Molly radar went off, and I'm not proud of it, but all thoughts of Murphy's predicament vanished. Of course, as soon as I saw her, I did my best to pretend like I hadn't. I laughed too loudly at Anthony's joke and punched Murphy's arm a bit too hard after retelling the story of Hank's toe rescuing us. All the while I watched Molly out of the corner of my eye. She made it to the front of the line and caught the small pill cup that came flying toward her. She dumped them unceremoniously into her mouth and chased them down with water like a pro. Then she turned and our eyes met. I froze, my heart stopped beating, and the world around us came to a screeching halt. If meeting her eyes made my heart feel like it was about to explode, what would actually kissing her feel like? Then it was over. She turned back to her friend, and I looked down at my feet as though they were the most interesting things in the world.

My distraction cost me as my own cup of pills collided with my forehead. Nurse Betsy raised an amused eyebrow from her perch behind her desk, but thankfully didn't comment. Anthony stepped away from us, pulling his shirt over his head as a squirt bottle full of green flame retardant followed him into the spray area. I swallowed my pills while Murphy went into a separate room to upload his daily time-travel report.

No sooner had he disappeared than there was a commotion outside the cabin. We all turned, and Nurse Betsy lost her friendly smile as Mr. Blue entered with two TTBI officers behind him. It wasn't Brawny and Burly from drop-off, but these guys with their dark suits and no-nonsense expressions were just as intimidating. Mr. Blue nodded at Nurse Betsy and led the two men into the room Murphy had just disappeared into, shutting the door behind them with an ominous click that I felt in my bones. Anthony came out a minute later, the sharp smell of the flame-retardant spray quickly overtaking the otherwise pleasant pine smell of the office.

"What happened?" he asked when he saw me. I wasn't sure what my expression had looked like, but I tried to reorganize it into something more acceptable. Murphy had told me something he shouldn't have, and here I was probably wearing a similar expression to the one my dog wore when he pooped on the floor. Not good.

I jerked my head at the closed door. "We need to wait for Murphy. Some guys from the TTBI just showed up to talk to him."

"You don't need to wait for Murphy," Nurse Betsy cut in as she kindly but firmly guided us toward the door. "He'll come back to the cabin when he's finished."

I hesitated, and she furrowed her brow as her arms crossed over her chest. "You heard me," she said. "Hustle or you'll be late for lights-out."

I thought about protesting, but Nurse Betsy wasn't someone you argued with. Anthony and I ran back up the hill, barely making it inside before lights-out. There was just enough time for Hank to send me an alarmed look when he noticed Murphy's absence. I shook my head, and was saved from an explanation when Murphy walked in five minutes later. His face was white and pinched and did absolutely nothing to reassure me. He threw on his pajamas and crawled into his bunk, rolling to face the wall without saying a word to any of us. I think Hank and I were the only ones who noticed, but as I lay floating above my bunk, I kept replaying the conversation with Murphy over and over again in my head. Well, that and my moment of eye contact with Molly. As it was, I didn't slide into sleep until well after midnight.

It felt like only moments later that I was woken up

by a hand covering my mouth. Fearing a repeat of initiation night, I panicked, sat up swinging, and walloped Hank in the face with my flailing fist. Even though it must have hurt, he didn't cry out. He just clutched his eye for a minute, breathing hard, before slapping me on the back of the head and motioning for me to follow him. A quick glance at my watch showed that it was 3:00 a.m., and I stopped feeling bad for hitting Hank. I lay there a second, debating ignoring him and going back to sleep, but instead I slipped on my vest, unstrapped myself from the bed, and tiptoed past a sleeping Eli and into the silent woods. When we were a safe distance away, Hank sat down on a stump, grinning up at me.

"I guarantee I have a killer black eye tomorrow. Thanks for that. You're lucky the ladies love a bad boy."

"Sorry," I huffed, "sort of." I sat down across from him, my back against a tree. A mosquito buzzed obnoxiously in my ear, and I slapped at it as I glared at Hank in the moonlight. His pajama pants were too short by about five inches, and he was right, he was going to have a killer black eye. I'd never hit anyone before. Did this count since I'd done it when I was still half asleep?

"Why was Murphy late coming back from the nurse's cabin?" Hank asked. "I about pooped myself when you and Anthony walked in without him."

"These two TTBI agents showed up with Mr. Blue while we were there. I'm guessing to talk about his time traveling this afternoon," I said, stifling a yawn that felt like it was capable of cracking my face in two. My eyes felt gritty, and I hunched my shoulders against the cool night breeze as I scowled at Hank. "Please tell me you didn't wake me up in the middle of the night and drag me out here to ask a question you could have asked in the morning?"

Hank shook his head and thrust something under my nose.

I blinked down at the paper, trying to figure out what was written there. No luck. "What is it?" I asked.

"It's a plan to save Murphy," Hank said, as though this should have been obvious. "What did you think it was? A treasure map?"

I shot him an exasperated look. "In case you hadn't noticed, it's the middle of the night. This could be the Declaration of Independence for all I know." I peered back down at the paper again and gave up. "Just tell me. What's the plan?"

"Well, he disappears when he time travels, right?" Hank said as though he was talking to someone who wasn't all there.

"Right," I replied warily.

"Well, we need to find some way to keep him from

doing that." Hank grinned as though he'd just cured cancer.

"That's it?" I asked. "Your plan is to stop him from time traveling?"

"Well, it's a little more elaborate than that," Hank said, "but I figure with your brains and my ingenuity, we'll think of something. I already listed ten different ideas."

"So just to clarify," I said, "you dragged me out of bed in the middle of the night to show me a list I can't even read?"

Hank nodded. "Yes."

"You're insane."

Hank shrugged. "Debatable. I couldn't sleep, so I decided to use the time to brainstorm. You snore, by the way. Not sure if you knew that. Anyway, it was the only thing I could think of. I can't exactly bring this up around the other guys, and Murphy is so edgy about the whole thing. Plus, isn't there something, I don't know, *cool* about a late-night meeting in the woods?"

"No." I frowned. "This is how horror movies start. Two kids alone, in the dark, in the woods."

Hank waved a hand dismissively. "You worry too much. Just tell me what you think."

"What's this first one say?" I asked resignedly, squinting down at the paper.

"Tackle Murphy," Hank said. "I figure those fancy-pants time-travel specialists have probably tried all sorts of crazy stuff, but I'm betting nobody has tried the obvious stuff! Number seven involves a massive amount of marinara sauce, so that one might be a bit tricky. For number nine we're going to need to get our hands on some superglue."

I stared at him for a second, realized he was serious, and shrugged. "If you say so, but I'm only agreeing because I don't have any better ideas."

"That's the spirit!" Hank grinned as he sprang to his feet. "Now let's get back to the cabin. I'm getting eaten alive." I nodded, shuffling obediently after Hank, his list of ideas crammed in my pocket. I doubted any of them would work, but I was willing to try.

Dear Mom and Dad and whatever snoopy TTBI agent screens this letter before you read it,

I know I promised to write more, but things have just been so busy these first few weeks. I'll try to do better. I've made some good friends. There is this kid named Hank, and he's absolutely nuts, but in a good way. Although he seems to be getting nuttier as camp goes on. Yesterday, he managed to spill an entire jar of marinara sauce on my head right before I ██████████ ███████████████████.

█████████████████████████████████████

███████████████████████████████

██████████████████████ Isn't that crazy? There is another kid here named Emerson who I think you'd both approve of a bit more than Hank. He's kind of a klutz though. Three days ago he was messing with some superglue during one of our survival crafts and managed to get about half of our hands stuck to this big rock. Of course, I time traveled then and ████████████ ██████████████████.

██████████████████████████████

Other than that he's pretty cool. He and I entered the tetherball tournament two days ago and got third place. We would have probably lost our last match if Gary's glove hadn't flown off right when he was about to hit the ball. His hand got stuck, and we had to cut the ball down so he could walk around with it attached to his hand for the next four hours. Whatever, we still got third. Miss you guys. Thank you again for letting me come to camp. It's been great. I'll write more soon. Although I'll be seeing you when I travel ████████████ ██████████████████████ so try not to worry too much!

Love, Murph

CHAPTER NINE

Seeing Hank's list in the light of day didn't make his plan any more impressive. If anything, every time he pulled out the crumpled piece of paper to peer down at the ridiculousness written there, I cringed. Besides that, Murphy didn't really appreciate our efforts, although so far we'd been able to disguise most of them as accidents. That part at least was easier than I'd hoped. At Camp O there was almost always some minor catastrophe that needed to be handled, and it wasn't uncommon to see a pack of counselors running from one end of the camp to the other carrying some bizarre piece of specialized equipment to deal with a camper's out-of-control RISK factor.

Our most recent attempt to keep Murphy from time traveling had been particularly disastrous and had landed all three of us extra KP duty, a fact that Gary felt the need to gloat about and rub in our faces at every opportunity. Well, that and that Hank had managed to attract an entire hive of bees with the honey we'd smeared all over the place. The extra KP duty meant that we were fifteen minutes late leaving the dining hall.

"It's pointless to head back to the cabin now," Hank said. "By the time we got our suits on we'd barely have a chance to swim, and I'm sure the tetherball court is packed."

"Well, what do you want to do, then?" Murphy asked. "And don't say archery, because the last time we did that you got distracted and almost shot Emerson."

"I did not almost shoot Emerson," Hank said. I raised what was left of my right eyebrow at him, and he smiled. "Okay, okay, my arrow got a little close. But those two girls from the Swallowtail cabin did come over and talk to us afterward."

"They were worried you'd poked out Emerson's eye," Murphy said. I snorted and rubbed gingerly at the newly healed gash. I really hoped that eyebrow grew back.

"Let's head to the lake," Hank said. "There might

be a few fishing poles left we can sign out." He tapped his pocket conspiratorially and winked at us. "I just stocked up on my special bait." Hank refused to use a worm, something about having one named Walter the Worm as a pet when he was a kid, and used a hot dog instead. It was usually a few days old and pretty funky by the time he threaded a chunk on his hook, but he caught more fish than the rest of us, so what did I know?

"Sounds good," Murphy agreed. We could hear the laughter, shouts, and splashes of other campers before we saw them as we descended the steep concrete steps down to the lake. Shaped like a long, narrow kidney bean, one end was roped off for swimming, with a sandy beach sloping gently into the water, but farther on was the boathouse, with canoes and fishing poles.

Hank's sharp elbow connected with my ribs, and he pointed excitedly toward the lake. I winced. If he kept this up I was going to develop a permanent bruise there.

"What?" I asked, rubbing the offending spot.

"Wait," Murphy said, slapping a hand over his eyes. "Let me guess. The girls are swimming."

"Wrong," Hank said. "But close." I glanced out at the lake and spotted a small grouping of canoes on the far end, all filled with the bright-orange T-shirts of the Monarch cabin. When I looked back, Hank was already charging down the remaining steps to the lake and heading toward the boathouse at a run.

"Do we follow him?" Murphy asked.

I shrugged. "He hasn't killed us yet."

Murphy snorted and shook his head, but we followed Hank. By the time we got there he was already on his way back out, holding two paddles and a bucket.

"Where are you going?" I asked, craning my neck to see into the boathouse where the canoes were usually tied up.

"They've all been checked out already," Hank said. "It took some sweet-talking, but Greg, the counselor for the White Oaks, said that we could use one of the retired canoes."

"Retired canoes?" Murphy repeated. "Where does a canoe go to retire?" Hank ignored him, already striding around to the back side of the boathouse. We hurried after him and found Hank standing with his hands on his hips surveying the waist-deep tangle of weeds and grasses that stretched out behind the boathouse and up the hill. It took me a second to spot the overturned canoes, their chipped wooden bottoms looking like little islands in the sea of green.

"Took you two long enough," Hank said, stooping to grab the rim of the one closest to us. He waited until

Murphy and I had each grabbed an edge and nodded. "On the count of three, lift. It will be easier to slide into the lake than carry it. One, two, three!" The decrepit old wood creaked in protest, but the canoe flipped, and Hank let out a shriek that made me jump backward. I looked left and right, certain that a rabid bear or something equally terrifying must be charging toward us. Instead I saw Hank clinging to the low-hanging roof of the boathouse as he did his best to get his long spindly legs up around his ears. And then I looked down. Underneath the canoe was a huge pile of snakes. There had to be hundreds of them, most no more than a foot or so long, all slithering and tangled together like knotted string. I screamed and jumped onto the closest thing available, which happened to be Murphy's back, as the snakes disentangled themselves and slithered away into the grass.

We stood there a few more seconds, frozen, as we looked at the canoe-shaped patch of dead grass that had apparently been hosting a snake party. Hank dropping down from the roof snapped us out of it. It took me another minute before I finally climbed down off Murphy's back.

"Did I just die and end up in an Indiana Jones movie?" Hank asked, shaking his head. "Geez, I'm going to have nightmares about those things for weeks!

Well, hustle to it, boys. This canoe isn't going to drag itself." It took him a second to notice that Murphy and I hadn't moved. "What's the holdup?" he asked, looking from Murphy's white face to mine and back again.

"We're still doing this?" Murphy asked, his voice a squeak. "After the snakes?!"

Hank looked around the now vacant grass and shrugged. "Well, I wasn't planning on bringing them with us. Now hurry it up, or we won't even make it to the girls before it's time to come in."

Maybe it was the shock, or just pure stupidity, but Murphy and I numbly grabbed ahold of either side of the canoe and followed Hank to the lake. Before I knew it, we were in the water, Hank in the front, Murphy in the middle, and me in the back as we rowed out toward the bobbing herd of non-snake-infested canoes on the far side of the lake. My stomach did that weird little twist of excitement thing it always did when I thought I might get to see Molly, and I felt grateful that I'd remembered to switch out of my vest and into the ankle weights I used for swimming. Not that the vest was that bad—it beat my old shoes by a mile—but still, it was nice not to have it on for a change.

It was that preoccupation with Molly that kept me from noticing the water coming in until there was a solid six inches of it sloshing around my feet.

"Hank!" I yelped. "We need to turn back. We have a leak!"

"I got it covered," Hank said, tossing the bucket I'd noticed earlier to Murphy. "Greg mentioned these might not be exactly seaworthy. So get bailing, Murph. You should be able to bail faster than it comes in. The hole is small."

"The hole?" Murphy said, "You knew this thing had a hole, and you didn't tell us?"

Hank shrugged and grinned over his shoulder. "Hey, guys," he said. "The canoe has a hole."

"Think anyone will notice if we drown him?" Murphy muttered with a dirty look at the back of Hank's semi-invisible head.

Before I could reply we had coasted right into the middle of the Monarch cabin's canoes, and I stopped worrying about the water around my feet.

"Hello, my beauties!" Hank called, standing up so that we rocked wildly from side to side. The girls turned, and I saw Molly sitting in the front of her canoe, a black baseball hat pulled low over her dark wavy hair.

"What are you guys doing out here?" asked a blond girl. "I thought you three had to scrub tables?"

I winced. I'd been hoping that no one else had noticed the incident with the honey.

"Uh, Hank?" Murphy said. "We have a problem."

"What my time-traveling friend meant to say was that you all look wonderful today," Hank said. "I don't know if I've ever given all of you a proper introduction, but we are three of the Red Maple men. I'm Hank, and this is Emerson and Murphy, and we are here to assist if any of you ladies have need!"

"Assist us?" a pretty redhead I think was named Abby said, with a meaningful look at our ancient canoe. "I think you might want to assist yourself."

"Nonsense!" Hank said. "But if you don't need help, then how about some entertainment?" He immediately broke into the chorus of an old Justin Bieber song, and even though he looked ridiculous, considering his invisible arms and neck, I had to admit that he wasn't half bad. The girls all watched with the same peculiar look on their faces, like they were trying hard not to laugh out loud.

"Hank! Emerson!" Murphy said, and there was something in his voice that finally succeeded in tearing my eyes away from the girls. I turned to find Murphy bailing hard, but without any noticeable effect. The water was almost up to my seat. Not sure what else to do, I cupped my hands together and started splashing water out, succeeding in getting more on Murphy and Hank than actually out of the boat. By now the girls were doubled over laughing, their faces red and their eyes streaming as our sad old canoe gave up the fight and sank completely. To his credit, Hank went down singing.

As we swam back to shore, the girls paddling around us in a loose circle, I had a hard time being as mad at Hank as I probably should have been since thanks to his stunt, all the girls, including Molly, now knew my name. They laughed and joked with us the entire way back, and I decided that being Emerson, that kid who sank the canoe with Hank, was a big improvement over being Emerson, that weird kid who floats.

CHAPTER TEN

A few weeks later I came into our cabin after my nightly visit to Nurse Betsy's to find Eli standing like a conductor in the middle of our cabin, tossing a football back and forth from one boy to another. I grinned, ducked the flying ball, and hurried into the bathroom to brush my teeth.

Hank crept in and quickly checked to make sure the showers were empty before walking up to stand at the sink next to mine. He had his *up to something* look on.

"What?" I asked, wondering if he'd come up with some new scheme to save Murphy. So far, nothing we'd tried had worked, and I knew Hank was just as tempted as I was to break our promise and tell the other guys.

"We're sneaking out tonight," he whispered.

"If you want to talk about a new Murphy plan, just tell me now," I hissed. "As much fun as stomping around the woods in the middle of the night with you is, I think I'll pass."

Hank shook his head. "It's not just us this time. It involves girls. The Monarch girls, to be exact." I shifted my train of thought away from Murphy.

"I'm listening," I said. Hank gave his teeth one last scrub, spit into the sink, and leaned forward to inspect them. Unfortunately the bottom half of his face went invisible at that moment, defeating the purpose of the gesture.

"Dang it," he muttered. "I really hate when that happens." He turned to me, and I realized that I no longer found it weird to talk to someone without a completely visible face. Odd how that had happened. Hank was smiling—even though his mouth was invisible, there was something about the way his eyes crinkled that made it obvious.

He leaned in conspiratorially. "So tonight we're going to meet the Monarch girls down by the lake for a bonfire. I'm checking *bonfire with hot chicks* off my life list, and so are you. I set it up with that cute blonde who had the purple feathers from initiation night. Remember? Her name is Kristy, and she is smoking hot."

"I thought you liked Molly," I whispered as Eli's laughter drifted in from the cabin.

"I do like Molly. That's not what I meant. She is *literally* smoking hot. If you touch her you could get like third-degree burns or whatever. French-kissing her would be like licking a frying pan. Crazy, right?"

"How are we going to sneak out?" I asked, my insides doing a funny little jump at the idea of seeing Molly.

"You leave it to me," Hank whispered. "I think Eli might be onto us, though, so we're going to have to be ninja sneaky. All you have to do is wait for my signal and trust me."

I cocked an eyebrow at him. "Ninja sneaky? Have you been hanging around Zeke too much? That's his line, dude."

"Dude?" Hank grinned. "I think you've been hanging around me too much." He ran back into the cabin, calling for Eli to throw him the football. I turned back to the mirror to finish brushing my teeth and stared at myself for a second. The kid looking back at me was almost unrecognizable. Old Emerson had always had a sickly yellow look to his skin from spending too much time in a dark basement playing video games. Camp Emerson had a tan, freckles, and a gnarly scar above his eye. I smirked at the new Emerson in the mirror.

Hank was right. I had been hanging around him too much.

Eli did know we were up to something. After lights-out, he settled down at a small desk in the corner of the cabin to read by the light of a tiny lamp. Which wasn't that abnormal, but he kept scanning the room suspiciously, staying up long past when he normally went to bed.

Directly across from me I could see Hank lying stick-straight in the worst imitation of sleep I'd ever seen. Deciding that the signal might be a long time coming, I settled in to wait. Two hours later, just before midnight, Eli turned off his light and crawled into his own bunk. The minutes dragged on, and I fought to stay awake.

It wasn't until Eli began to snore quietly that I saw it. The signal. Unfortunately I saw it right as it smacked into my face. Hank couldn't see me in the dark, but I glared in his general direction anyway, then looked down at the object that had hit me. It was a bungee cord. I understood. A few careful knots tethered it to my ankle, and I untied all but one of my sleeping belts. I went to slip into my vest, but the hook it usually hung on was empty. I was just looking around for something to throw at Hank when an invisible hand grabbed the bungee around my ankle and unhooked the last belt tying me to the bed. Suddenly I was floating along the ceiling, being pulled rapidly toward the door. I remembered the cabin's ancient ceiling fan just in time and ducked, covering my head protectively with my hands.

In the glow of the moonlight shining through the window, I caught sight of Gary and Anthony crawling across the floor of the cabin on their bellies while Zeke slid along the wall, a tiny black-and-white shadow at his heels. Apparently Mr. Stink was not willing to be left behind on another late-night adventure. Murphy was nowhere in sight. One by one everyone slipped out the window, except me. I was left bobbing along the ceiling doing my lame abandoned-balloon imitation. Then Hank apparently remembered and yanked me unceremoniously through the window. I managed to grab ahold of the outside of the frame and hung there upside down while a now visible Hank reeled me in like some absurd fish.

When Hank finally had me at ground level, Anthony appeared and gingerly handed me my vest, careful, as always, not to get too close in case he caught fire. I wondered momentarily what it must be like to go through life like that. Could his mother even hug him without worrying about third-degree burns?

"How did you get my vest out here?" I whispered as I gratefully buckled its straps.

"Hank threw it out the window earlier in the night," Anthony explained.

I narrowed my eyes at Hank. "Don't do that again."

"Shhhhhh," Hank hissed, his fingers pressed to his lips. "Gary, did you get the stuff?"

Gary held up a red gasoline container. "Got it."

We'd discovered that Gary had sticky fingers in more than the literal way. So far it had just been extra servings of cake spirited off another cabin's tray and onto our own. This was the first big thing he'd taken. I stared at the gasoline can dubiously. It made me nervous, especially in his hands.

"Wait," I said. "Where's Murphy?"

"He didn't want to come." Zeke shrugged. "Said he'd rather sleep." His absence made me even more nervous about this adventure. Murphy had been all about checking things off his life list. Why would he pass up this opportunity? Did he know something that we didn't?

"Well, if he's not going," I said, hedging, "maybe I should stay here too."

Hank rolled his eyes in exasperation. "Murphy's coming. Just give me a second." He blinked out of view, and his T-shirt and shorts fell to the ground.

"Do you think he's naked so much because he likes it, or because of the whole invisibility thing?" I asked.

"I think he just doesn't care," Anthony said. "Remember when he went streaking through the dining hall last week? He was invisible, but he was still naked." I rolled my eyes at the memory. If Hank's ear hadn't showed up at the last second, he would have gotten away with it.

There was a muffled whine from inside the cabin, and a moment later an invisible hand boosted Mr. Stink out the window. I blinked—it wasn't every day you saw a levitating skunk.

Zeke smacked his head. "I knew I was forgetting something. Sorry, buddy." Mr. Stink glared at us before trotting over to Zeke, his black-and-white-striped tail held in an indignant arc over his head. A second later Murphy followed, being dragged by an invisible Hank.

"I told you I didn't want to come," Murphy muttered, rubbing the sleep from his eyes. The ratty black T-shirt he slept in hung on his thin frame, making him look even skinnier than usual. He'd time traveled earlier in the day, but I hadn't been there when it happened or when he showed back up. He hadn't been himself since. Not that I could blame him. It couldn't be fun never knowing if today was your last day.

"If you don't come, you can't check *bonfire with hot chicks* off your list," Hank wheedled, slipping his T-shirt back over his now visible head. "Besides, if you don't come, Emerson won't come. Do you want

167

the poor boy to be stuck at the adolescent life-list age of ten forever?" Murphy looked like he wanted to say something, but then he pressed his lips together and shook his head in resignation.

"Let's get this over with," he sighed.

Hank grinned and clapped him on the back. "Brilliantly positive outlook there, Murph! Let's go, men." He disappeared into the woods. The night was full of the sounds of crickets and frogs, and lightning bugs flashed and blinked around our knees like tiny UFOs as we crept through the sleeping trees down to the lake. We walked in single file, and I brought up the rear right behind Zeke. Mr. Stink was riding in his accustomed place, wrapped around Zeke's neck and shoulders like some exotic fur cape. I was absentmindedly wondering if my mom would ever let me have a skunk for a pet when all of a sudden Mr. Stink jumped to the ground and started chattering angrily, pawing at Zeke's pant leg. Zeke froze and sat down so fast that I tripped over him, yelping as I took a surprise header into the bushes.

"What's going on?" Hank asked as he circled back around, the beam of his flashlight throwing weird shadows off the surrounding trees.

"No clue," I grumbled as I picked myself up and attempted to brush the worst of the mud and sticks off my pajama pants. They were my best ones, specially chosen for this midnight meeting with the Monarch girls, and I was pretty sure I'd just ripped a hole in the knee.

Zeke turned his head in our direction, and I jumped as the flashlight lit up his face. His eyes had gone black, the pupils stretching and expanding until there was almost no white showing.

"Can you see?" Hank asked, catching on faster than the rest of us. Mr. Stink sat protectively on Zeke's lap, his head turning back and forth as he checked for danger. I'd known he was Zeke's service animal, but I'd never seen him in action before.

"Well," Zeke said, "right now I can only see through solid objects, which means that I can see what's on the other side of each of these trees, which does me absolutely no good, but other than that? No. I'm going to need someone to help me if we are going to make it down to that bonfire."

Anthony and Gary threw their hands up, making the universal *not it* gesture. Murphy stepped forward to grab Zeke's left arm while I grabbed his right. Together we helped him navigate his way through the trees and over fallen branches, Mr. Stink at our heels watching the whole process disapprovingly. Luckily Zeke's X-ray-vision episode lasted only a few minutes, and by the time we got to the edge of the woods by the lake he was able to walk on his own again.

Next to the lake was a large dirt circle with a stone fire pit built in the middle. Hank walked around it, hands on his hips as though surveying a ship, before ordering us to collect wood for the fire while he and Zeke rolled rocks over to use as makeshift seats. His job done for the time being, Mr. Stink wandered over to paw under a fallen log, presumably looking for a snack. Unfortunately the wood we collected was soggy from rain earlier in the day. But we doggedly built it into a pyramid shape the way Eli had shown us on one of our many survival hikes.

"I wish we had marshmallows," Anthony said as he stuffed twigs into the gaps between the larger logs.

"Got it covered." Gary grinned and produced a large bag of marshmallows from underneath his shirt. "There are benefits to having KP duty every other night."

"If you weren't such a pain in the rear, Eli might not stick you with KP duty so often," I pointed out.

Gary raised an eyebrow. "Behavior problem, remember? I have a reputation to uphold." He threw the bag of marshmallows at my head. I attempted to catch it, but they sailed right past my hands, bounced off my face, and hit the ground.

"Hey, Emerson," Anthony called, "we need more big pieces of wood. Could you find us a few?"

Before heading back into the woods, I picked up the bag and launched it at Gary. He was turned the other way, and it thumped off the back of his head. I would pay for that later, but it would be worth it.

"How are we going to light this?" I asked five minutes later, after adding my sticks to the pile. "Even I know that wet wood won't light."

"That's why we brought this," Zeke said, holding up the can of gasoline.

"Isn't that stuff pretty dangerous?" I asked, taking a self-conscious step back.

"Chill out, E-dawg. We only need a tiny bit," Hank said. He took the can from Zeke and proceeded to splash a small amount over the top of the wood. He noticed me still eyeing it warily, so he sighed and moved the gas can ten feet away, so it sat at the edge of the lake. "Feel better now, Emerson? You're as touchy as an overcaffeinated squirrel."

I snorted. "You see a lot of overcaffeinated squirrels?"

"Not anymore. My mom made me stop giving them Mountain Dew, said it was animal cruelty," he replied with a straight face. I stared at him, trying to decide if he was serious or just messing with me. It was a fine line with Hank.

"Mountain Dew?" Murphy asked.

"Oh yeah, they're fiends for the stuff. Real bad for their teeth though." He moved one last stick into place and motioned grandly toward the pile. "Anthony, would you do the honors?"

"With pleasure." Anthony grinned and shut his eyes. We took a step back as his right hand caught fire. He quickly thrust it into the pile of wood, which began crackling and snapping. Everyone cheered.

"Add a year, gentlemen," Hank said. "A bonfire with hot chicks has been achieved. Please congratulate me on turning one hundred and five."

"This doesn't count yet," Zeke said. "Unless girls show up, this is just a midnight bonfire with a bunch of dudes."

"True," Hank admitted. "And, may I say, excellent usage of *dude* there. I approve. Maybe I'm only one hundred four and a half then."

"Now all we need are the girls, and we can age that last half year," Zeke said as he fed a marshmallow to Mr. Stink.

"They won't be here for at least an hour," Hank said, grabbing the marshmallow bag and shoving four of them onto a stick before thrusting the whole thing into the fire.

"An hour?" Gary yelped. "Why did we rush out here, then?"

"Two reasons," Hank said, expertly blowing out a flaming marshmallow. "The first is that there is something magical about midnight. A one a.m. bonfire just doesn't have the same ring to it. And second, we have something important to discuss without the womenfolk around."

"Did you really just say *womenfolk*?" I asked.

"Affirmative, my faulty floating friend." Hank grinned. "Do you want to start or should I?"

I frowned at him, confused. "It would help if I knew what you are talking about."

"Right." Hank nodded, and he turned to the rest of the guys. "It's like this," he said. "Murphy's going to die, and we have to save him."

CHAPTER ELEVEN

I inhaled in surprise and choked on the marshmallow I'd popped in my mouth seconds before. Had Hank really just said that? Coughing and gagging, I turned to Murphy, who looked just as shocked as I was. There was a moment of stunned silence before every guy in the Red Maple cabin started talking at once. Hank motioned for us to be quiet and walked over to throw an arm around a very angry Murphy's shoulders.

"Sorry, man," he said. "Had to be done. We are all your friends, and we all want to help. Emerson and I found out a few weeks ago," he went on. "I thought maybe we could keep our promise and figure out a solution on our own, but so far all we've managed to do is come up with a bunch of ideas that haven't worked. So we are bringing in the big guns. You guys. We need to prevent Murphy from time traveling, because sometime between now and the last day of camp he's going to time travel and not come back. So start brainstorming, boys. We have a job to do."

"Stop it," Murphy snapped, shrugging out from under Hank's arm. "I don't want your help. Don't you get that? If I wanted to sit around talking about dying, I would have stayed home with my parents." Everyone stared at him. Soft-spoken Murphy had never yelled.

"We're just trying to help," Hank said, completely unfazed by Murphy's outburst. "It's what friends do. You don't really have an option."

Murphy sighed. "I get that, but you have to see this from my point of view. What you just did, Hank, could get *all* of you guys in serious trouble. And on top of that, what you are trying to do could potentially ruin the entire reason I came here. I don't want to think about dying. I want to live . . . as much as I can before . . ." He swallowed hard and looked down. There was an awkward silence as everyone processed this. I remembered how I'd felt the day Murphy had told me his secret, like I'd just swallowed a poisonous snake, my stomach in knots as my brain tried to make sense of it all. Gary's face in particular looked almost

175

pained as he worked through what Murphy said.

"Am I the only one who's confused?" Zeke finally said. "You're telling us that you've known Murphy was doomed since almost the first week of camp?"

"Friends keep friends' secrets," Hank said.

"They are supposed to," Murphy said with a look at Hank. "Traitor."

"Why'd you tell them and not us?" Anthony asked, sounding more than a little hurt. "We're your friends too."

"In my defense," Murphy said, "I really only told Emerson. I'd just come back from"—he swallowed hard and blinked—"well, from a really bad time-travel trip, and I told him. I shouldn't have. Trust me. I regret it. But Mr. I'm-Invisible-When-Naked-and-I'm-Naked-All-the-Time over there overheard everything."

"Wait a minute," Anthony said with an accusing glare at Hank, "is that why you and Emerson have been acting so weird?"

"Acting weird?" Gary asked. "Dude, Hank invented weird."

"Thank you," Hank said with a gracious dip of his head in Gary's direction.

Murphy scowled at Hank, probably remembering all the random times we'd tackled him, dumped stuff on him, or attempted to grab him before he time traveled. "I figured as much," he said. "Did you ever think that in your well-meaning but misguided attempts to save me . . . you might just be what kills me?" Hank's mouth snapped shut on whatever he'd been about to say, a look of gobsmacked horror on his face. "I'm kidding," Murphy relented. "Kind of. But you all need to just forget what you heard. It's bad enough that I have the TTBI crawling all over camp every time I travel. If they find out what Hank just did"—he winced—"what I did by confiding in Emerson in the first place, you can kiss the rest of your summer good-bye."

The top of Anthony's head had caught on fire, but he didn't seem to notice as he shook it back and forth. "Hank's right. You have to let us help. You're our friend."

"If you really want to help, then help me check a few more things off my life list," Murphy said. "That's all the help I want. I think I have at least a few more weeks, and I don't want to die having only reached the age of eighteen."

"But—" I began to protest. Murphy held up a hand to silence me.

"No buts. I'm here to live. Not to talk about dying. Got it?"

I didn't get it. Not one bit. If I knew I was going

to float away, I'd do everything I could to stop it. Life was too precious not to fight for. Why wouldn't Murphy fight?

"We got it," Hank said, but from behind Murphy's back he gave a big overexaggerated wink. Every guy in the circle nodded, but while Murphy relaxed, convinced we were agreeing to go along with his wishes, I knew that those nods were for Hank.

"You might not die," Gary grumbled. "You might just get stuck somewhere. I get stuck places all the time. Getting stuck sucks."

"You should make that into a bumper sticker." Hank grinned.

"I might." Gary nodded. "It has a certain ring to it. Just for the record, though, I'm not going to jail or whatever for this."

"Your loyalty is heartwarming, Gary," Hank said. "Really. You could have been a collie in a past life." I looked from Hank's grinning face to Gary's scowling one to Murphy's angry one and then at the rest of the guys illuminated in the flickering light of the fire. Anthony seemed lost in thought, while Zeke hadn't taken his eyes off Murphy, his thick glasses reflecting the crackling bonfire as he absentmindedly stroked a sleeping Mr. Stink. And in that moment, seeing the familiar worry and determination spread across my friends' faces, I felt better. Hank and I weren't in this alone, and for the first time in a while, I felt hopeful.

"So, what's left on your life list?" Zeke asked Murphy, interrupting my thoughts.

"Let's take a look," Hank said, pulling from his pocket the small notebook where he'd been keeping track of our respective life-list ages. I peered over his shoulder at Murphy's list. Murphy was officially eighteen, four years older than everyone but Hank. But Hank didn't count, as he'd had a head start.

Murphy Swift
~~Go to summer camp and make friends~~
Lasso a pig
~~Zip line~~
~~Perfect the swan dive~~
~~Hold breath underwater for two minutes~~
French-kiss a girl
Learn to juggle
Skinny dip
Capture a flag
Win capture the flag
~~Complete ropes course~~
Catch a five-pound bass

~~Learn how to build a fire~~
~~Learn how to do a backflip~~
Shave hair into a Mohawk
Be in a movie
Jump off a bridge
~~Hit the bull's-eye in archery~~
~~Dive to the bottom of the lake~~
Canoe down a river
Skydive
Run a marathon
Jump over a fire

There were thirty more things, but a lot of them involved stuff like climbing Mount Everest and exploring the rain forest. Mr. Stink waddled over to inspect the list and sneezed.

"Bless you," Hank said, turning to Murphy. "So where do you want to start? I'm partial to the Mohawk idea myself." Murphy was about to respond when he froze, the blood draining from his face as he clutched his stomach and disappeared.

Panic clawed at my insides as I stared at the spot he'd been in moments before. What if this was it?

"He'll come back," Zeke said as though he'd read my mind.

"How do you know?" Hank asked.

"Don't you remember?" Zeke asked. "He was wearing a black T-shirt and flannel pants." When no one said anything he sighed. "Initiation night? Future Murphy saved Emerson's life? Remember? He was wearing that exact outfit. I can't believe I didn't notice it earlier."

"Phew," Hank said, sinking down onto one of the rocks perched around the fire. "That's a relief. But, just to clarify before he comes back, we *are* going to bust our butts to save him. Right?"

"Right," everyone said in unison, even Gary, which honestly was a bit of a surprise.

Before we could say anything else, Murphy appeared with a small pop. He caught sight of us and doubled over, laughing.

"What's so funny?" I asked. My heart hammered in my chest, stubbornly refusing to relax even though Murphy was obviously back and fine.

"*We* were!" he howled, his face beet red. "I forgot how incredibly stupid we looked in those dresses. Emerson, you had that bow on your butt, and Gary, those ruffles." His laughter was contagious as we relived the night that had cemented our friendship. The moment was bittersweet, though, at least for me. Murphy had saved my life that night, and while life listing was great and all, it wasn't going to save his.

"Speaking of dresses," Hank said when we'd all

managed to catch our breath, "I think I hear the girls now." We fell silent in anticipation, scanning the woods for the first sign of the Monarch cabin. The yellow arc of a flashlight cut through the trees, and my heart skipped a beat at the thought of seeing Molly. A second later, I registered that the voices I was hearing were male . . . not female.

"It's Mr. Blue!" Hank hissed. "Quick, get rid of the gas. Put out the fire. Hide the marshmallows. We need to get out of here!" Zeke raced over and upended the gas can into the lake. Its oily contents spilled out, spreading across the surface of the water in iridescent swirls. I registered the fact that gasoline floated with a detached feeling of surprise before the panic of the situation jolted me into action. Not sure what else to do, I shoved the entire bag of marshmallows down the neck of my shirt, where they proceeded to spill, dumping the white fluffy lumps out across the ground. Dropping to my knees, I began picking them up by the handful and chucked them toward the lake.

"We can't put the fire out," Murphy yelped. "It's huge." He was right. Now that the damp wood had finally caught, the fire was almost up to my chest and crackling merrily.

"I got this," Anthony said. Bending down, he grabbed

the pyramid of sticks in his arms as though he were a kindergartner collecting blocks, took a few quick steps, and tossed them into the lake. As soon as the burning sticks hit the water there was a loud whoosh and the entire lake went up in flames. For a few brief seconds the surrounding forest was lit in an eerie red glow as the fire raced along the surface of the water, burning off the gasoline Zeke had dumped in earlier. Mr. Stink squeaked in terror and vaulted himself into Zeke's arms, and we all leaped backward with yells of alarm. And then, just as fast as it had lit, it went out, throwing us into darkness again. I blinked in amazement. I'd had no idea that water could catch fire.

"What just happened?" Gary asked, sounding as shocked as I felt.

"Holy crap," Anthony said. "I've never lit a lake on fire before."

"Any chance they didn't see that?" Hank asked, whipping his head back toward the woods, but it was too late to run.

Mr. Blue came barreling out of the woods with a very angry Eli trailing behind him. He stopped short to stare for a long moment at the smoking lake, and I forgot to breathe for a second. Then he looked at us. Then back at the lake, where the half-melted gas can still floated on the surface of the steaming water, condemning us. Mr. Blue's jaw clenched. We were so busted.

The next morning Mr. Blue handed us each a toothbrush and a cup of bleach. The smell coming from my cup reminded me of the sharp antiseptic smell of hospitals, and I wrinkled my nose in distaste.

It was time to face the music, meet our maker, take it like men. Whatever. I was pretty sure that it was going to be bad. Scratch that. I was positive. After we'd gotten caught lighting the lake on fire, we'd been marched back to our beds with promises of punishment the next morning. Eli was so disgusted he wouldn't even look at us. It was worse than if they'd just yelled and punished us right then. I looked over at the dark circles under my friends' eyes and knew that I wasn't the only one who had lain awake all night imagining the horrible things that might happen to us today.

"You want us to brush our teeth with bleach?" Gary asked. "Isn't that, like, child abuse?"

"Oh, you won't be brushing your teeth with that toothbrush. Follow me, gentlemen." Mr. Blue turned and headed straight into the bathroom we shared with the White Oak cabin. We filed in after him until we were standing shoulder to shoulder surveying the grim scene. Seven toilets sat in a low row down the middle of the room like squat porcelain soldiers. We had all learned quickly that summer that if you had to poop, you did it fast, and you hoped your neighbor did too. Also—no eye contact. Personally I was a big fan of doing my business in the middle of the night. Hank, however, had no problem with the setup and would settle himself on a porcelain throne while we all brushed our teeth and attempt to carry on a full conversation with one of us. Gary was right. Hank was epically weird.

"You will be cleaning the bathroom, gentlemen," Mr. Blue instructed. "Top to bottom. And not just this bathroom either. You will also be cleaning the bathrooms of the Silver Birches, Pines, and Redwoods."

"We have to clean all of them with *these*?" Hank held up his toothbrush.

"With those, Mr. Roberts. It's an old army tradition. I want every grout line scrubbed, every toilet bowl, every sink, and every shower drain. If these bathroom floors aren't clean enough to eat off, you'll be doing it again tomorrow."

Anthony's hand caught fire and the toothbrush he was holding melted into a puddle at his feet. The rancid smell of burned plastic almost overshadowed the room's usual smell of mold, urine, and feet, but it wasn't much of an improvement.

Mr. Blue handed him a new toothbrush. "Make sure you get that plastic off the floor before it sticks." He turned on his heel and marched out past a fuming Eli.

Eli looked at each of us, forcing us to meet his eyes. "You are all lucky Mr. Blue didn't call your parents and boot your butts out of here. We've had to return the flag we captured to the White Oak cabin, which puts us in last place. I've never had a cabin in last place before, especially not for doing something as idiotic as setting the blasted lake on fire! Instead of doing the ropes course and going swimming with the Monarch cabin today, I have to sit around and babysit while you scrub toilets."

"The Monarch cabin?!" Hank yelped. "Why didn't you tell us?"

"Because it was supposed to be a surprise!" Eli practically snarled. "Now the only surprise you geniuses will have today is how much fungus is growing on the shower drain. Nice one." He banged out the door of the bathroom, only to return a moment later with a desk chair. He threw himself into it and folded his arms menacingly. We stared at him.

"Get a move on!" he bellowed. We did. Two hours later we were almost done with our first bathroom. My hand was cramping, my knees were raw, and I'd barely avoided throwing up twice from the sheer nastiness of it all. The only things left to do were the toilets. We'd all avoided them in the same way people avoided week-old roadkill, but now it was time to get down to the real dirty work.

We stood in a line staring at the pea-green porcelain as though the toilets might attack at any moment. "Each of us only has to do one full toilet and part of another," Hank reasoned.

"Let's get this over with," Zeke said, dropping to his knees and dipping his toothbrush in his bleach cup. The first step had been taken, and we got to work.

"I shouldn't have to do any of the toilets," Murphy grumbled. "I didn't even want to go."

Something occurred to me, and I narrowed my eyes at him. "Did you know about this?" I hissed. "And you didn't warn us?"

"There's a law, remember?" Murphy muttered under his breath so only I could hear.

"Laws, shmaws," I snapped.

"Less chatter, more scrubbing," Eli called absentmindedly from where he sat reading a *Sports Illustrated*, a sleeping Mr. Stink curled up on his lap.

"I'm serious," Murphy said.

"I am too," I said. "Did you know or not?"

Murphy sighed, his voice dropping so low I could barely hear him. "All I knew was that it wasn't going to end well. Trust me, if I'd known Hank was going to blab to everyone about me, I would have done something to stop it."

"But you wouldn't have done something to stop this?" I asked, holding up my frayed toothbrush.

Murphy shrugged. "Probably not. Time-traveler laws are not something you mess with, and I'm already skating on thin ice." He shuddered, and I wondered if he was thinking about the parade of menacing TTBI agents that had come through Nurse Betsy's office to check up on him since the beginning of camp. Remembering them made my anger fizzle away, and I frowned down at my half-cleaned toilet and the surrounding floor. What did everyone do when they took a pee here? Close their eyes and spin? Yuck.

"You are going to let us help though, right?" I asked as I gingerly scrubbed at the dried-on yuck on the underside of the toilet seat.

"If you mean with my life list? Yes." Murphy nodded. "If you mean ruining the rest of my summer with crazy plans to save my life that won't work anyway? Then, no."

"Is there a suck list?" Gary asked from the other side of Murphy. "If you gain a year for everything on your life list, you should lose a year for everything on the suck list."

"What else would go on the suck list?" Anthony asked.

"Getting kneed in the family jewels comes to mind," Gary said. "But I'm sure if I thought about it, there are a lot more."

I snorted, and Gary scowled at me. "What's so funny, floaty?" he asked.

I shook my head, not taking my eyes off my toilet. "Just thinking about the bumper sticker idea from last night, you know, getting stuck sucks? I was trying to think of one for cleaning a toilet with a toothbrush."

"Dude," Gary said, shaking his head. "Why would you ever want to advertise that we did this?"

"Good point." I nodded, but there was something about that getting stuck thing that wouldn't leave me alone. It was like my brain had an itch, and no matter how many times I tried to think about something else, I kept coming back to it. I glanced away from my toilet over at Gary, whose gloved hands were busy working on something encrusted on the outside of his toilet. And like a puzzle piece clicking into place, I got it. Getting stuck sucked, but what if you were stuck in the present? What if you weren't able to time travel because you literally had someone stuck to you, anchoring you to the here and now? The idea rolled around in my brain as I continued to work. It seemed crazy, and I knew Gary would never go for it in a million years. But what if it was just crazy enough to work?

Before I could think any more about it, the door to the White Oak cabin flew open and two guys came in. They stopped short when they saw us and then burst out laughing. Doing my best to ignore them, I scrubbed harder, anxious to finish my toilet and be done with it.

Moments later the rest of the White Oak guys filed in to see what the commotion was about. Now we had an audience. Great.

"Could this get any worse?" Anthony muttered at my elbow.

"Did you really just say that?" I groaned, looking over at him. "Never say that. That's like inviting fate to crap on your head."

"I think that is a good idea, don't you, boys?" One of the White Oak guys had overheard me. And just like that, it got worse. A chubby kid named Gus stepped forward, and even though he was still ten feet away, the smell of day-old BO and dirty gym socks wafted off him in waves. I wondered if his RISK factor was somehow related to that smell, and I stifled a gag as he sauntered over to the one toilet we hadn't cleaned yet, yanked down his pants, and sat down. Murphy looked like he was about to cry, and even Hank looked a little green.

"I am never, ever, EVER, lighting a lake on fire again," Anthony said, sounding ill.

I looked over at Eli for help, but he was laughing so hard he'd fallen out of his chair, upending Mr. Stink. The little creature picked himself up and looked over at us, his nose twitching, before scurrying through the door to hide under Zeke's bed. It was too stinky in here even for a skunk.

"Well," Eli choked out, "I think you learned your lesson."

MOM! DAD!

I know that you are probably pining away for your favorite son, but I don't miss you at all! Kidding! Mom, I've had dreams about your meat loaf, and I'm not even joking. My cabin rocks. I think you'll be happy to know that I'm not the freakiest freak here—that goes to this kid Anthony, who self-combusts. Now aren't you grateful that your kid doesn't go around lighting things on fire? And no, Dad, that time in the garage with your car doesn't count. (It wasn't really even big enough to be considered a fire.)

Just yesterday we were in this crazy

nature scavenger-hunt competition. The entire camp was in on it, which was sweet because the girls' cabins barely ever do stuff at the same time as us, and I had a chance to show off some pretty slick moves if I do say so myself. Dad, I owe you one for teaching me how to do blindfolded backflips. Anyway, we had to find all this nature stuff, like a live salamander, the branch of a buckeye tree, an empty bird's nest, ten walnuts . . . you get the idea. We would have had a shot at winning if Zeke hadn't misread the list and told us that we had to find a live snake instead of a salamander. (In hindsight, we really shouldn't have given the kid with the X-ray-vision impairment the list.) We spent a good hour flipping over logs and rocks trying to find a snake, and we even looked behind the boathouse where we'd seen a whole boatload of them a few weeks before. (Literally, Dad, a boatload of snakes. Creepiest thing ever.) When Emerson finally found one, he screamed like you wouldn't believe. The only guy brave enough to pick it up was Murphy,

and he time traveled right when he was about to grab it. Which reminds me, when you send your next care package, could you put some duct tape in the box? Don't worry, I'm not going to duct tape myself to the wall again. I remember what happened last time. I also need some rope, my bike lock, and the trick handcuffs out of my old magic kit. Don't ask.
LOVE YOU!

Hank

PS Mom, I totally get now why you are always complaining to me when you have to clean the bathroom. You think that's bad? You should try scrubbing a toilet with a toothbrush. Again, probably best if you don't ask.

CHAPTER TWELVE

Despite the rotten ending to Hank's bonfire scheme, it did succeed in taking some of the weight of Murphy's secret off my shoulders. Besides, we knew we had at least a few weeks until Murphy disappeared for good, thanks to future Murphy conveniently showing up one day when we were all swimming and letting slip that he was from the last week of camp. Present Murphy acted like he was mad at his future self for it, but really, I could see he was relieved to know that he was guaranteed more time. He wasn't the only one. Even though it felt like we were working with borrowed time, every guy in our cabin was fully committed to doing anything we could to save Murphy. Unfortunately, with

Murphy so set against getting any help from us, it was nearly impossible to talk to the other guys about how we were going to do that.

Four days after the horror of the toilet scrubbing, we were sitting in a loose circle on the shore of the lake, our towels wrapped around our shoulders as we attempted to eat the ice cream sandwiches Eli had brought out for us before they melted. It wasn't going well, and long sticky drips kept running down my hand. The day was bright and hot in that muggy way summer always was in July. We had gone for a long swim down in the lake, taking turns diving to the bottom to see who could bring up the biggest rock without drowning. It was a lot more fun than it sounded when Hank first suggested it. Eli had gone back up to the dining hall to grab one more ice cream sandwich, since Mr. Stink had gotten to Zeke's before Zeke had, and I found myself wondering longingly if there were any extra ice cream sandwiches up there.

"What time is it?" Gary asked. He was stretched out on the sand, his gloved hands behind his head.

"Three," Hank said. "Two more hours until dinner-time."

Gary cracked open an eye to look at Hank, whose head was conspicuously absent, making it appear that his ice cream sandwich was being devoured by thin air. "If I didn't know any better," he said, "I'd think you could read minds."

"Who needs to read minds when they can hear your stomach grumbling clear across the lake?" Hank asked. Mr. Stink finished off the last of his pilfered ice cream sandwich and waddled over to sniff at mine, giving two short sneezes that covered what was left of it in skunk spit. I sighed and fed the rest to him. Smart skunk.

"Hey, Murph," I said, glancing over to where he sat staring at the water, his ice cream sandwich melting unnoticed onto the sand. "If you aren't going to finish that, I'll take it off your hands."

"What?" he asked, distractedly.

I rolled my eyes and opened my mouth to reply just as Murphy blinked out of view, his ice cream sandwich falling with a plop onto the sand.

"It's about dang time!" Hank said, jumping to his feet. "Quick, someone throw the rocks down."

"What?" I asked, already moving to grab the familiar bag from where Eli had left it.

"Battle plan. Strategy session. Meeting of the minds," Hank said, as though it should be obvious. "Murph has been watching us like a hawk ever since the bonfire, and Eli is almost worse. If we are going to save his skinny butt, we need a game plan, and a good one. I'm hoping you geniuses have been brainstorming."

"I know I have," Zeke said, shooing Mr. Stink away from the circle of rocks and Murphy's ruined ice cream.

"And?" Hank prompted.

Zeke shrugged. "I've got jack squat. But I have noticed something kinda interesting. You know how Mr. Stink acts right before I have an episode?" I nodded, thinking of the fuss Mr. Stink had put up last night when we were on our way back to the cabin from dinner. It had attracted a few of the girls from the Monarch cabin, who wanted to croon and cuddle the cute little skunk. Which, of course, Eli wouldn't allow, since Mr. Stink was on duty. Hank had been asking to borrow the little guy ever since, because, apparently, skunks were real chick magnets.

"Well," Zeke went on, "Mr. Stink does something weird right before Murphy disappears. At first I thought it was just a fluke, but about ten seconds before Murphy travels, Mr. Stink sneezes. Every time." I snapped my head to look at Mr. Stink, who still had the remains of my ice cream sandwich on his whiskers. He *had* sneezed right before Murphy disappeared.

"Are you sure the rat doesn't just have allergies?" Gary asked.

"I'm sure," Zeke said, running a protective hand down Mr. Stink's back.

"Well, that's a start," Hank said.

"You already tried superglue, right?" Anthony asked. "I mean, I'd like to think that Emerson didn't get half of us stuck to a rock just for kicks."

My face flushed and I shook my head. "Sorry about that."

"Maybe he should cut out gluten, dairy, and sugar," Gary said. "Oh, and artificial colors. My mom tried all of those with me at some point in an attempt to fix me."

"Not a bad idea," Hank said. "Although it might be hard to pull off without him noticing."

"Yeah," Gary said, "since, you know what you can eat on that diet?"

"What?" I asked, genuinely curious.

"Nothing," Gary said.

"Does he really think we are just going to stand by and let this happen?" Anthony asked.

Hank shrugged. "I have no idea. But as long as we don't sit around talking about him dying, I think he'll be okay."

"You mean like we are now?" Gary asked.

Hank nodded. "Exactly. He's more worried about his life list at the moment, so if we focus on helping him with that, he might not notice us trying to save him."

"Fat chance," Gary muttered.

Hank ignored him, and we spent the next few minutes furiously brainstorming ideas to save our friend. I stayed quiet, mulling over my *getting stuck sucks* plan that I'd thought up while scrubbing the toilets. One glance at Gary made it crystal clear that he would never agree to it. Gary wasn't the same scowling kid his parents had dropped off at the beginning of camp, but he wasn't exactly Mr. Sunshine either. Zeke had just suggested that Murphy take up yoga when Eli strode up with Zeke's replacement ice cream sandwich. Before he could even comment on the conspicuous circle of red rocks with a ruined ice cream sandwich sitting beside it, Murphy was back.

Eli took one look at his pale face and threw a companionable arm across his shoulders and squeezed.

"Welcome back," he said. "Would you like a new ice cream sandwich? I think I saw a few more in the freezer."

Murphy nodded, sitting down to pick up the red rocks with shaking hands. Eli turned and headed back up the hill at a trot. When all the rocks were picked up, Murphy looked around at us and raised an eyebrow. "What?" he asked. "Did I miss something important?"

"Yup," Hank said, bounding to his feet. "We found a bridge that's begging to be jumped off. Want to gain another year?" He didn't have to ask twice.

The bridge turned out to be about a five-minute hike up the small river that fed into the lake, and I grabbed Hank, pulling him back to walk with me while everyone else went on ahead.

"What's up?" he asked. "Don't worry. The water's deep under the bridge. I checked."

I shook my head. "It's not that. I have an idea to save Murphy."

"Then why didn't you speak up in the strategy meeting?" Hank said, sounding slightly annoyed. "You sat there like you'd swallowed your tongue."

"I was thinking."

"Well, you make thinking look painful," Hank said. "What's the idea?" I quickly filled him in on my *getting stuck sucks* plan.

"Now do you see why I didn't bring it up in the meeting?" I asked.

Hank nodded. "Yes. You didn't want Gary to kill you. Excellent thinking. The problem with that plan, though, is that it's only going to work once. If we stick Gary to Murphy and it actually prevents him from time traveling, we'd have to convince Gary to stay stuck to Murphy for the next few weeks."

"He might do it," I said.

"Or he might tell us to get lost," Hank said. "Besides,

Eli and Mr. Blue would have to report it to the TTBI, and who knows what would happen then. So let's keep this plan in our back pockets until we've tried everything else, and it's absolutely necessary."

"How will we know when that is?!" I asked.

"Well," Hank said, "let's just keep Gary close to Murphy the last week of camp."

"You say that like it's going to be easy," I said, thinking of how difficult it was to get Gary to do anything, let alone get him to do it without him realizing what was going on.

"We will cross that bridge when we get there," Hank said with a wink. "But right now, we have another bridge with our name on it. Operation Check Things Off Murphy's Life List has begun, and if we don't hustle we're going to miss out!"

Three minutes later we launched ourselves off a bridge into a river, which finally answered the question parents had been asking kids for ages. If all the rest of your friends jumped off a bridge, would you? Yes. Yes, we would. Unfortunately, it turned out to be illegal to jump off that particular bridge. Although in our defense, there wasn't a sign or anything. And even though Eli made us rake the sand around the lake for goose poop as our punishment, we all agreed that it was worth it.

Hi guys!

How's Europe? Bring Mr. Stink and me back something cool. It's the least you can do after going on such an awesome vacation without us. Next time you send a package from Germany, though, don't write the word GIFT on it really big. It didn't help it get through customs faster like you thought. Apparently GIFT in German means "poison" . . . so let's just say the chocolates you sent had seen better days when they finally made it here. No worries, though. The guys helped me eat them anyway.

Mom, you were totally right about needing to pack a few pairs of backup glasses. I broke one pair last week when Emerson and I tackled our friend Murphy so we could handcuff him to a pole. It's kind of a long story. They probably would have been fine if Murphy had landed on them instead of Emerson. (That weighted vest he wears is no joke!) Anyway, I saved the pieces, and I bet Dr. Frank can fix them. Miss you guys!

Zeke

CHAPTER THIRTEEN

It didn't take long for the tiny red check marks next to the items on Murphy's life list to multiply, although after our bridge stunt, Eli was a bit more watchful. While he fully endorsed the whole life listing idea, and let us post them on our bunks, he did make us take jumping over fire off our lists. I was secretly a little relieved. Kids in weighted vests weren't exactly known for their jumping abilities. And while all those little red check marks were great, what was even better was the ever-growing list of things we tried out to save our friend. None of them had worked yet, but we were all sure that one of them was bound to work eventually. Yoga turned out to be the most fun, since Monarch cabin also attended the class every afternoon during free time. Molly always sat in the very front row, bending herself into weird positions with ease.

Every other day or so mail would be delivered to our cabin in the afternoon. It was our scheduled "downtime," when we were supposed to relax. No one ever did. Usually we filled the hour with a card game Hank had invented called Pickle Paddle Punk, where you had to do everything from name brands of peanut butter to speak in a German accent until someone drew a queen or jack. Honestly the game made absolutely no sense, and I had a sneaking suspicion that Hank just made it up as he went along, since he'd never successfully been able to explain the rules, but it didn't matter. The game made us all laugh so hard we were in danger of peeing ourselves, and it was in the middle of one of these games that mail always seemed to get delivered. I'd open the letter my mom sent every few days and glance at the usual pleadings to be extra careful, to double-bungee myself, etc. She'd end every letter with the hope that I wasn't too homesick. That last part always made me smile a little as I tossed her letter into the pile beside my bed.

Home had been filled with all sorts of special classes and accommodations as I maneuvered my RISK factor with all the skill and grace of a tap-dancing hippo.

I'd expected that camp would be a lot of the same—just another school dressed in camp clothing—but it wasn't. By this point in our lives we all knew how best to survive our particular RISK, and the counselors at Camp O didn't waste our time going over the same lessons we'd had forced down our throats our entire lives. The only reminder that we were actually spending our summer in a government-approved accountability camp was Nurse Betsy, who would pop into a cabin occasionally to log some bit of information on our condition. Here, where being a RISK was nothing special or even impressive, I felt normal for the first time in my life. This feeling of normalcy, of belonging, of having friends I could laugh with, was what I would miss. Homesick? Nope. Campsick? I'd feel it the moment I left this place.

I wrote a few letters home like everyone else because Eli made us, but I kept my descriptions of camp life to surface details, like what we'd had for dinner the night before and how long we'd gone swimming for that day. I'd learned a long time ago that the less my mother knew, the better.

The days of summer flew by in such a whirlwind of activities and fun that I was shocked when the mail delivery included a letter from her detailing how excited she was to see me soon. I blinked at her familiar swirly handwriting in surprise. We'd been preparing all week for our two-day end-of-summer camp-out, as well as the last capture-the-flag battle, but I guess I hadn't really put it all together. The realization that camp was almost over put a sick feeling in the pit of my stomach. Not only was I having more fun here than I'd ever had in my life, but the end of camp meant that the deadline to save Murphy was almost up. My *getting stuck sucks* plan was beginning to look like the only viable option, and I had no idea if it would even work.

"Pack check in two minutes," Eli called from the front of the cabin, jarring me from my thoughts. I jerked my head up and turned to look at Eli. The poor guy was having a rough morning. Today his arms were only about half their regular length, giving him the appearance of a gangly T-rex. He clapped his hands impatiently. "We leave in five, and you beauty queens are about to make us late!" I threw my bag over my shoulder and jumped from my bunk.

Lugging my pack to the center of our cabin floor, I plunked it down between Murphy and Anthony, whose bag was smoking a bit. He didn't seem worried, so I tried not to be.

"All right, men," Eli said with a familiar grin. "We have to hike over ten miles to reach our campsite, and I don't want to make it out there and find out somebody forgot their toothbrush." He raised an eyebrow at us, and we groaned.

"Too soon," Zeke moaned.

"Too soon?" Eli smiled wickedly. "It's been weeks since I watched you six scrubbing the inside of a toilet."

"Stop talking about it," Anthony muttered. "Just thinking about it makes me want to yak."

"If I ever have to smell anything that toxic again, I will slice off my nose," Murphy said.

"That's actually not a bad look," Hank said. "My uncle Gilbert has a permanently invisible nose and the ladies love him." He frowned. "Or was that Uncle Julius?"

"Sorry, men," Eli chuckled, cutting Hank off before he could really get going. "I couldn't resist. But back to the packs—when I say the item, you produce it. Got it? I want to get this finished. We're burning daylight." We nodded, and I loosened the drawstring on the gigantic backpack I'd been issued. The thing was built to strap around the waist as well as the shoulders and was reinforced with metal poles. Of course, we'd had to put a few extender straps on mine so that it would fit over my already bulky vest, but that was all just par for the course. The pack was the faded green of an old army blanket, and I wouldn't be surprised if it had been originally manufactured for use in World War II. As I opened it, I got a whiff of the musty fabric again and changed my assessment; it was probably issued during World War I.

Eli pulled a list out of his pocket with some difficulty, as his arms didn't quite reach that far at the moment. What must it be like to never know what physical obstacle you might face each morning? At least with my RISK I knew what to expect, and I'd spent a lifetime learning how to maneuver and survive it. Eli began to read off the list of required items. On cue I produced my sleeping bag, flashlight, roll of toilet paper, swim trunks, underwear, socks, toothbrush, soap, canteen, and my meds for the next two nights.

"That's all the standard-issue stuff," Eli said, flipping his paper over to the back side. On it was listed each of our names with our own unique requirements.

"Emerson, do you have your carabiners, bungee cords, tether, and ankle weights?" Eli asked.

"Yes, sir," I said, producing the extra straps, clips, and weights.

"Hank, do you have the glow-in-the-dark spray paint?"

Hank nodded, producing a small yellow spray bottle. "Got it, sir."

I shot him a questioning look, but he waved me off.

"Zeke, do you have your saline, backup glasses, and supplies for Mr. Stink?"

Zeke nodded. It went on like this, making sure that Anthony had his flame-retardant spray and his special burn ointment, that Gary had an extra set of gloves as well as a bottle of corrosive acid, gauze, safety glasses, and ointment.

I hadn't realized that everyone had something they needed to bring with them. It made me feel better about my pack full of straps. That is, until Murphy produced his bag of red rocks, and my stomach clenched.

A quick glance at Hank's frowning face confirmed that he was on the same page as me. I glared down at the floor. Trying to stop Murphy's time traveling was like trying to make Hank stop disappearing or Gary stop sticking. Our RISK factors were so interwoven with the fabric of who we were that they couldn't be separated from us. Still, I wasn't ready to give up. There were a few more days left of camp. We would save Murphy. We just had to.

"The things they carried," muttered Zeke, and I shot him a questioning glance. He shook his head. "Nothing," he said. "Just this book my dad told me about. It was called *The Things They Carried* and was about this guy in some war. Don't remember which one, but he talked about what each of the army guys carried with him into war. How what everyone carried really defined who they were."

"Tim O'Brien," Eli said as he checked off the last of the things on his list. He glanced up when no one said anything. "That's the author of that book. I had to read it for school. But the difference between you guys and those guys back in the Vietnam War is that the things you guys carry with you, the physical things, don't mean squat. This," he said, holding up his list, "doesn't define you. What you carry here," he said, thumping his heart, "is what matters." He looked down to sign off on the list. It was funny. Eli had been saying stuff like that since the first day of camp, but this was the first time I'd kind of believed it. Eli slid the list into an envelope labeled "Nurse Betsy" in large black handwriting before turning back to us. "We have to hike past the dining hall before we can leave, to collect our food supplies for the night." He stood, shouldered his pack, and headed out the door. We hustled out after him.

"This is going to be a blast," Hank said, catching up to me. His legs were invisible, so he appeared to be floating.

"I hope so," I said, unwilling to admit to anyone but myself that I was a little worried about this trip. Bunk beds, lack of air conditioning, and a communal toilet line was roughing it in my opinion. This was going to be a whole new ball game.

As the dining hall came into view, I spotted a group

of girls packing various food items into backpacks just like ours. My Molly radar went off, and I found her among her Monarch cabinmates instantly. Although, it was kind of easy—she was the only cocker spaniel wearing a backpack.

Unfortunately, Hank spotted them too. "Is that who I think it is?" he asked dramatically, a hand held over his heart.

"Here we go again," Zeke groaned as Hank took off and raced ahead to the dining hall. The girls were up on the deck that surrounded the cabin, and I saw a few of them elbowing one another as Hank came barreling down the hill on invisible legs.

We followed Hank down the hill, and I relished the feel of the wind whipping past me as my feet practically flew over the uneven dirt. It was a feeling I'd never had before coming to camp, when my every step had been dragged down by my lead shoes. It had rained the night before, giving the morning a freshness that made me feel alive. Murphy and the guys fell back behind me, and for the first time in my life I wasn't just keeping up, I was leading the pack. I slowed down when I reached the bottom of the hill and jogged up to the dining hall. I expected Hank to leap onto the deck and start bowing or something equally ridiculous, but I was wrong, at least about the jumping-on-the-deck bit. Hank slid to a stop in front of the dining hall, tossed off his backpack, and fell to his knees.

"What light through yonder window breaks? It is the east, and the Monarch girls are the sun!" he cried.

"Is that Shakespeare?" Zeke asked. "Because he is *not* smart enough to come up with that on his own." The girls of the Monarch Cabin were all crowded around the deck railing, peering down at Hank and doubling over with laughter.

"Arise, fair sun, and kill the envious moon," Hank called, his head thrown back dramatically.

Suddenly Kristy, the blonde who had been covered in the purple feathers on initiation night, pushed her way through the gaggle of girls and grinned down at Hank. "Oh Romeo, Romeo! Wherefore art thou Romeo?"

"Oh!" Hank cried. "Speak again, bright angel, for thou art hot."

"Okay," Anthony said, "I know Shakespeare never used the word *hot* like that."

At that moment Hank's legs reappeared, and half his head vanished.

"Enough, Romeo," Eli called, biting back a grin. "We have to pack our food, and as much as I enjoy a good tragic love story, we need to get a move on."

Kristy winked at Hank, pulled the red ribbon from her ponytail, and flung it dramatically down. Hank snatched it from the air, kissed it, and bowed grandly. The girls on the porch applauded, and I noticed that Molly was herself again. She was red-faced from laughing, and in that moment, I wished that I had Hank's guts, that I had been the one who made her laugh. Maybe good things only happened if you were willing to make yourself look like an idiot. I frowned, not sure how I felt about that.

"Come on, ladies," said their tall brunette counselor as she grinned at Eli. "We have a long hike in front of us."

"Are they doing their camp-out tonight too?" I asked Eli. "Are we hiking with them?"

"Not a chance," Eli said. "They hike to the opposite side of the lake we camp at."

"Oh," I said, slumping a little in disappointment. Hank tied the red ribbon around his arm and stumbled back over to us, a goofy grin on the half of his face that was still visible.

"Were you in a Shakespeare play or something?" Zeke asked. "How did you know those lines?"

"Google." Hank shrugged. "It is one of the greatest love stories of all time. I figured it was worth learning a line or two. I can quote *Twilight* too. Want to hear?"

"I'll pass," Gary said. "I already just threw up in the bushes over there. Seriously, man, hadn't you seen a girl before coming to this camp?"

"Of course I've *seen* girls," Hank said, "but these are *our* girls. You know?" He never took his eyes off the Monarch cabin as they marched past us and up the trail into the woods.

"I don't think they're ours," Murphy said wryly. "I think they are just girls who think you're a wacka-doodle."

"Not like ours possessive," Hank huffed in exasperation. "Ours as in, *like us*. You know? They don't look at us like we're freaks."

"Because they're freaks too." Murphy grinned.

"We're all freaks here," I agreed.

"Which means none of us are," Eli said as he thrust packages of marshmallows, sticks of butter, bags of onions, and bricks of frozen hamburger meat to each of us.

"I get it about the girls," I said, picking up the conversation again. "But did that little speech or whatever that was mean that you like Kristy now?" I was really hoping he'd given up on Molly, all too aware that I couldn't compete with Hank on my best day.

"I don't know." Hank shrugged. "I like to keep my options open. She is pretty cute, but how would I ever kiss her without my lips getting third-degree burns?"

"No clue," I chuckled.

"Invest in a lot of aloe," Anthony suggested. "I'd be happy to slip you some of my burn cream too. My doctor gave me a prescription for the good stuff."

Gary grinned at Hank wickedly. "You're assuming you could keep your head visible for the whole kissing process, which I doubt. If you look like you do now, she'd probably miss your lips."

Hank frowned and walked over to the dining hall window, so he could see his reflection. Only half his face stared back at him from the smudged glass. "Please tell me my whole head was there for that performance?" he groaned, looking at me.

I smiled. "Most of it. You lost it right at the end."

"Kristy didn't seem to care," Murphy said. "She still gave you the ribbon."

"I just wish I could tell when it happened," Hank moaned. "I always have to go by other people's reactions. Usually the screaming and the running are pretty good clues."

"Let's go, Casanova," Eli said, heading off into the woods.

"You mean Shakespeare, good sir!" Hank called back, his momentary melancholy forgotten.

And so we hiked. For ten long, hot miles, with heavy packs, and surprisingly, I didn't hate it.

When we finally arrived at our campsite, we

discovered that it wasn't much more than a small clearing of dirt around a fire pit with a few logs laid haphazardly for seating, but to us it looked like an oasis in a desert. Too exhausted to take another step, I dropped my pack and rolled my shoulders to work out the knots.

Eli stomped around, surveying the scene with a satisfied look on his face. His mood had improved tremendously since his arms had regained their normal proportions. His hair was now a brilliant orange, but I doubted he even knew it.

"Home sweet home," he crowed. "We only have another hour of usable daylight, so let's get to work." We gaped at him like he'd sprouted an extra head.

"Are you crazy?" Gary asked. "I've never been so tired in my life, and now I have to work?"

"Welcome to your end-of-summer Camp O campout," Eli went on, ignoring Gary. It was a tactic he employed well whenever Gary started whining. "Gary and Emerson, you guys go dig the latrine." He handed us a shovel. "Zeke, could you and Mr. Stink find us some firewood so we can cook dinner tonight? Make sure it's dry. Murphy, you stay here and help me get the tents set up. Hank and Anthony are in charge of filling up the water containers." He tossed them what looked like two deflated plastic bags. "Smog Lake is that way," he pointed. When he noticed Anthony's hesitation to touch the bags, he smiled. "Don't worry. These are flame resistant. We won't make that mistake again." Anthony smiled in relief and bent to pick up one of the containers.

I raised my hand. Eli saw and rolled his eyes good-naturedly. "Emerson, this isn't school. You don't have to raise your hand."

"Right." I nodded. "Sorry. But, um, what's a latrine?" I waited for everyone to start laughing at my stupidity, but nobody did. Apparently no one else knew what a latrine was either.

"It's a fancy word for a large hole in the ground we can defecate into." Eli grinned.

"We have to dig the toilet?" Gary squeaked, his face turning red. "Why can't we get the firewood or water?"

"No switchbacks," Hank said, grabbing the containers and bolting toward the lake. Everyone else took their cue and scattered like cockroaches.

"Perfect," Gary grumbled. "I think I escape KP duty, and I get put on CP duty instead."

"CP?" I asked as I followed him into the woods.

"Crap patrol."

"Did you know that the guy who invented the toilet was named Thomas Crapper?" I asked.

"He didn't invent it," Gary muttered. "He just made

them more popular. He had a showroom for toilets. He also made manholes."

"Wait a second, how did you know that?"

"Wikipedia." Gary shrugged. "The suspension room at my school has this ancient computer with everything on the web blocked, except for Wikipedia. It's not incredibly entertaining, but it beats counting ceiling tiles. There are thirty-eight tiles in that room. In case you cared."

"Right." I nodded, even though I'd never been in the suspension room in my school. I wasn't even sure if my school had one. "Wait up a second," I said, stopping to look around. "We shouldn't put it too far away from camp, or we might get lost in the middle of the night trying to find it."

"Good point," Gary agreed grudgingly. "Where do you want to dig the stupid thing?"

"Over there?" I asked, pointing at a small grouping of bushes that might provide some privacy. I snorted; compared to the toilets back at camp it would be a boatload of privacy.

"Whatever," Gary said. I'd never dug a toilet before, but I figured the deeper, the better. Gary grumbled the whole time, but it really wasn't that bad. When we were finished, I found a decent-looking stick to shove into the ground next to our hole.

"What's that for?" Gary asked.

"Toilet paper holder," I explained.

"Good call," Gary admitted as we headed back to camp. The small dirt circle had been transformed. Eli had a fire started, the three tents were set up, and Hank and Anthony were just hauling back the last plastic container of water.

I sank down onto one of the logs perched around the fire and stretched out my aching legs.

"Emerson, Gary, I'm glad you're back," Eli called from where he was busily poking around in his pack. "I need that shovel." He held out his hand, and I glanced at Gary. Unfortunately, his hands were just as empty as mine.

"We forgot it back at the latrine," I admitted.

"Well, one of you better go get it," Eli said without looking up. A quick glance at Gary's *if you think I'm going back you're crazy* expression made it obvious who that would be. With a groan, I got back to my throbbing feet and stumbled into the woods by myself.

CHAPTER FOURTEEN

The sun was just starting to set, and the clammy air of the afternoon was cooling off as a crisp Michigan night began to fall. The trees around me threw long shadows, making the woods seem both eerie and beautiful at the same time. I had just spotted our latrine and the abandoned shovel lying beside it when suddenly there was a faint popping sound to my right. I yelped and jumped sideways as something crashed to the ground mere feet from me. Before I could get myself together enough to run, the thing that had fallen picked itself up, and I blinked in surprise at Murphy.

My hand pressed reflexively onto my chest, where I could feel my heart hammering hard.

"How did you get here?" I asked, turning to look back toward the fire pit, where I'd seen Murphy only moments before helping Eli with the fire.

"Emerson!" Murphy cried as though he'd seen a ghost. Rushing forward, he grabbed my shoulders and gave me a shake. If he hadn't already freaked me out by practically appearing out of thin air, the look on his face would have terrified me. "Quick," he gasped. "What year is it? Do you know who I am yet?" He shook his head in frustration and gripped my shoulders even harder. "I'm not making any sense, am I? What I mean is, have we met yet? Where are we?"

And it clicked. This wasn't *my* Murphy. This was a time-traveling Murphy. I squinted at him in the moonlight. He was thinner than the Murphy I'd just left at the campsite, the skin on his face stretched tight over too prominent bones, and he had the musky smell of someone who hadn't bathed in weeks. Murphy shook me again. "Hurry," he said. "I don't have long."

I looked over his shoulder, worried something or someone was after him by the way he was talking, but all I saw were empty, shadowy woods.

"Emerson!" Murphy cried. "Answer me!"

"Okay, okay," I said, shaking my head in a vain attempt to focus. "The year is 2018. I do know you. And we're at Camp Outlier, on our end-of-summer camp-out."

"Then it's not too late," he gasped, seeming to sag a little in relief. He straightened again a moment later and the grip on my shoulders tightened painfully, his wide, frightened eyes staring into mine. "Listen to me," he whispered, glancing around nervously. "It hasn't happened yet. But when it does, you need to make sure that the TTBI doesn't find out that you talk to those guys. They can't know. Do you understand?" Murphy was trembling, his thin frame seeming to almost vibrate as he stared into my eyes.

He was making no sense, and I tried to wrench out of his grasp. Something about this Murphy felt all wrong. "No, I don't understand. What are you talking about? What guys?"

Murphy shook his head. "I know you don't. How could you? What I'm saying isn't going to make any sense, not for a few more days." He bit his lip, thinking, before shaking his head again. "No. I can't tell you any more. I'm sorry."

"Because of the time-traveler laws?" I asked, desperate to understand.

Murphy shook his head angrily. "If I explained

everything, it might change what you do, how you react, and that would make everything worse. Just do what I said, okay? After it happens, don't let the TTBI find out that you talk to those four guys. They tell you something that sets off an awful chain of events that I don't have time to explain right now. Promise me."

"What four guys?!" I asked frantically. "And when is this mysterious *it* supposed to happen?"

"You'll know. Now promise." And he looked so terrified, so desperate, that there was no other answer I could give my friend.

"I promise," I said automatically.

Murphy held on to me for another second before stepping back. "Thank you," he said just as his edges blurred, and he vanished.

I stood blinking for a full minute after Murphy disappeared, my breath catching in my lungs like I'd just run a marathon in my steel shoes. Forgetting all about the shovel, I turned and stumbled back to the campsite. Feeling numb, I collapsed on a log next to Hank. My eyes went automatically to where Murphy sat on the other side of the fire, completely unaware of what had just happened. Hank glanced at me and did a double take.

"Dude, are you all right?" he asked. "You look like you've seen a ghost."

All I could manage was to shake my head. I felt like I'd been hit by a stampeding elephant. Everything future Murphy had said was swirling around my brain in dizzying circles, his strange request replaying over and over again until it was nothing but a jumble of mangled words with no real meaning.

"Is it about Murphy?" Hank hissed, following my gaze to where Murphy was laughing at something Anthony had just said.

I nodded.

"Are you boys hungry?" Eli asked, and I jumped, tearing my eyes away from Murphy for the first time.

"We'll talk later," Hank whispered in my ear, and I nodded, doing my best to rearrange my features into some semblance of normalcy. Beside me, Hank's stomach snarled, and I realized that I was hungry too—starving, actually. All we'd eaten on our hike were some soggy peanut butter and jelly sandwiches, and even they seemed like a distant memory.

Eli began rummaging around in his pack. "Grab the food from the dining hall out of your bags. If you want to eat, we need to cook it. Emerson, I need that shovel."

I blinked at him stupidly, pulled from my preoccupation over Murphy.

"You know," Eli prompted impatiently, "the one you just went to retrieve from the latrine?"

"Oh, that," I said, my face turning red. "I got, um, got distracted, and I forgot to grab it."

"Distracted initiating the latrine?" Zeke asked, eyebrow raised, and everyone laughed.

Eli rolled his eyes in exasperation and turned to Gary. "Can you go grab it, Gary?"

Gary looked like he wanted to refuse, but then he shoved to his feet. "Emerson, you couldn't be any more of a RISK reject if you tried," he snapped irritably. Everyone froze. I could see my own expression of hurt and disgust mirrored on the faces of my friends. Being called a RISK reject was one of the worst things you could say to a RISK kid. It came from a time before RISK kids were government-protected, when people born with a RISK were literally rejected from society. They weren't allowed to go to regular schools or be around normal people. Parents who knew their kid was a RISK went to extreme and sometimes dangerous measures to hide it. Thankfully, that was a long, long time ago, but calling someone a RISK reject still held a strange, painful power. Probably because there were pockets of the population who were *still* scared of kids like us, scared of us injuring their own kids by accident, or scared that by helping us the schools wouldn't have the resources left to help their normal kids, and they'd let their fear turn into something ugly. The term was awful, but it didn't stop people from saying it when they didn't think you could hear them.

"What?" Gary asked defensively, looking from one shocked and angry face to the next.

Eli shook his head sadly. "Gary, please go get the shovel. And if I hear that word again, you will be speaking with Mr. Blue."

"Geez." Gary frowned as he turned to stomp into the woods. "I didn't know you were all so sensitive." Eli ignored this comment and began assigning us each jobs. Mine was cutting the potatoes into chunks. As he handed me a paring knife, he gave my shoulder a reassuring squeeze, and I made an attempt to smile. Gary's comment had hurt, but that wasn't why my face felt pinched. My meeting with future Murphy was gnawing at me, refusing to be ignored even as Eli handed us each a piece of tinfoil with a hunk of raw hamburger meat in the center.

"These are called hobo pockets, gentlemen. Add whatever ingredients you want inside the foil, wrap it up, and stick it in the fire." I looked uncertainly down at my hunk of raw hamburger and couldn't help but think it looked like a pile of red worms, all oozy and tangled with one another. But I was hungry, so I scooped potatoes, onions, and celery onto it. Eli cracked open a can of refrigerated biscuits and plopped a wad of sticky dough onto the top of the pile. I was getting more and more skeptical of this meal, especially when Eli dumped water on top of the whole mess, but I wrapped it up and thrust it into the fire just like the rest of the guys.

While our meal cooked, the sky around us darkened, and the night insects started their familiar whirring concert. I slipped on my Red Maple hooded sweatshirt and sat on a log next to Hank. I tried not to stare at Murphy, but my eyes kept getting drawn back to him, comparing his smiling face to the terrified one from the woods. Was the Murphy from the woods taller? He'd seemed older. Just then Murphy caught me staring, and I quickly looked back into the fire. The whole thing made me feel like I'd swallowed the container of night crawlers Eli had packed to use for bait the next morning.

When it came time to pull my hobo pocket from the fire, I burned the tips of my fingers. It had bloated out to twice its original size, like a small sliver spacecraft. I carefully peeled back the hot foil to discover a golden-brown biscuit inside with the bits of onion, potato, and hamburger embedded in its fluffy underside. I stared at it in open amazement. Hank didn't bother to be amazed; he just dug in, groaning in appreciation. I bit into my own, but even though it was delicious, I was too preoccupied with thoughts of Murphy to really taste it.

"You gonna eat that?" Hank asked with a jerk of his head at my half-eaten meal, his mouth still stuffed. When I didn't say anything, he grabbed it and dug in. Before I could figure out how to pry his hands off the remains of my dinner and somehow get him alone to tell him about Murphy, Eli plunked down a gigantic bag of marshmallows, a stick of butter, and a box of Rice Krispies cereal in front of me.

"Open these, will you?" he asked distractedly as he unstrapped a battered pot from his pack.

"Not that I'm doubting your culinary abilities or anything," Hank said to Eli, eyeing the bags I was opening skeptically, "but don't you need, like, a pan or something for Rice Krispies treats?"

"These aren't Rice Krispies treats," Eli explained as he set the pot directly in the burning embers of the fire and proceeded to dump the ingredients inside. "These are Rice Krispies blobs." He left the pot over the fire a few minutes, gave it a couple of stirs, and then began ladling large sticky mounds of the stuff onto our pieces of foil. I grabbed a glob of the warm marshmallow mush and shoved it in my mouth. It was like biting into heaven, if heaven burned your tongue a little bit. Hank reached over to grab some of the mess off my foil, and

I smacked his hand. I was worried and stressed, but he was not getting any of this. No way.

I looked across the fire for Gary, waiting to see what snarky comment he was going to make about the messy dessert. But, to my surprise, Gary wasn't there.

"Hey, Anthony," I called. "Where did Gary go?"

Anthony looked around, as though Gary might be hiding under the log he was sitting on, and shrugged. "I don't think he ever came back from getting the shovel."

Eli looked troubled as he glanced around for his missing camper. "Any volunteers to go look for him?" he asked.

There was my opportunity. I shoved the last lump of gooey treat into my mouth and stood up, hauling Hank with me. "Hank and I will look for him."

"We will?" Hank asked around a mouthful of marshmallow.

I shot him a *shut up and go with it* look and nodded. "We'd love to."

"Oh," Hank said, finally catching on. He grinned at Eli. "Emerson's right. We'd love to."

Eli squinted suspiciously at both of us. "Why does that make me nervous?" he asked. I didn't say anything, willing Hank to stop looking so dang guilty. Finally Eli nodded and jerked his head toward the woods. "Be quick about it."

"Got it!" I said, and grabbed Hank before he could say something stupid or suspicious or both. The darkness of the woods surrounded us as soon as we were a few steps from the fire, and I flicked on the flashlight I thankfully still had in my pocket from my last trip to the latrine.

"I kind of hope we don't find him at the latrine," Hank said. "Gary won't appreciate it if we butt in on him taking care of business. Get it? Butt?"

"Shut it," I said. "We need to talk."

"Oh yeah!" Hank said as he sucked the last of the marshmallow off his fingertips. "What happened to you in the woods? I haven't seen someone that freaked since my uncle Duke set off a firecracker in his own armpit."

"He set a firecracker off in his armpit?" I asked, momentarily distracted.

Hank nodded. "It was an accident, obviously. Almost blew his whole arm off. Surgeons had one heck of a time reattaching it. The thing kept going invisible on them, so finally—"

"I got it," I interrupted. "We need to talk about Murphy."

"He seemed fine to me," Hank said, craning his head to look back at the campsite, where we could just see Murphy perched on a log next to Anthony.

"Not our Murphy," I said. "I ran into a different

230

Murphy in the woods. A time-traveling Murphy."

"Really?" he asked, his joking manner conspicuously absent. "From the past or the future?"

I furrowed my brow, recalling the odd conversation I'd had. "I'm pretty sure it was the future," I said. "He kept talking about how something was going to happen, and that when it did happen that I should make sure the TTBI never found out what these guys said. I don't really know. He was all jumbled and panicked."

Hank's eyebrows jerked upward in surprise. "Really?"

I quickly recounted what Murphy had told me, trying my best to repeat what he'd said word for word.

"But," Hank said, frowning, "what in the world does that even mean? When *it* happens? What's *it*? What guys? What are you supposed to make sure the TTBI doesn't find out?"

"That's the problem," I said, "I have no idea."

Hank wrinkled his nose. "Think we should tell our Murphy about this?"

I shook my head. "I think he has enough to worry about right now. If we tell him his future self is running around the woods breaking the laws he's so terrified of, he'll really flip."

Hank nodded. "Good point." Then his face brightened, and he grinned. "You said it was future Murphy, right?"

"Right . . . ," I said, wondering where he was going with this.

"Well, maybe this means we succeed." He grinned. "That we, or maybe just you, figure out how to save Murphy. Who knows! Maybe plan *getting stuck sucks* actually works! I think it's time we kept Gary close."

"I agree," I said. "But to do that we still need to find Gary. Remember?"

A moment later, I spotted the stick I'd stuck beside our latrine. "This is it," I said, gesturing to our hole.

Hank eyed it skeptically. "Those pea-green toilets are looking pretty good right now, aren't they?" he said.

"Hank, focus," I commanded, glancing around at the dark trees. "Gary isn't here. Do you think he got lost? What if he ran away like he's always threatening?"

Hank cupped his hands to his mouth and bellowed, "GARY! DUDE! WHERE ARE YOU?"

I cringed as his voice shattered the silence. "Should we go tell Eli?"

"Not yet." Hank frowned. "It didn't bother you? What he called you earlier?"

I shrugged. "It's Gary."

"It doesn't matter." Hank shook his head. "He should know better." He was just about to go on when I heard something.

"Listen," I whispered. We froze, straining our ears,

but the only sound was the buzz of night insects. I began to think that I'd only imagined the noise when the faint cry came again. We took off toward the sound, stumbling over tree branches and through foliage. A minute later we burst from the underbrush to find Gary standing under a tree, his pants around his ankles. I skidded to a stop behind Hank and burst out laughing. Gary glared at us furiously from red-rimmed eyes, his face puffy and tear streaked, and my laughter died instantly on my lips.

"What's wrong, dude?" Hank asked as we approached. Gary tried to reach down to grab his shorts again using only the back of his hand, and I noticed for the first time that his other hand was stuck to the tree.

"What do you think is wrong?" Gary snapped. "I'm stuck, and I've been hanging out in the dark getting eaten alive by mosquitos in very unfortunate places."

"Well, how did that happen?" I asked as I inspected the hand stuck firmly to the tree.

"I ripped off my gloves when I left that lame campfire. Those things get itchy and sweaty. Well, I stopped to take a pee, slipped, and got stuck," Gary muttered. "Could one of you please pull up my pants?"

Hank shrugged and yanked Gary's pants up.

"So how do we get you unstuck?" Hank asked.

"You need the corrosive acid in my pack," Gary said

with a sniff. "I'll lose some skin, but I won't be stuck to this tree anymore."

"Got it," Hank said, turning and dashing back into the woods. Glancing around, I saw a decent-sized rock and took a seat. If the situation were reversed, I'd want someone to wait with me. Gary ignored me, glaring at the hand stuck to the tree as though he were contemplating chopping it off.

"So why did you leave the campsite?" I asked after the silence had stretched for a while.

"I was just going for a walk," Gary grumbled.

"But there were Rice Krispies blobs," I said. "Why would you miss those to stomp around in the dark by yourself?" Gary didn't say anything for a while, and I shifted uncomfortably.

Finally, he sighed. "No one wanted me there after what I said. I'm tired and hungry, and it just kind of slipped out. Which is crazy, because I've never called anyone that in my life. I mean, I'm not a *complete* jerk." He looked at me and then down at the ground. "Sorry."

"It's fine." I shrugged, trying not to let my surprise register on my face. I'd never heard Gary give a sincere apology for anything. Ever.

"It's not fine." He frowned. "I hated it when people called me that, and I turned around and did it to you." He would have gone on, but the sound of people stomping through the underbrush stopped him.

"Gary? Emerson? Where are you guys?" Eli's voice called.

"We're over here," I yelled. Gary scrubbed at his face furiously with the sleeve of his T-shirt, trying to erase the evidence of his tears. Moments later the Red Maple men came crashing into view.

Eli approached Gary and clapped him on the shoulder. "We were worried about you, buddy. Hank said to bring the acid. Are you sure you want to use it?"

Gary nodded. Eli pulled from his pocket the small blue bottle I'd seen Gary pack and shook it.

"You need to have safety glasses on when you use that stuff," Gary said.

"Got it covered," Eli said, pulling two sets out of his pocket. He slid a pair on and carefully put the other on Gary. "Murphy," he called over his shoulder. "Can you get the first aid kit ready? We're going to need ointment and some gauze. Emerson, grab that bucket of water from Zeke and bring it over here."

Gary had his eyes squished shut, and even in the dim moonlight I could tell his face was a sickly grayish color. Eli was talking quietly to him, but I couldn't hear what he was saying. I took the bucket from Zeke, brought it over, and took a step back. Eli unscrewed the cap of the bottle and poured it carefully onto the tree so that the sickly green acid ran down around Gary's fingers. Gary let out a strangled cry as the wood around his hand started smoking. The smell of chemicals and burning skin filled the air and made my stomach roll. Eli grabbed Gary's arm and yanked. Gary's hand popped free, and he quickly plunged it into the bucket, silent tears streaming down his face. The water seemed to help, because after a moment his face relaxed.

"Murphy, the ointment and gauze, please," Eli said. Murphy handed over the supplies, and Gary brought his hand out of the water. I stared in horror at the blistered and peeling skin. He saw my glance and tried to shrug nonchalantly.

"It's not a bad one," he reassured me. "Probably only a second-degree burn. No big deal," he said as Eli gently smeared ointment over his palm using a small rubber spatula and then wrapped it with the gauze.

"You have to do that every time you get stuck?" I asked, noticing the mottled and scarred skin on Gary's other hand for the first time.

"Only if I'm stuck to something impossible to move, or I can't wait around to get unstuck," Gary said, wincing as Eli finished the bandage.

"Show's over, boys," Eli said. "We are already past lights-out. I want to be up early tomorrow. We're fishing for our breakfast, and if we don't catch any fish, we don't get any breakfast." Eli marched us back toward our campsite in somber silence. As I crawled into the tent I shared with Hank and Murphy a little while later, I found myself unable to get the image of Gary's scarred hand out of my mind. I hadn't realized that undergoing that kind of pain was part of his daily life. It explained a lot about why Gary was the way he was.

CHAPTER FIFTEEN

Eli woke us up by shaking our tents at 6:00 a.m. "Get up, you lazy bums!" he yelled. "The fish won't catch themselves!"

My eyes felt scratchy and my muscles ached as I emerged from the tent into the chilly morning. Now that summer was coming to an end, the nights were cooling off, and little drops of condensation beaded over the surface of our tents. My breath fogged in front of me, and I ducked back inside the tent to shrug into my sweatshirt.

Eli had just snapped the last fishing pole together and handed us each one. Together we trudged down to the lake to catch our breakfast. The water was like glass, and I guess it was pretty, or at least I would have thought so if I wasn't still half asleep. I settled down on the dock between Hank and Murphy, threaded a worm onto my hook, and tossed my line in. It was a familiar movement now, but the first time I'd had to impale a worm I'd vomited. Not one of my finer moments. Hank slid his usual chunk of hot dog out of his pocket to use as bait, and we sat in companionable silence for a while as the sun started to rise slowly over the trees, making the lake sparkle in the early light.

Now that I was fully awake I couldn't shake the heavy weight of guilt that sat in the pit of my stomach. Here I was sitting next to Murphy, and I had this huge secret I was keeping from him. I reminded myself again that the only thing telling Murphy would accomplish would be to freak him out. I glanced around to see where Gary was, and relaxed when I saw him perched five feet down, next to Zeke. Mr. Stink sat between them, appearing for all the world like he was listening to their conversation. Keeping Gary close to Murphy was going to be tricky, but if Zeke was right, Mr. Stink would give me at least a few seconds' heads-up.

Hank kept his eyes on his line, waiting for the telltale tug that meant a fish was on the other end. "If I manage to catch a five-pound catfish, I'll be able to cross something else off my list," he said, breaking the sleepy silence.

"You don't have to give the fish to a girl for it to count?" Murphy grinned.

"Now, why would I give a fish to a girl?" Hank asked, glancing away from his bobber. "Girls like flowers. Or chocolate. Not fish. Never fish."

Murphy laughed. "Noted. It's just that a lot of the things on your life list seem to be about girls."

"Those are just the newest additions to the list," Hank explained. "I started life listing when I still believed girls were crawling with cooties."

"What do you mean?" I asked. "Don't you just make your list and that's it?"

Hank shook his head. "Nope. I always have one hundred things on my list. In fact," he said, frowning, "since I crossed off bridge jumping, I'll have to add something new."

"Really?" I asked, surprised. "Why?"

Hank shrugged. "I saw this *Dateline* special once on this guy named John Goddard. He made a life list of one hundred and twenty-seven goals and accomplished one hundred and nine of them before he died. I liked that he didn't finish his list. In fact, he just kept adding to it every year. It means he was living it up, setting goals and accomplishing them right up until the very end. So every time I cross something off my list, I have to add something else."

"I don't know if that makes any sense," I argued. "Isn't the whole point of a list to finish it?"

"Nope. The point is to *never* finish. To live a big life. Think of it this way," Hank said. "If I had set a list of only one hundred things, I would have reached it by now, and then what? If I have it my way, I'll die with a list of one hundred more things I wanted to do."

I shook my head, resigning myself to the craziness that was Hank logic. "So, what's next on the life list of the great Humble Henry?" I asked.

"Well, like I said, there's catching a giant catfish, French-kissing a girl, riding a bull, getting a tattoo, skydiving, being in a movie, and chopping down a tree."

"Impressive." I nodded. "Murph, what about you?"

"I'm feeling pretty good about my life list these days." He smiled. "Besides, I already crossed the biggest one off," he said.

"What's that?" I asked.

"Experience an amazing last summer," he said sadly, "but camp is almost over. Can you believe that we have less than a week left?" Murphy hid it well most of the time, but today he looked scared and sad.

It was that look that almost made me tell him about

my encounter with his future self the night before. Part of me wanted him to know that there was still hope. That my crazy last-resort plan might actually work. But something about the way future Murphy had looked made me keep my mouth shut.

"So what's next on your list?" Hank asked. "We still have plenty of time to check things off."

Murphy smirked. "Lasso a pig."

"Why a pig?" I asked.

He shrugged. "Cows seem overdone. So I figured, why not a pig?" Before I had a chance to answer, my bobber plunged under the water and my pole jerked. Hank hooted, and I reeled for all I was worth.

The rest of our morning consisted of swimming in the lake, exploring the neighboring trails, and learning more survival skills from Eli. By one in the afternoon we were packed up and hiking toward our next camp-site. I found myself glancing into the surrounding woods every few minutes, wondering if I'd get another glimpse of future Murphy, but the only things I saw were a few deer and one very chubby squirrel. Eventually, I relaxed and just enjoyed the hike.

A few hours later our trail converged with another small trail, and we stopped for a water break. I'd barely pulled my canteen out before voices floated down the other trail. I turned to look just as the girls from the

Monarch cabin rounded a bend. Hank hooted trium-
phantly and pumped his fist in the air. The Monarch
cabin's tall brunette counselor was leading the way,
her hair braided into long pigtails and a bandanna
around her head. When she caught sight of Eli, her
face lit up.

Eli had a similar expression on his face. Hank
moved next to me, probably preparing himself for some
kind of grand gesture, but Eli put a restraining hand on
his shoulder.

"Let me show you how it's done," he said, striding toward the pretty counselor. "Hello, ladies." He
smiled graciously, inclining his head to the Monarch
girls. "Anna," he said, greeting the girls' counselor. She
smiled as he grabbed her hand, and in one smooth
move dipped her backward and kissed her. The girls
shrieked in delight. When Eli finally put Anna back on
her feet, she was grinning from ear to ear. Eli turned
back to us. "Any objections to hiking with the Monarch
girls for a few miles?"

"Do you think he could teach me how to do that?"
Hank asked, awed.

"I don't think you're his type," Gary said, smirking.
Hank punched him in the arm good-naturedly, and we
followed the girls down the trail.

The girls were funny, and they smelled nice, like

flowers or something. I wondered how that was possible after sleeping in a tent and hiking all day. Zeke in particular was living it up as the girls fawned over how cute Mr. Stink was, crowding around to pet him and feed him bites of their granola bars. And I wondered again if there was any way I could talk my mom into getting me a cute service animal, although the only service animal that would be of any use to a kid who floats was probably a gorilla trained to sit on me in case of emergency. Not quite the chick magnet I was hoping for.

Molly was walking a few feet in front of me, and I watched the back of her head for the first half hour of the hike. I probably would have continued that way for the rest of the day if Hank hadn't intervened.

"You're being creepy," he muttered under his breath as he dropped back to talk to me.

"What?" I asked, pulled from my thoughts. I'd been mulling over my encounter with future Murphy again, while simultaneously noting the way Molly's hair bounced while she walked.

"Creepy," Hank repeated. "A Grade A stalker, my friend. It's like you're trying to memorize the back of her head or something."

"I'm not even going to pretend to know what you're talking about," I said, shifting the heavy pack on my back to lessen the pressure it put on the straps of my vest.

Hank rolled his eyes. "You'll thank me for this later," he said, and before I could ask what he meant, he'd shoved me. For a guy with noodle-thin arms, he was alarmingly strong, and I stumbled forward, colliding with Molly. She cried out in surprise, and I reached out instinctively, catching her arm before she could fall, barely stopping myself from tumbling headfirst into a nearby bush. When it was clear we weren't in danger of face-planting, I mumbled an apology and shot Hank the dirtiest of dirty looks. But, being Hank, he just winked before turning back to Kristy.

"It's no big deal," Molly said, pulling my gaze away from Hank's shameless flirting. She'd moved over on the trail, and I hurried to walk beside her, aware that my left armpit was sweating about three times worse than my right one was. I kept it clamped at my side and tried desperately to remember if I'd put deodorant on this morning. Molly jerked her head toward my vest, snapping me out of my panicked realization that I had *not* put deodorant on.

"It must be hard to hike in that thing," she murmured.

"It's not that bad." I shrugged, hoping I sounded nonchalant even though she was absolutely right. I racked my brain for something clever to say. The silence between us was starting to feel awkward, so I glanced over at her. "So, um, turning into a dog randomly must be kind of interesting." Which was the least clever and most obnoxious thing I could possibly say. I'd officially blown it. I gave myself a mental kick in the head, and then another for good measure.

But to my utter shock, she laughed, and the ice was broken. I'd always imagined that talking to a girl like Molly would be hard, a constant battle to think of funny or intelligent-sounding things to say, which was clearly something I sucked at. But after my less than suave start, things went really well. She honestly didn't seem to mind that I'd asked about her RISK factor, and I found myself laughing as she described the time she'd accidentally been taken to the humane society, and her parents had to pay an adoption fee to get her back. Not wanting to be outdone, I pulled out my story about bobbing around on the ceiling of our mall when I was five, and she actually smiled. Of course, I left out the part about all the screaming and vomiting I'd done while the fire department tried to fish me down with ropes, but still, she smiled. It wasn't a smile like she'd given Hank when he did his *Romeo and Juliet* performance, but I'd never had a girl look at me like that before. It made me want to say something to make her do it again. When it came time for our cabin to head down a different trail, I held up my hand for a high five, of all things, which she didn't see since Hank chose that exact moment to do an uncanny imitation of a chicken. To save face I just turned it into a pathetic wave. Lame.

Our second campsite was next to a wide stream. Actually, it might be considered a river, I wasn't really sure.

"Hey, Gary," I called. He was attempting to tie his shoe with one bandaged hand and one gloved one. It wasn't going well. "Is that a river or a stream?"

Gary considered the body of water in front of him. "River. It's deeper and wider than the average stream."

"Thanks!" I grinned as I helped Hank set up our tents. He shot me a questioning look. "He's like a walking Wikipedia," I explained.

"He's a Garypedia," Hank said.

Anthony wrinkled his nose. "That sounds like some sort of bug."

"G-man?" Hank said, testing out potential nicknames the same way people tested flavors of ice cream. "G-fact, G-brain, G-pedia."

"Any of those beats Sticky, or Superglue, or Spider-man Reject," Gary said, giving one of his rare smiles.

"Spider-man Reject?" I asked.

Gary's smile disappeared, and I regretted asking. "Kids find out you have sticky hands, and they expect you to climb walls or whatever. When you get stuck to that wall, well, out come the flattering nicknames."

"There is a kid in the Silver Birch cabin nicknamed Spider-man," Zeke piped up. "But instead of spider webs spraying from his wrists, he's a magnet for actual spiders. He's always covered in the creepy things."

"I'm glad I don't share a bunk with that kid." Gary shuddered.

"So what are the plans tonight?" Murphy asked Eli. "Do we have to catch our dinner again?"

"Not this time," Eli said, checking his watch. "Mr. Blue should be dropping off fresh supplies and the canoes in about an hour. The White Oak cabin was here last night and already dug the latrine and gathered firewood, so you guys just need to go refill our water supply." He pulled out the two empty water containers and tossed one to Hank and the other to Murphy. "Follow the river to the right. About a half mile up is a farm owned by a man named Mr. Bickle. He lets us use his well, so we don't have to worry about boiling our water."

"Got it." Hank nodded. The containers took two guys to carry when they were full, so we all decided to go with. It was better than sitting around debating who'd developed the worst BO (it was Gary by a land-slide).

We spotted the farm just as the sun was starting to set. A gigantic red barn was perched next to the river, its paint faded and chipped. Farther on I could see pens of fluffy white sheep and morose-looking cows. It was a real honest-to-goodness Old MacDonald–type farm. I hadn't known that places like this still existed.

We found the pump just where Eli had said it would be and quickly filled both plastic containers. We were heading back toward the river when Hank stopped, throwing an arm out to stop Murphy.

"Do you see what I see?" he asked, pointing to a small pen in the distance.

"See what?" Zeke asked, squinting. "I can't see squat."

"You say that like we should be shocked," Gary said. He elbowed past Murphy to look, shielding his eyes from the glare of the setting sun. "It's just a bunch of pigs. Haven't you ever seen a pig before?"

Hank let out a war whoop and dropped his half of the water bag I was helping carry. Grabbing Murphy's arm, he took off across the field at a full sprint toward the pen.

Unable to hold it on my own, I dropped the other half of the water container. It sloshed over my feet, but I barely noticed.

"What is he doing?" Zeke asked. "Did I miss something? What did he see?"

"A pig," I said dryly as I watched the two figures race across the field. "Murphy wants to lasso one. It's apparently on his life list."

"Who lassos a pig?" Zeke asked.

"This I have to see," Anthony said, tearing off across the field. I followed. I had to see it too.

CHAPTER SIXTEEN

When I reached the pigpen, Hank and Murphy were already perched on the top fence rail, a look of anxious excitement on their faces as they surveyed the grunting and snorting pigs. I looked down at the pen's occupants and wrinkled my nose. Somehow I always pictured pigs looking like Wilbur on the cover of *Charlotte's Web*, all pink and clean. These pigs were no Wilbur. Huge and hairy, they stood knee-deep in what I was pretty sure was years of fermented pig poop. Periodically one of them would snuffle its face through it as though searching for buried treasure. I began reconsidering the idea of bacon.

"I'm going to lasso that one," Murphy said, pointing

to a smallish-looking pig near the back of the pack. He was the runt of the litter for sure, and I had to commend Murphy for not trying to go after one of the gigantic male pigs snuffling around. They had to weigh three hundred pounds apiece. Mr. Stink hopped out of his spot in Zeke's messenger bag and trundled over to investigate the pen. He took a few tentative sniffs before backing away in disgust.

"You don't have a rope," Anthony pointed out. "And do you even know how to lasso?"

Murphy frowned. "No, but it doesn't look that hard. I mean, you make a loop, you throw it, and you pull. Right?"

"That's the spirit!" Hank said, slapping Murphy on the back so hard he almost fell off the fence.

"Wait, do *you* know how to lasso?" Anthony asked Hank.

Hank grinned. "I'm from South Dakota, remember? We learn to lasso before we learn to walk."

"You still don't have a rope," I pointed out.

"I got a rope," Gary said, walking up. He hadn't sprinted across the field like the rest of us. Gary avoided running the way I avoided the dentist. "Saw it hanging off the side of that barn."

Hank reached down, plucked it from Gary's gloved hands, and began tying one end into a slipknot.

I rolled my eyes in exasperation at Gary. "Why did you bring him that?"

Gary shrugged. "I don't know. I've never seen anyone lasso a pig before?"

"That's because people don't lasso pigs!" I hissed.

"Hey, Emerson," Hank called, straddling the fence. "If Murphy manages to lasso the little guy, we should totally bring him back to Camp O as an end-of-summer prank. We could grease him up and let him loose in the White Oak cabin, get a little revenge on that Gus guy for his toilet stunt. What do you say?"

"Wouldn't work," Zeke called. "They'd never be able to tell the difference between the pig and Gus."

I laughed despite my growing anxiety over the situation. "That would be fun to explain to Eli," I said. "Just help Murphy lasso the dumb thing and let's get out of here. If that farmer catches you two, we'll be in serious trouble." There wasn't a sign posted anywhere stating "Don't Lasso the Pigs," but I had a feeling that it might be one of those unspoken rules.

"Right," Hank said, swinging his leg back over as he did something complicated with one end of the rope. "Okay, Murph, all you have to do is hold on to the loop and swing it like this. Don't move, Zeke," he commanded, letting the rope fly. It whizzed through the air with an audible swish and settled around Zeke's shoulders. Hank pulled and the rope went tight.

"Sure," Zeke said as he shrugged out of the rope, "lasso the kid who can't see it coming."

Murphy's forehead was scrunched in concentration as he watched. "I think I can do that." He nodded. "Hand it here." Hefting the rope in his hand, he began swinging it around his head in a large loop, his eyes focused on the little pig. The rope went flying through the air in a graceful arc, and if I hadn't been so worried about the whole thing, I might have been impressed.

The rope came down. But it didn't come down on the tiny pig he'd been aiming for. It came down on one of the gigantic hairy behemoths standing just to the left of the tiny pig. The rope slipped around the muscled neck, and Murphy yanked backward.

"You actually got one!" Zeke yelped. Murphy looked slightly stunned by his success, but the massive pig he'd lassoed looked even more surprised. It froze for a moment as the rope tightened. And then it backed up, squealing and screaming in protest. I nearly jumped out of my skin. If I didn't know any better, I would have thought we were killing it instead of slipping a rope around its neck. I guess that when your future was someone's Christmas ham, you saw death threats everywhere. The pig took off, and Murphy went flying off the fence, his hands still holding tight to the rope.

254

Hank made a grab for him but missed and fell into the mud instead.

The rest of the pigs squealed and scattered, running a few ambling steps before stopping to stare at us from a safe distance. But not the monster Murphy had lassoed. He took off like a rocket for the opposite end of the pen, pulling Murphy face first through the muck. Without even consciously deciding to do it, I found myself vaulting over the railing and into the pen, my feet landing with a sickening squelching noise in the shin-deep mixture of poop and mud. Hank stumbled to his feet beside me. Without a word, we took off after our friend. Shouts came from behind me, and I knew the rest of the guys were on our heels. The pig was still screaming bloody murder, dragging Murphy along behind it, his body flopping in a way that looked painful. The pen was deceptively large, and the pig seemed to have no intention of slowing down.

"Let go of the rope!" I called. Murphy just yelled back inarticulately.

"We need to stop the pig," Hank shouted.

"How do we do that?" I gasped.

"How should I know?!"

The pig finally reached the end of the pen, and with nowhere to go it slid to a stop and gave its head a vigorous shake. To my utter relief, the rope slipped off its neck. That relief evaporated as a second later it whirled and came charging right at us. Someone screamed, but I was too freaked to know if it was me or one of the other guys. Murphy was just picking his head up out of the mud when he saw the pig and flopped facedown again, covering his head with his hands. The pig charged right over the top of him. I dived to the right as Hank dived to the left, and the pig barreled between us, coming so close to me that I felt the stiff bristles of hair that covered its muddy side brush against me. Glancing back over my shoulder, I saw the mammoth pig scattering the rest of the guys like bowling pins before rejoining its fellow pigs on the other side of the pen.

I scrambled to my feet and slipped and slid over to where Murphy was still lying facedown in the muck. Maybe this was it, I thought frantically. Maybe this was why Murphy didn't survive camp, because his idiot friends let him lasso a pig. What were we thinking? Stupid life list. Stupid Hank. Stupid pig. Large muddy hoofprints covered the back of Murphy's arms and shirt as I reached down to flip him over.

"Don't be dead, don't be dead," I said, not sure if it was a prayer or a command.

Murphy was coated so completely I couldn't tell where he stopped and the mud started, and I stared down at his still form for a second, my heart somewhere near my tonsils. Then his eyes opened, and he blinked up at me out of a muck-covered face.

"Hey, Emerson?" He coughed.

"Yeah?" I asked anxiously.

Turning his head to the side, he spit out a mouthful of mud. "I don't recommend lassoing a pig." I sagged backward, plopping down into the mud in relief just as everyone else caught up with us. Together we pried Murphy from the muck. He left a Murphy-sized impression behind, like he'd decided to make a snow angel, only in pig poop instead of snow.

"Are you okay, dude?" Hank asked. "Why didn't you let go?"

Murphy spit again, wiping at his mud-encrusted face with an even muddier hand. "I couldn't. The dumb rope was wrapped around my hand."

"Rookie mistake," Hank said, shaking his head. "You never wrap it around your hand."

"That would have been good to know *before* death by pig," Murphy pointed out. Hank shrugged apologetically.

"It bites getting stuck to stuff, doesn't it," Gary snickered. "Although I have to say, I've been stuck to a lot of things in my life, but I was never stupid enough to stick myself to a pig."

Hank raised an eyebrow at Gary, taking in his

almost spotless appearance. While the rest of us were liberally painted with who knew what, Gary was clean from the knees up. Hank bent down and grabbed a handful of muck.

"Hey, Gary," he called, "catch." He lobbed the blob of muck at Gary, who tried to catch it but only managed to explode it all over himself. He had such a shocked look on his face that I burst out laughing. Which was a mistake, because part of Hank's next poop bomb landed in my mouth. I gagged, spitting out gobs of the stuff. And then a full-on war broke out. Everyone was scooping up piles of mud and pig poop and chucking it at one another. I got a few good ones in after I discovered that my aim improved when I packed the stuff like a snowball before launching it. Zeke lobbed one at me, and I ducked so it nailed Hank in the back of his head instead. Hank turned to return the favor and slipped, landing on his face in the muck. Again.

"Well, this is a new one," drawled a voice behind us. We froze, and the handful of pig poop I was clutching fell from my hand with a splat. As one, we turned to see a man in worn blue jeans and a faded flannel shirt leaning against the fence, an amused look on his weathered face. Murphy scrambled to his feet, but instead of dropping his handful of muck he plopped it onto Gary's head. Gary hunched his shoulders as it slid down the back of his neck and into his shirt but didn't retaliate.

The man pushed his cowboy hat back and surveyed the six of us. Except for our eyeballs, there wasn't one square inch of us that was clean. I made a vain attempt to wipe some of the mud off but gave up when I realized I was just making the situation worse.

"Can you boys please explain to me why you're scaring the daylights out of my pigs?" he finally asked with a jerk of his head toward the pen behind us. I glanced over my shoulder. The creatures in question stood huddled in a corner staring at us in bug-eyed terror.

"We could," Hank said after a moment. "But it's a long story. Can I just cut to the part where we say we're sorry and get out of your pigpen?"

The man nodded. "That'll work." We slipped, slid, and squelched over to the fence and ducked underneath. Gary managed to shove one last handful of muck down Hank's pants as he was bending over to climb under the fence—a maneuver that earned him a very dirty look.

"Are you some of them Camp Outlier kids?" the man asked.

"If we are, would we get in trouble?" Murphy asked.

The man chuckled. "As far as I can see, you didn't

actually hurt anything, just redistributed the pig poo, so I guess not. I'm Arnie Bickle. I'd invite you into my house for a bite to eat, but to be perfectly honest, y'all smell horrible."

"That's an understatement," Gary muttered as he tried to unsuccessfully get a glob of the stuff out of his ear.

"We need to get back anyway," I said. "Our counselor will be wondering what happened to us." Everyone mumbled their agreement and apologies as we slunk across the field to retrieve our abandoned water containers. Mr. Stink chose that moment to rejoin us, his black-and-white fur spotless as he inspected us with distaste. When Zeke offered him his usual spot in the messenger bag, he declined.

"I hope that was worth the check on your stupid life list," Gary muttered as we watched Mr. Stink trot ahead of us, his tail held in a disgruntled arc above his head. "We just grossed out the skunk. Again."

CHAPTER SEVENTEEN

O ne of the water containers had spilled, so we had to go back to the pump to fill it. We made a halfhearted attempt to rinse off some of the mud in the icy water from the pump, but it was hopeless. The stuff seemed more like glue than mud, and all we accomplished was getting even muddier.

I had pig poop in more places than I wanted to think about, and every few minutes on the walk back to camp one of us would gag a little from the smell. To make matters worse, the flies that had been swarming the pigs had decided to follow us home, and they buzzed around our heads in obnoxious circles.

"I can't take it anymore," Hank finally proclaimed

as he swatted at a particularly large horsefly that had already bitten him twice. Before I could protest, he'd dropped his end of the water container again and slid down the three-foot embankment into the river we'd been following.

"Holy crow," he yelped, making the universal *this water is freaking cold* face, before gritting his teeth and submerging to scrub vigorously at his hair. The mud washed off him in murky swirls before being whisked away in the current. He emerged a second later with a triumphant whoop and glanced back up to where the rest of us stood in muddy, fly-covered misery.

"Well?" he asked. "What are you waiting for?" Dropping my end of the container, I slid cautiously down to the river with the rest of the guys. The water was like ice, and I sucked in an involuntary breath as I eased myself in. Thankfully, the river never seemed to get much deeper than a few feet, so I didn't have to worry about my vest dragging me straight to the bottom, and soon I was scrubbing the muck off along with everyone else.

"You know what?" Hank said after a minute. "The river is flowing in the same direction as camp."

"Your observation skills are astounding," Gary said dryly as he rubbed at his ruined T-shirt.

"Why, thank you, my sticky friend." Hank grinned. "But my point is that we could just float back to camp.

It beats walking in wet shoes."

"What about the water bags?" I asked.

"I bet they float," Hank said, already scrambling up the riverbank. Without hesitation he gave the two water bags a shove, sending them rolling down the bank to crash into the river. They disappeared from sight, and I glared up at Hank, who was already sliding back into the water. A second later though they bobbed back to the surface, already zooming down the river.

"Boys," Hank called. "Follow those bags!"

Gary muttered under his breath, but he paddled after them obediently. Sloshing through the waist-deep water, I grabbed onto the closest container as it zoomed by. In a pinch, it would work as a flotation device if the water got too deep. Zeke quickly scooped up Mr. Stink and deposited him onto the second bag. He looked unhappy about the new arrangement, but he dug his claws into the thick plastic and held on resolutely to his makeshift boat.

Five minutes later, I spotted our camp as we rounded a bend in the river. Parked next to our fire pit was the battered blue pickup from our infamous dress-filled initiation night. Eli was perched on the tailgate next to Mr. Blue and Nurse Betsy. They saw us, and Eli hopped off the tailgate to meet us. I was suddenly really happy that we hadn't walked into camp covered in pig poo.

"Red Maple men," Eli said as we emerged from the water to assemble dripping in front of him. "Was the hike too much for you?"

"We just felt like swimming." Hank shrugged.

"In the future, you don't go swimming without me," Eli said sternly, his eyes darting toward Mr. Blue. Looking back at us, he raised his eyebrows significantly. "If you drown, I need to know about it. There's paperwork involved."

"Sorry," we mumbled. I turned to walk back to our tent for some dry clothes, but Eli's hand on my shoulder stopped me. He was looking closely at Murphy, who had just taken his shirt off to wring it out.

"Are those hoofprints?" Eli asked. Murphy craned his head to get a look at his back, where two large hoof-shaped bruises stood out against his white skin.

"Maybe?" Murphy said, shooting a *help me* look at Hank.

"Well, you see . . . ," Hank jumped in.

Eli held up a hand, stopping Hank. "Hold it right there. I just decided that I don't want to know. Murphy, put your shirt back on. Nurse Betsy is here to see you and Gary." Eli sniffed. "And why do you all smell like dog poop?"

"It's pig poop," Hank said. "If you want to be accurate. Because . . ."

"Stop," Eli said. "I don't want to know. Remember?" Mr. Stink clambered off the water bag onto the shore and shook himself vigorously, spraying tiny water droplets onto our legs. He looked up at Eli as if to say, *see what I have to deal with?* then gave three quick sneezes.

"He sneezed!" Hank said, turning to look at Murphy with wide-eyed terror. Realizing a moment too late what was happening, I lunged for Gary, but I'd barely grabbed his arm when Murphy disappeared.

"What's the big idea?" Gary snapped, shrugging me off. "You should have grabbed Murphy, you big doofus."

"Sorry," I muttered, letting go of him to step back. "I jumped in the wrong direction."

Gary rolled his eyes. "Real smooth, Emerson." I nodded, glancing over at Hank, who looked just as upset with himself as I felt.

"Eli, do you have the red rocks?" Mr. Blue asked as he walked up to us, not taking his eyes off the spot where Murphy disappeared.

"Yes, sir," Eli said. "Emerson, go grab Murphy's pack and bring it over here." I flew back to our tent and grabbed the pack. Eli dug around in the depths of Murphy's bag for a second, spilling ratty T-shirts and wash-worn shorts onto the ground before finally producing the bag of red rocks. In a matter of seconds he had the stones placed in a circle around the small puddle of water that marked the spot Murphy had been just moments before.

"That should do it," Mr. Blue said. "Eli, notify me on my radio when he returns. Nurse Betsy will just have to check him when he gets back to camp tomorrow. Hopefully the TTBI doesn't mind waiting until you get back from camp for him to log his report, but that might be wishful thinking." Eli nodded. I stifled a shudder at the memory of the ever-unfriendly TTBI officers. They didn't show up every time Murphy logged a time-travel episode, but they'd popped into enough of our activities to make everyone pretty twitchy about them.

"I'll watch the rocks," Anthony volunteered.

Eli nodded. "Thanks. The rest of you need to change. I'm hoping that stink is just in your clothes and not in your skin."

"You and me both," Gary muttered.

"Not you, Gary," Eli said, grabbing his shoulder. "Nurse Betsy needs to look at that hand." Gary nodded and began unwrapping the muddy bandage from his injured hand as he walked toward Nurse Betsy. I watched him go, wondering if his hands were really going to be able to save Murphy. I swallowed hard. That is, if Murphy came back.

Fresh clothes did improve our smell somewhat, but

I was ridiculously happy that the Monarch cabin wasn't anywhere nearby. My vest had gotten the brunt of the poop bombs, so while everyone else bustled around setting up camp, I used a stick to pick the tiny bits of pig muck out of the crevices of the vest. I felt twitchy and anxious, and my eyes kept returning to that circle of empty red rocks. Had it been a mistake not to tell Murphy about my encounter with his future self? Hank seemed to be thinking the same thing, because he was unusually quiet as he gathered firewood. A half hour later Nurse Betsy left Eli with Murphy's pills and drove away in the pickup truck with Mr. Blue.

Two hours and three fire-roasted hot dogs later, I spotted Hank jumping up from his spot by the circle, where he'd been on watch. Murphy had returned. Relief flooded me, and I jogged over.

"Welcome back," I said, clapping Murphy on the shoulder. He looked pale and tired, the way he always looked after time traveling.

"So what did I miss?" he asked.

"We ate hot dogs," I said. "Hank tried to teach Zeke how to do a backflip. It didn't go very well, mainly because Hank's legs were invisible."

Hank shrugged. "Besides my utter failure as a backflip teacher, it was pretty much the usual. Anthony started a small fire, but we put it out pretty quickly.

Then he chucked these little balls of fire at rocks we threw into the air until he missed and almost hit Zeke, who, of course, couldn't see them coming. Then Eli yelled at us, and we had to stop. Nurse Betsy looked at Gary's hand, which thankfully wasn't infected by some strange swine disease. Emerson didn't do much of anything besides pick pig poo out of his vest. Eli told us that we smelled bad about a million times. Like we didn't already know that. Oh, and we made s'mores."

Murphy's stomach growled audibly.

I threw an arm over his shoulder and led him back toward our campfire. "Eli saved you some hot dogs, and Gary even offered to cook your marshmallows to help you catch up on the contest."

"What contest?" Murphy sniffed.

"To see how many s'mores you can eat. Gary has already had ten, but I think if he has one more he's going to yak."

Murphy nodded and smiled. It wasn't a real smile, though, not an *I just lassoed a pig* smile. Not that I could blame him.

The next day we packed up our camp and piled into the canoes Mr. Blue had left for us. The river we'd floated down the day before led straight back to Camp O, and the day flew by in a frenzy of paddling and tipped canoes. The sun was just starting to set when we rounded the last curve of the river and glided into Camp Outlier's lake.

"All right, men," Eli called as we paddled toward the dock. "We normally would head straight to the dining hall, but you guys still smell horrendous, and Mr. Blue set up a surprise for everyone tonight. You have five minutes to hit the showers. Use soap. Lots and lots of soap." We retrieved our packs and jogged up the hill toward our cabin. Our showers were fast, punctuated by Eli periodically bellowing "SOAP" at the top of his lungs from the cabin, as though we'd forget. As we scrubbed, hopefully washing the last remains of Farmer Bickle's pigs down the drain, we debated with Hank about whether or not Murphy and I aged a year by surviving three flipped canoes in one day, even though it wasn't on our original list. In the end we had a vote, and Murphy and I both aged one year.

Mr. Blue's surprise turned out to be fireworks to celebrate the last week of camp. After dinner, Eli handed out some faded green army blankets to sit on, and we followed the crowd of campers down to the lake.

"We should try to snag a spot next to the Monarch girls," Hank whispered.

"Excellent," Murphy said, perking up. "Where are they?"

"I don't see them," Zeke said, squinting. When someone snickered, he flapped an impatient hand at us. "I know, I know," he grumbled.

"There!" Gary pointed. We followed his finger and spotted the girls just settling onto their blankets next to the boathouse. Hank grabbed my arm and started pushing his way diagonally through the crowd, heading straight for them. When we finally made it, Hank lay his blanket down with a flourish.

"Hello, gorgeous," he said, grinning breathlessly at Kristy. "Fancy meeting you here."

"Fancy that." Kristy smirked. She looked over her shoulder at Gabby, a girl with tiny wings, and said, "Pay up." Gabby sighed and handed over a wad of dollar bills. Kristy pocketed the money and scooted over on her blanket, patting the spot next to her. Hank didn't waste a second moving over.

"Come on, boys," he called. He turned back to the girls, his classic Hank smile firmly in place. "Any objections to sitting boy, girl, boy, girl? I figure that if it's good enough for kindergarten, it's good enough for camp."

One of the girls made a joke about how eating Play-Doh was also good enough in kindergarten, but that didn't mean it was still a good idea. But since they didn't seem completely against the idea, the rest of our cabin found seats next to the girls.

Kristy watched the entire process with an amused expression, but then coughed, waving her hand in front of her face. "My gosh, did you guys bathe in cologne?" She wasn't exactly wrong.

"The alternative was much less appealing," Murphy said. I wasn't sure if it was because his Red Maple sweatshirt was just as new as ours, or because he'd successfully lassoed a pig, but he seemed to ooze an almost Hank-like confidence that night. It was quite the change from the quiet and withdrawn Murphy we'd had to coax to eat a s'more the night before.

"I like it," Molly said, sitting down next to me.

"It's Hank's," I admitted. "I was ambushed getting out of the shower. We all were. He was trying to kill the pig smell."

"Pig smell?" Molly asked, confused.

"Hey, Murph," I called. "Molly wants to know about the pig smell. Show her your back."

Murphy shrugged and yanked up his shirt, revealing two perfect hoof-shaped bruises. The girls gaped at them and then demanded the story. Murphy's storytelling was impressive. Of course, Hank pretending to be the pig made the whole thing funnier. We were laughing so hard that we almost didn't hear the first firework explode above us in an umbrella of falling white light. We got quiet to watch, our heads craned back to take in the night sky. Molly's hand was just sitting there on the blanket an inch from mine. Was her hand there because she wanted me to hold it? Was this some sort of a signal? I glanced over to Hank for guidance, but he was turned away from me, an arm slung casually over Kristy's shoulders. Murphy was no help either, his head bent as he whispered conspiratorially with Gabby. I couldn't see the rest of the guys. I was on my own.

The next firework went off, and I tilted my head back to watch the blue arc of lights. Molly leaned over, her breath warm against my ear as she whispered, "I like that one the best." Goose bumps prickled up my arms and neck. Her lips had practically touched my ear, and I wished I'd remembered to bring Q-tips to camp. I nodded. Even though the night was cool, I was suddenly overheating, and I shucked off my sweatshirt. Then I went for it. Snaking my hand across the blanket, I grabbed Molly's. It wasn't until I had her cool fingers entwined in mine that I realized my hand was sweating. Great.

An orange firework exploded overhead, but I was barely watching anymore. Every fiber of my being was attuned to the skin on my hand, the skin touching her skin. Was I squeezing too tight? Not tight enough?

Why had no one ever taught me the proper pressure for handholding?

I jumped as the soft skin under my palms suddenly turned into curly fur. Molly had turned into a cocker spaniel. She looked at me and whined.

"It's okay," I whispered. She made a funny little dog whimper and licked my face.

"Doesn't count!" Gary called from the other side of the blanket. I scowled at him and fought the urge to wipe the dog drool off my cheek. He was talking about our life lists, of course. Every single one of the guys had *French-kiss a girl* on their list. Except for Zeke, who had already done that. Twice. Although no one really believed him. When the grand finale of fireworks burst over the lake, everyone applauded, and Molly barked happily. Out of the corner of my eye I saw Hank lean in to kiss Kristy, but she ducked, successfully avoiding his puckered lips. I guess Hank wasn't going to add another year tonight, either.

It wasn't until we got back to our cabin that night that I realized I'd forgotten my Red Maple sweatshirt down by the lake. Resolving to look for it the next day, I fell asleep imagining what would have happened if Molly hadn't turned into a cocker spaniel.

CHAPTER EIGHTEEN

And seemingly in the blink of an eye, we were down to our last full day of camp. I couldn't quite believe it, and neither could Murphy, who had been convinced that he'd be long gone by now. I found myself hoping that maybe he'd been wrong, and this was all one big mistake. Maybe the future wasn't one where I attended his funeral, and instead his parents would show up tomorrow to take him home. But deep down I knew that was just wishful thinking. It was weird—usually summers dragged for me. I emerged from them pale and bleary-eyed from too many electronics and too little light. This summer I hardly recognized myself. As I stood in front of the mirror washing my hands, the face staring back at me looked older, definitely tanner, and had more than one scar to show for my life-listing endeavors. Oh, and I had a Mohawk. That one hadn't been on my life list, but it had been on Murphy's, and we'd all decided to join in. I liked this version of myself.

"You ready, dude?" Hank asked, coming to stand next to me so he could peer in the mirror and smear black face paint under his eyes. He already had his camouflage gear on, and his blond Mohawk was spiked up with way too much hair product. He turned his head this way and that, admiring the effect.

"Ready." I nodded, grabbing the tub of black paint and spreading it liberally on my own face. Tonight, I was going to help Murphy cross *Win capture the flag* off his life list. It was just an added perk that I would get to check it off my own list too.

"Red Maple men, huddle up!" Eli bellowed from the cabin. Hank and I both turned and ran for the door, getting in a minor shoving match to see who could get through first.

"So tonight, we end this thing," Eli said, when we'd all found our seats. "Redwood has three flags and we have two, so we need to capture their flags tonight or they win automatically. If our luck holds, they were too cocky to move their flags from the area Zeke, Murphy, and Emerson scouted out at the beginning of the summer. But I'm not taking any chances."

He surveyed us for a second, his hand on his chin, then nodded.

"Anthony and Gary, you guys will stick with me to protect our flag down by the lake. Zeke, you go with Hank, Emerson, and Murphy to take a crack at getting Redwood's flags."

"Could Gary come with us?" I asked. Gary turned to me with a raised eyebrow. We were all friends with Gary, but he wasn't necessarily someone who got picked first for a team. Even in this crowd.

"Yeah," Hank agreed, a little too quickly. "Can we have Gary?"

Eli raised surprised eyebrows, then looked at Hank suspiciously. Finally he gave a curt nod and Zeke and Gary switched places. I let out a silent sigh of relief. It was getting harder and harder to keep Gary within sticking distance of Murphy, but with the clock ticking down until the end of camp, Hank and I weren't taking any chances.

"Remember the rules, Hank," Eli warned as we turned to go.

"I know, I know," Hank interrupted, flapping a hand at him dismissively. "No naked. I remember." Since Hank's stunt at the beginning of the summer, Mr. Blue

had changed the rules so that all flags had to be captured while visible.

"Good." Eli nodded. "I'd hate for your bare butt to
disqualify us."

"Do we have a plan for how to actually get the
flags?" I asked Hank as we headed out the door.

"Nope," Hank said a little too quickly. Just then
Zeke walked up and wordlessly gave Gary the rope
he'd been holding. Gary nodded and looped it around
his waist, purposefully avoiding my eyes.

The exchange was too smooth, and I narrowed my
eyes and turned to Hank. "There *is* a plan, isn't there?
I said accusingly.

"Don't worry about it," he said, clapping me on the
shoulder reassuringly.

My eyes went from Gary's rope to the backpack
conspicuously perched on Hank's back, and I frowned.
"Too late." I had a bad feeling that rope was going to
end up tied to my ankle while I tried not to puke, but
I decided to drop it. I wasn't about to give them any
ideas. Besides, this game felt bigger than life at the
moment. I think we all believed that if we won capture
the flag, we'd somehow be able to save Murphy. Like
the two things were one and the same, even though we
all knew they weren't.

When the bell rang five minutes later signaling the

start, we took off. The cabins that had been eliminated cheered as we charged into the woods. The Redwood guys were hooting and hollering like they'd already won, and even though I tried not to let it psych me out, it did a little bit.

Hank was ahead of us as we barreled through the trees.

"Which way did you say it was?" Murphy whispered as we ran.

"Right up the hill," I said. "Somewhere near that log with the poison ivy that we hid inside." Hank slammed on the brakes, and Gary, Murphy, and I almost took him out trying to stop.

"Wait a second. You *all* hid in a log?" he laughed. "I never heard that part of the story! Was that cozy or what? Were you face to face? Butt to butt? Oh gosh," he choked out. "Head to butt?" My face turned bright red, giving him a clear answer, and he practically howled with laughter. I fought the urge to kick him.

"Shhhhh," Murphy hissed as we continued to creep up the hill. I'd just caught sight of the infamous poison-ivy log when the soft murmur of voices met my ears. Hank must have heard the same thing because he finally stopped giggling and got his game face on. As though we'd planned it, we all dropped to our hands and knees to crawl through the underbrush. As I crept along over fallen branches, my fingers sinking into mud, I tried to imagine myself doing this at the beginning of the summer. And failed. Old Emerson *never* would have done this. Not for a flag. Not for anyone. I had to push those thoughts aside, though, as we got closer to the voices. The sky was already getting dark, but I could make out the silhouettes of three guys. I recognized two of them as Chad and Max from our initiation night. They stood casually leaning against a tree. Peering up, I could just make out three flags suspended in the branches near the top—the Redwood flag as well as the two they'd managed to steal from other cabins. Unfortunately, they'd taken all the lower branches off the tree, making it impossible to climb.

"Okay. guys, it's now or never. Let's get started," Murphy whispered, squinting up at the flags.

"Get started with what?" I asked.

"Emerson," Gary said, already tying a rope around my ankle. "I hate to do this to you, but it's the only way. Either you float or we fail." My stomach flopped uncomfortably, but I'd had a feeling it was going to come to this.

"You can do it," Hank said encouragingly. "Murphy and I will create a distraction while you guys go for the flags. We won't be able to keep them away for long though, so make it fast."

"I don't know," I said, hedging and glancing back up at the tree. I turned to Murphy hopefully. "Can you guarantee I don't die?"

Murphy shrugged. "I know you show up at my funeral. Does that count?"

"That's morbid and awful." I frowned.

"And it's not going to happen," Hank chipped in, giving me a conspiratorial wink. I was too nervous to wink back. My idea for saving Murphy was raw at best, and downright stupid at worst. Hank was, of course, fazed by neither of those two things.

"Here," Gary said, slipping off one of his gloves to grab the rope with his bare hand. "I'm stuck, possibly for the next week. There is no way I can let go." He had a grim determination on his face, and I nodded.

"Fine." I squared my shoulders. "I got this. But I am going to triple-knot that thing before I take off my vest." While we prepared, Hank yanked off the back-pack he'd been wearing and pulled out a crumpled-up wad of pink fabric. My jaw dropped in surprise when he untangled it to reveal his prom dress from initiation night. It had lost one of its shoulder bows, and the tiered ruffles were ripped and stained.

"You kept that thing?" I asked.

"Yup. Thought it was too hideous to part with." He

grinned. "Lucky for Murphy, I kept his too." He reached into his backpack and pulled out the tattered remains of Murphy's brown polka-dot prom dress and tossed it to him. "Suit up."

Murphy grinned and yanked it over his head.

"Hank, you make one ugly girl," Gary said appraisingly when the boys were ready. He'd already helped me take off my vest and was sitting on my chest, human-paperweight style, to keep me from floating away, the rope firmly stuck to his right hand.

A minute later Hank looked at us and wiggled his fingers around in what I assumed was some kind of signal. Gary nodded, flapped his arms like a chicken, and made a peace sign on his forehead. It looked like a bizarre version of a baseball signal, but it worked, because Hank and Murphy disappeared quickly into the thick underbrush. Before I could ask Gary where they were going, he held a finger up to keep me quiet. I nodded and waited for Hank and Murphy's distraction.

A shrill whistle came from our left and a second later Hank strutted out of the bushes in his prom dress like he was walking a runway, not through the middle of the woods. The Redwood guys stopped talking and stared.

"Oh, boys!" Hank called in a falsetto.

"What the . . . ," Chad said. Hank wiggled his fingers at the boys, turned, and flipped up his dress.

"Is he seriously mooning us?" Max snorted.

"Is only half his butt visible?" the third guy asked.

"Look alive," Chad said, scanning the woods. He's the distraction." I fidgeted nervously under Gary. They were onto us. Hank continued wiggling his solitary white butt cheek at the boys, and even from where I lay with Gary sitting on my chest, I could hear them start to crack up.

"That's by far the ugliest distraction I've ever seen," Chad chuckled. "I'll stay here. You two go catch that knucklehead and throw him in jail." The two boys charged after Hank, who dropped his dress and took off. I tugged urgently on Gary's arm. Now was our time to move, right? But Gary shook his head at me, motioning impatiently for me to keep quiet. A few seconds later, I found out why. Chad gave a surprised shout as Murphy came charging out of the woods, his brown polka-dot dress flapping around his knobby knees as he made right for the tree. Chad turned so fast he tripped, and Murphy went crashing into the underbrush uttering war whoops, Chad hot on his heels.

It was our turn. Gary leaped off me, and I popped into the air. Clamping my hand over my mouth to stop myself from screaming, I rushed toward the sky. Gary reached the tree a second after I jerked to the end of my rope, and I had to throw my hands in front of my face to keep from losing an eye on one of the few remaining branches. The flags were right in front of me, and I set to work untying them, doing my best not to look down. Whoever had put them up here had quadruple-knotted the suckers, and I was forced to use my teeth as well as my hands.

"Hurry up!" Gary said from below me. "They could be back any second!"

"You telling me to hurry isn't going to make me go any faster," I snapped. I was still working on the first flag when I heard the shout. Turning, I spotted the Redwood guy named Max sprinting at full speed toward us. I looked back at the flags, realized that they were tied to a pretty flimsy-looking branch, and snapped the entire thing clean off the tree.

"Go!" I bellowed. Gary went, but he unfortunately didn't take the time to reel me in first. I found myself flying through the tops of the trees as Gary sprinted away. I threw my arms over my face and ducked as tree branches whizzed past my head, scratching my skin like a bunch of angry cats. Someone was screaming, an ear-piercing screech, and I only registered it was me when I saw Hank come flying out of the woods, his pale legs pumping hard under his tattered dress, my vest thrown over his shoulder. He looked up and yelled something at me. Unfortunately, I couldn't really hear him over all the screaming I was doing. I clamped my lips shut.

"Do you have the flags?" Hank called again. I had a moment of panic that I had dropped them, but I looked down to realize my hand was still clutched in a death grip around the stupid tree branch with all three flags. Unfortunately looking down also gave me a good view of the ground thirty feet below, and I almost passed out. Camp Outlier had changed me a lot that summer, but it hadn't managed to take away my fear of heights. I puked. Pretty spectacularly. It missed Gary and Hank and splattered somewhere behind them. Looking back, I saw Max yelp in disgust as he dodged the airborne vomit.

"Nice one!" Gary called, as though I'd done it on purpose. I wiped my mouth off on my sleeve and ducked as I was dragged through a pack of thick pines.

"Get me down!" I howled.

"No time!" Hank called back just as Murphy darted from the trees, three Redwood guys in full pursuit. The race was on, and I had an aerial view.

The lake loomed in the distance, and I whooped as

we burst from the trees and into the open area by the dining hall. The other cabins were playing a game of softball, but when they spotted us they started cheering. There was so much adrenaline pounding through my system I felt like I was about to burst.

The Redwood guys were gaining, but we had a chance to make it. We hurtled down the hill toward the lake, Gary with his Emerson kite, Hank and Murphy in their ridiculous dresses, and a pack of furious Redwood guys inches behind. Right when I thought we were goners, one of the Redwood guys tripped, tumbling down the hill, and knocked over two of his buddies on the way down. They cried out, but I barely heard it over the excited cheers of Eli, Zeke, and Anthony as they came barreling toward us. They tackled Gary the moment he made it past the boathouse and into Red Maple territory. I felt a sharp jerk on my ankle as I was pulled to the ground. Eli threw my vest around my shoulders, and I hoisted the tree branch above my head victoriously. Our entire cabin roared in approval, and I thought my face might split from grinning.

"Emerson!" Hank bellowed. I turned just in time to see Mr. Stink sneeze. Murphy stopped cheering as all the blood drained from his face.

"Now!" Hank yelled.

Grabbing Gary's free hand, I yanked off his glove

and smashed it onto Murphy's bare arm. Murphy's eyes widened in surprise, and then he and Gary disappeared. There was a horrible gut-wrenching pull, like someone was trying to yank my spine through my belly button, and everything went black.

CHAPTER NINETEEN

My insides coiled and writhed like snakes, and I doubled over. I was on fire, and I was freezing. There was nothing around me but a swirling blackness, and I tried to scream, only to discover that I couldn't. Every fiber that made me me was being torn apart from the inside out. Then just as suddenly as it had begun, it stopped.

I stood blinking in the middle of a bright wood. Sunlight shone down through the thick leaves that canopied above my head, and the heady smell of pine, dirt, and impending rain filled the air. The place was both familiar and oddly foreign, and I turned, trying to figure out how I'd gotten there when only a second before I'd been standing at the side of Camp O's lake. I was still trying to figure it all out when something clubbed me hard in the left eye. The punch radiated from my teeth to my toes in a way I would have found astonishing if it hadn't hurt so freaking bad. Glancing up, I saw Gary launch himself at me again. I barely had time to register the furious look on his face before my knees hit the hard forest floor.

"Easy!" someone yelled. Through my one good eye I saw Murphy grab Gary's shoulder and pry him off me. It was only then that I realized that Gary's hand was still stuck firmly to Murphy's arm. I got up gingerly, my hand covering my throbbing left eye.

"What is going on?" I asked, taking in the forest, a furious Gary, and a white-faced Murphy.

"What do you think is going on?!" Gary bellowed. "You gigantic floating moron! You stuck me to Murphy, and now we've time traveled!"

"Really?" I asked stupidly, glancing at Murphy for confirmation.

He grimaced. "I'm afraid he's right." He wrinkled his nose as he looked down at Gary's hand still stuck firmly to his skin. "I didn't think it was possible. My mom and dad have been touching me a bunch of times when I time traveled, and they never came with me. It must be something with your RISK factor. Man, I'm glad I didn't rip Gary's arm off or something when I traveled."

I felt my face go white as I looked at Murphy in horror. "That could have happened?!" I gasped. "I never thought of that!"

"Clearly!" Gary snapped. "You didn't think through any of this. And here I thought being sticky couldn't get any worse. Good to know the universe still has the ability to mess with me."

"How in the world did I come?" I asked. Then I remembered the rope. A quick glance confirmed that it was still tied firmly to my ankle, the other end grasped in the very hand that Gary had used to deck me.

"What were you playing at, sticking me to Murphy?" Gary yelled. "I never wanted to time travel! And I *especially* never wanted to time travel with a *doomed* time traveler!" He tried to twist away from Murphy, presumably to finish the thorough butt kicking he'd started, but Murphy held tight.

"I'm sorry," I sputtered, scrambling to my feet. My fingers fumbled clumsily to fasten the remaining buckles on my weighted vest that had, thankfully, traveled with me. Eli had thrown it over my shoulders seconds before Murphy had time traveled. Before *I* had time traveled—the thought made my insides flop. My face was throbbing, and I was pretty sure I was going to have an impressive black eye. "It wasn't supposed to work this way," I explained. "I thought you would keep Murphy in the present, not that he would take you with him."

"You were planning this?!" Murphy and Gary yelped at almost the exact same time.

I nodded guiltily. "I had the idea a while ago, but Hank and I weren't sure it would work. It was supposed to be a last resort if we couldn't figure anything else out."

"Is that why you wanted Gary to help us get the Redwood's flag?" Murphy asked as he thought through the last couple of hours.

I shrugged. "I've been trying to keep you and Gary as close as possible. It hasn't been easy."

"So now instead of just Murphy getting stuck somewhere, we get stuck too?" Gary yelled.

"We might not get stuck here," Murphy said. "We could time travel back. Or," he said, shrugging, "we might just die."

"Not helpful, Murph." I frowned. "Speaking of here, *where* is here? Where are we?"

"No clue," Murphy said, glancing around.

"*When* are we is the question you should be asking," Gary grumbled. I shot him a nervous glance, but he made no move to come after me again.

"Different question, same answer," Murphy said.

"That's the real bummer about my condition. The not knowing."

"Is there any way to tell if this is the time you, um, don't come back?" I asked, swallowing hard as the realization of what I'd just done finally set in.

"Weren't you listening?" Murphy groaned in exasperation. "I! Don't! Know! Should I spell that for you?!" Suddenly there was a loud crack and the tree behind me sent an explosion of splinters down on my head. I turned in confusion to inspect the huge chunk that was now missing from the bark of the tree, only to find myself flat on my back in the next second as the rope still tied around my ankle went tight, ripping my legs out from under me. There was a heavy thud and Gary and Murphy landed next to me. Gary's hand was still firmly stuck to the rope connected to my ankle, and when he'd dived to the ground, he'd brought us both with him. I made a mental note to untie that rope as soon as possible. A second later, there was another resounding bang and a tree to my right let out its own shower of splintered wood. This time I knew what had blasted it. A bullet. And it had hit in the exact spot Murphy's head had occupied only moments before. Rolling to my stomach, I threw my hands over my head, pressing myself against the ground. I was going to die. I knew it with every fiber of my being. The sound of three more

291

bullets slamming into the surrounding trees echoed out into the forest, and I squeezed my eyes shut.

"Hold it!" bellowed a deep voice. The gunshots stopped as abruptly as they had started. I didn't move, inhaling the earthy smell of the forest floor as I waited to see what would happen next.

"Did you hit it, Jerry?" called another voice.

"I don't think that was a deer," said the first voice. "Did you see the way it dived to the ground?"

A deer? I thought foggily. Why would they think we were deer? Prying one eye open, I saw that Gary and I were wearing head-to-toe camouflage, and Murphy, well, Murphy was wearing camouflage too, but his was underneath a hideous eighties prom dress. A brown polka-dot prom dress with white puffed sleeves. If I squinted, I could see what they meant. With his spindly frame and that dress he *did* look like a deer. The underbrush to our right suddenly rustled and four men wearing bright-orange hunting gear stomped out, large rifles clutched in their hands. They glanced around the forest, and I knew the exact second they spotted us because their faces drained of color simultaneously. Not that I blamed them—realizing that you'd been shooting at kids instead of a deer had to be jarring. Although probably not as jarring as actually being the one shot at.

Realizing the danger had passed, Murphy and Gary got shakily to their feet. I didn't. My muscles had turned to squishy puddles of mush, and all I could manage was to sprawl on the ground panting as the panic slowly drained from my veins.

"Emerson, are you okay? Were you hit?" Murphy asked as he reached down to flip me over. I allowed myself to be rolled like the stump of wood I was and stared up into the terrified faces of my friends and a very worried hunter.

"Were you hit?" Gary repeated.

"No." I shook my head and reached out a hand to Murphy, who grabbed it and hauled me to my shaky feet. "But you almost were." The image of that bullet smashing into the exact spot Murphy's head had been only moments before replayed in my mind again, and I had to swallow the urge to vomit.

"What are you kids doing out here? This is private property," one of the men said as he turned Gary roughly so he could see him. "Did any of you get hit?" He ran his eyes over each of us as his companions hurried over. If I had to guess, I would say they were all in their late forties. Three of them were built the same, with receding hairlines and round beer bellies cinched into hunting pants. The fourth man was leaner, with spidery wrinkles around his mouth and narrowed eyes.

"What are *we* doing here?!" Gary fumed. "What are *you* doing shooting at us?"

"It's deer season!" the shortest of the four men explained, his bearded face red with anger. "Any fool who stomps around the woods dressed like you three deserves to be shot at!"

"Frank," the first man admonished. "They're just kids. Relax. If you have another heart attack I'm not carrying your butt to the truck." He turned back to us and took off his hat to run a hand over thinning hair. "You did give us a scare." He jerked his head at Murphy's tattered brown dress. "Is that a dress?"

"Who cares about the kid's stupid dress?" asked the short man. "They are on private property. If they'd gotten shot, we wouldn't be liable. I have signs posted all over the place against trespassers."

"We're sorry," I stuttered, taking an involuntary step back that almost sent me sprawling when my feet got tangled in the rope still attaching me to Gary. I bent to untie it.

"Don't do that," Murphy said, yanking my arm away. I glanced up at him in surprise, but I let go of the thick knot of rope.

"Why?" I asked.

"Because if I travel back to Camp Outlier, I'm guessing you'd like to come with?" he whispered.

I gulped and nodded. The thought of Gary and Murphy disappearing and leaving me behind had never occurred to me. Now that it had, I really wished it hadn't. I felt twitchy and my heart was pounding entirely too hard. Although that could have been an aftereffect of almost dying; I wasn't experienced enough with being shot at to really know.

"Did you just say Camp Outlier?" cut in the fourth man. He was the thin one, and up until this point he'd been standing behind the other three staring at us. It was a look I didn't exactly like. Those beady eyes moved from the rope around my ankle to Gary's hand stuck to Murphy's shoulder and then back to me.

"He did," Gary snarled. "And when we get back there, we're going to make sure our parents know about this. Trespassing signs or not, we could sue you rednecks for everything you're worth!"

"Gary, that's enough," Murphy warned, taking a step back. "Let's just leave these nice men to their hunting and go."

"Are you kidding me?" Gary yelped, whirling to face Murphy, which was a bad idea, seeing as his hand was still connected to Murphy's shoulder. The result was a head-on collision that left them both blinking and rubbing their foreheads. Gary recovered first and glared at Murphy. "Sorry," he muttered. "I forgot. But I couldn't have heard you right. Did you really just call these four hilljacks *nice men*?" Just then the rope still stuck to Gary's hand released with a pop that made us all jump.

"It's about time," Gary said, flexing his fingers. He stared glumly at the hand still stuck to Murphy and gave it a halfhearted yank. It didn't budge. Murphy sprang into action, and before Gary could protest, Murphy had taken his newly freed hand and smashed it onto my bare forearm.

"Hey!" Gary said. Murphy didn't respond. He just stood there, his lips pressed firmly together as he stared at the men. "Oh, right," Gary said, rolling his eyes. "Can't leave good old Floaty McFloaterson behind when we time travel back. Although"—he glared at me— "I'm kind of tempted at the moment." He cocked his head to the side as something occurred to him and turned excitedly toward Murphy. "Wait a minute. Do you think this means you survive? You were supposed to die here, right? I mean, two seconds and your brain would have been splattered all over that tree." He jerked his head toward the tree in question. "So everything's okay, right?"

Murphy's face had gone white, and he was shaking his head at Gary, his eyes wide. The message he was trying desperately to send was crystal clear—*Shut up, Gary. Shut up now.* Unfortunately, Gary was too riled up to notice. I did, though, and I shot a nervous glance at the thin man. He was smiling at us in a way that made my skin prickle uncomfortably.

Oblivious, Gary turned back to the men. "What year is it? We need to figure out if we time traveled to the future or the past." Murphy dropped his head into his hands in defeat, and a sick feeling of dread crept over me at the look that had come over all four men's faces.

The thin man grinned, pulled a pack of cigarettes out of his pocket, and placed one between nicotine-stained teeth. He turned to the first man. "Are these three what I think they are?"

"Run!" Murphy yelled, already turning, but the thin man snaked his hand out and grabbed me by the shoulder. Since Gary's hand was stuck tight to my arm, this brought Gary and Murphy up short too, and they stumbled backward into me. I tried to reach out to steady them, but the man's grip on my arm was like iron.

He turned to his buddies. "Say hello to our early retirement plan, boys." The shorter of the other three men had pulled his rifle up, and although he didn't have it pointed at us, the threat was there.

"What are you talking about?" Gary asked nervously, his eyes flicking from the gun to the man holding it.

"Don't you know?" the thin man sneered. "Ever since the RISK Reduction Act got passed, RISKs like you can't just go wandering around wherever you please. We gots to keep the general public safe. It's the law. There's a hefty reward for bringing in rogue RISKs."

"What?" I spluttered, glancing to Murphy for some kind of direction.

"Dangers to society," added the short man. "Isn't one of their kind responsible for exploding the Washington Monument?"

"It was Lincoln's Memorial," the first man corrected. "Speaking of, what if one of them catches fire or expands or makes us go blind or somethin'? I've heard that some of them can do that."

"I don't think these three can," the thin man sniffed. "They don't seem higher than level threes. Although," he said, plucking experimentally at my vest, "this one might be something else altogether. What's the vest for, boy?" He reached for the front clip of my vest, and I panicked and jerked backward. My arm popped loose from the man's grasp, and we seized our opportunity and ran. All the fear of the last few minutes pounded through my veins, and I found myself dragging Gary and Murphy along behind me as I wove under low-hanging branches and around overgrown trees. A gunshot rang out, and a tree to our left practically exploded as it got hit by buckshot at close range.

"Don't shoot them, you idiot!" bellowed the sandy-haired man. "Catch them!" The sound of running feet came from behind us, but I didn't slow down to look. I barely registered that we were running downhill until a lake loomed in front of us. I could feel the men gaining on us, and I knew that it was only a matter of time before they caught up. Suddenly Murphy groaned, doubling over so abruptly that he knocked me and Gary off-balance. I threw my hands out instinctively to catch myself, but a moment before I face-planted into the ground, everything around me went black. For the second time in my life I felt the twisting pain of being yanked through time. A moment later I hit the ground, rolling in a tumble of flailing arms and legs with Gary and Murphy.

"They're back!" someone shouted, and an instant later we were being untangled by the helpful hands of the guys of Red Maple as Eli's anxious face peered down at us. I whipped my head from side to side, half expecting the four men and their guns to show back up at any second. Instead, I saw Camp O's lake. It was too much. All of it. The time travel, the men, the guns, time traveling again. Leaning over, I hurled. Everyone leaped back with exclamations of disgust as the contents of my stomach splattered onto the ground for the second time that day. I spit and wiped my mouth on the back of my hand, looking up just in time to catch Molly's eyes staring at me from a group of girls. And for the first time, I didn't even care.

"Are you okay?" Mr. Blue asked, helping us the rest of the way to our feet.

"No!" Gary exclaimed. "We're not! Do we look like we're okay? We just got shot at! Murphy almost died! We all almost died. And then, just when we thought it was safe, it wasn't! It got worse! Worse than getting shot at! I didn't even know that was possible! We were in the future and there were these guys, and—" Gary's rant was cut off abruptly as Murphy slapped a hand over his mouth.

"We're fine," he said, his white face and wide frightened eyes exposing the lie for what it was.

"Tell him the rules," Mr. Blue said quietly under his breath, with a nervous glance over his shoulder. "The TTBI will be here any moment."

Murphy's face went even whiter than before, and Mr. Blue shook his head apologetically. "I'm sorry. But as a government-approved camp, we have to report anything abnormal. Time travelers aren't supposed to pick up hitchhikers."

He turned to the group of gawking campers and raised his hands, a smile back in place and his voice booming. "Everyone please report back to your cabins," he said with a forced cheerfulness I doubted anyone really believed. "The situation is being handled, and everyone is all right. We will convene to formally announce the winners of the boys' capture-the-flag game at eight o'clock, when you meet at the dining hall for some of our famous chocolate chip cookies." Reluctantly the crowd dispersed, our fellow campers climbing the hill with worried murmurs and glances over their shoulders at us.

"Are you guys seriously okay?" said a voice at my elbow, and I turned to see Hank, his brow furrowed as he looked at us. "All three of you look like you've seen a ghost. You weren't even gone that long. What happened?"

"That's enough, Mr. Roberts," Mr. Blue said, a firm hand on Hank's shoulder as he guided him none too gently away from us. "Please join the rest of your cabin." He glanced over Hank's head at Eli. "I will bring these three up after the questioning."

"The questioning?" Gary said, looking from Mr. Blue to Murphy and back again, his brow furrowed. "What questioning?" Just then the sharp wail of a siren cut through the air, and Murphy jumped.

"I will try to delay them," Mr. Blue said quietly. "Give you guys a second to pull yourselves together."

With that he turned and jogged up the hill, where three men in dark suits were just getting out of a large white SUV that sported flashing red lights and the initials TTBI across the side.

"Come here," Murphy whispered, pulling Gary and me a few feet away from my puddle of puke. Gary's hands were still stuck tight to our arms, and we stumbled into the shelter of a nearby pine.

"What's going on?" Gary asked.

"Just shut up, will you?" Murphy snapped, glancing nervously behind us to where we could just make out Mr. Blue talking to the suited men, who seemed to be ignoring him as they strode purposefully down the hill toward us. "You've already broken enough laws as it is."

"I didn't break a law," Gary sputtered indignantly.

"You did," Murphy snapped. "When you time travel you cannot, under any circumstances, tell people you're a traveler. It's one of the first laws of time travel. If those guys up there find out, we all get thrown in jail."

"How was I supposed to know that?" Gary protested.

"You weren't," Murphy said, his voice barely a whisper as Mr. Blue and the men got closer. "Because it's impossible for someone to time travel with someone else. Or at least it's supposed to be. Now listen and listen good. When the TTBI gets down here, we can leave out that Gary said we're from the future, but we will have to tell them what happened. It's the law. It's why I have to log my time-travel episodes with Nurse Betsy."

"But," I protested, "I thought you weren't allowed to talk about your time travels?"

Murphy nodded. "Not to the general public, but the government? That's a different story. Whatever you do, don't tell them that you planned to stick Gary to me. Then they'll know that I told you I wasn't going to survive the summer. We have to convince them that it was just some freak accident."

"But—" Gary protested.

"No *buts*," Murphy said, cutting him off. "If the TTBI even suspects that I blabbed to you guys, they will lock us all up and throw away the key. We're young and a liability. These guys don't mess around. People are sent away and imprisoned for life as safety precautions. Let me do all the talking. I'll just tell them about our jump, and hopefully we can leave it at that." He studied each of our faces to see if we were getting the message. As I stood there processing his words, all the mysterious pieces of the Murphy puzzle slammed into place with the violence of a head-on collision. Shutting my eyes, I dropped my head into my hands to think as the conversation I'd had with future Murphy played over again in my mind, the way he'd been so panicked, so desperate. He'd said that I'd know when *it* happened. I turned wide frightened eyes on Murphy.

"No," I said.

"What do you mean, no?" Murphy said.

"I mean that we can't tell them anything. You came from the future and warned me about this on the first night of our camp-out."

"I did what?" Murphy asked, with another panicked glance up the hill, where Mr. Blue and the TTBI men were closing in fast.

"Just trust me," I said, desperate now that I realized what was at stake. "Whatever happens, we can't tell the TTBI what those guys said. Don't ask me why. I have no flying clue." I looked at Murphy. "But future you was pretty freaked about the whole thing, and I think we need to listen to him." Murphy stared at me for a second, his lips pressed in a thin line, and then he nodded. I turned to Gary, who finally grumbled his consent, and I sagged a little in relief. Murphy glanced nervously over his shoulder and leaned in closer, his voice low. "Then we need to have our stories straight. When those guys ask, we time traveled to a forest. Nothing special or distinctive about it, just a generic forest with pine trees. We don't know if it was in the past or the future because we saw no one and talked to no one. We walked around for a little bit and then we traveled back. Got it?"

Gary frowned, still looking unconvinced. I had no idea what my own face looked like, but it was probably a lot like the expression a raccoon wore right before an eighteen-wheeler hit him.

"Be believable," Murphy muttered under his breath.

"Boys," Mr. Blue said, walking up. "These gentlemen from the TTBI have a few questions for you."

I gulped, wishing I had a glass of water or a toothbrush to get rid of the acidic taste of vomit in my mouth, and turned to face the men. I could only hope that I was better at lying than I'd been at time traveling.

CHAPTER TWENTY

Two hours later I was sitting on the floor of our cabin with a gigantic bag of frozen brussels sprouts over my swollen left eye. I'd almost forgotten about the black eye Gary had given me until Nurse Betsy had pulled me aside and thrust the frost-covered bag into my hand. She'd warned me not to eat them, as though eating frozen brussels sprouts was some big temptation. It wasn't. The bag smelled like moldy feet. As I'd placed it onto my throbbing face, I'd been a little disappointed it wasn't a steak. Whenever a guy got a black eye in the movies, they held a raw steak to their eye. It made them look tough, rugged, and manly. Frozen brussels sprouts did none of those things.

I'd spotted Molly on the way up to our cabin, and she'd waved. It was a pity wave, though, for the public puking and the lame brussels sprouts bag defrosting on my face. Pity waves sucked. People who got pity waves never got kissed. Ever.

I eased myself back against my bunk bed and watched as the Red Maple guys got ready for bed. The atmosphere in the cabin was quieter than usual, and I could only assume that it was because Eli had given them strict instructions not to ask Murphy, Gary, or me about what had happened. Although from the furtive glances they kept shooting our way, it was obvious that they were dying to do just that.

The questioning from the TTBI had been intense and had taken so long that we'd missed the ceremony in the dining hall announcing the Red Maple cabin as the winners for the guys' capture the flag. A fact that should have really bothered me but didn't. It was weird, all summer I'd dreamed about winning, but now that we had, I could not care less. I shuddered, remembering the cool stare of the officers who had grilled us for hours about our time-traveling trip. We'd lucked out that Gary's hands had still been stuck to our arms. Otherwise they would have split us up for questioning, and our stories might not have matched up as perfectly as they needed to. For my part, I tried to keep things vague, playing up my disorientation and reminding the men multiple times that I was a puke risk by sitting with a trash can between my knees. Through it all, we'd stuck to the story Murphy had given us, trying to make it sound like we'd barely figured out which way was up before we'd traveled back to camp. The men watched our every move, studying our faces, trying to read something there. Finally, unable to separate us for further questioning, they'd relented and let us head back to our cabin. To our relief, Gary's hands had popped off on our way up the hill, freeing us to move like individuals again.

"Lights-out in five," Eli called from his spot near the door to the cabin as he watched us get ready for bed. Probably to prevent anyone from asking any questions they weren't supposed to ask. He was holding our capture-the-flag trophy, passing it from hand to hand, a worried frown on his face. Reluctantly, I got to my feet. The brussels sprouts smelled even worse thawed than they had frozen, and I chucked the soggy bag unceremoniously into the trash before climbing into bed and strapping myself down for the night, still wearing my capture-the-flag camouflage.

A minute before Eli turned the lights out, something soft and crinkly bounced off my forehead. With a surreptitious glance to make sure Eli wasn't watching, I unfolded the crumpled wad of paper. On it, written in a hasty scrawl, were the words:

Midnight meeting. Wait for my signal.—H

I looked up from the note and gave a slight nod just as the lights went out. It didn't even matter that the last time he'd arranged something like this I'd ended up scrubbing toilets with a toothbrush; I was desperate to talk with my best friend.

When the signal—an all too familiar bungee cord—was eventually whipped at my head, I managed to catch it before it clobbered me. Progress. I quickly unstrapped myself, and Hank expertly floated me across the room and through the window of our cabin, where my vest was waiting. The night was a cold one, and I shivered as I followed him into the woods. I'd lost my hoodie at the fireworks display the night Molly had held my hand, and I really missed it.

"Talk," Hank said as soon as we were out of sight of the cabin. So I talked, filling him in on everything from the hunters and Murphy almost getting shot to the interrogation from the TTBI guys. Hank stayed silent through the whole thing, an uncharacteristic frown on his face.

"So that was what future Murphy was talking

about," he finally said when I was done. I swallowed hard as I remembered how ragged and thin he'd been. Had not telling the TTBI about what happened in the future changed that somehow? Fixed it?

Suddenly there was a snuffling snort from behind us, and Hank and I both whirled as a tiny black-and-white creature waddled out of the shadows of the trees. My heart, which had momentarily stopped, restarted with a vengeance as Mr. Stink inspected my bare feet with interest. Zeke followed a second later with Anthony, Murphy, and Gary right behind.

"We saw you two knuckleheads sneak out," Gary said, arms crossed. "What's the big idea leaving us behind?"

"Is it about today?" Zeke asked, eyes wide. "Because we are dying to know what happened." He turned to me. "Did you plan on sticking Gary to Murphy all along? Why didn't you tell us during our brainstorming sessions?"

"Wait a second," Murphy said, with an accusing glare at Hank and me. "There were brainstorming sessions?"

Hank glanced around nervously. "Let's not talk here," he said. "Follow me." Ten minutes later we were down by the lake. The whole thing brought back memories of the infamous bonfire night, but Hank jogged right past the spot where we'd caught the lake on fire. He finally stopped in front of a small cave I'd never seen before. He ducked inside, and we followed.

The inside of the cave was tiny, about the size of the cab of a pickup truck, with a damp, musty smell to it. I caught more than one elbow in the head and jabbed a few people with my own as we shifted and shoved in order to fit. A moment later Hank produced a tiny electric lantern, and the small space was flooded with a warm orange glow.

"No fire this time?" Zeke asked, eyebrow raised.

Hank made a face. "Very funny, but we aren't here for your comedy routine. Which needs work, by the way." He jerked his head at me. "Go ahead, Emerson, tell them."

I glanced over at Murphy. "Are you okay with this?" I said.

Murphy sighed and shook his head. "No," he said. "But we've already broken about a million time-traveling rules today, so what's one more? Besides, the guys deserve to know what happened. I know you've all been worried about me this summer, and as pathetic as some of your attempts to keep me from time traveling were, I appreciated them."

311

"Just hurry up and get it over with," Gary said, leaning back against the wall of the cave, his arms crossed over his chest. "This whole thing gives me the creeps."

Murphy squared his thin shoulders. "Before we say anything, everyone has to promise not to talk about what gets said here tonight."

"Why all the secrecy?" Zeke asked, his brow furrowed. "You've hinted about future stuff before and it was never a big deal. Like how you told Emerson he wouldn't die when we floated him up in that tree on initiation night, or how you knew that it wasn't a good idea to have that bonfire by the lake."

Murphy shook his head. "That was different, all unimportant stuff, and really I shouldn't have even done that."

Gary elbowed me painfully in the ribs. "Hear that?" he muttered sarcastically under his breath. "Your life is unimportant stuff." I made a face at him.

"You saw those guys who showed up in the white SUV today," Murphy went on. "If they find out that Emerson, Gary, and I hid something that we saw in the future from them, and that we told you about it, we could all be imprisoned or worse."

"What's worse than prison?" Anthony asked as he calmly extinguished the small fire that had just broken out on his left elbow.

"You really don't want to know." Murphy shuddered. "My uncle was a time jumper too. More sporadic than me, and he tried to make some extra money betting. The TTBI caught up with him. . . . We never saw him again."

"They get it," Gary growled. "It's a big secret."

"Right." Murphy nodded. He went on to describe our near miss with the hunters, and what our conversation with them had revealed. When he was done, no one spoke for a minute.

"So they were going to turn you in? For money?" Anthony finally said slowly.

"That's crazy," Zeke said. "There are so many laws in place to protect people like us. Our government spends millions to accommodate our RISK factors."

"Yeah," Anthony said. "My school has to have all this extra fire-prevention stuff, and I have an aide who comes to every class with me trained in fire-extinguishing techniques. I heard my dad say once that it cost the government almost forty grand a year."

"That's probably part of the problem," Gary snapped. "Maybe everyone got sick of spending so much money on kids like us. Kids who are unpredictable and dangerous." When no one said anything, Gary huffed in frustration. "Don't you get it? We aren't anything special! What we can do isn't cool. We never got a letter from Hogwarts. There is no bald guy in a wheelchair going to show up at our door to recruit us to be part of his team of supermutants. Our parents weren't Greek gods who blessed us with cool superpowers. There is never going to be a moment where we realize that these things we can do are actually really great. We will never be anything but a burden and a danger." He motioned to Anthony. "Take good old fire butt, for example," he said. "He's a forest or building fire waiting to happen." He went around the circle, pointing at each of us. "Hank, we love you, man, but you are going to disappear at the wrong time someday and get hit by a bus or worse. Emerson is going to float straight to the moon if he ever forgets that stupid vest of his, and Zeke can't see squat, so he'll probably walk in front of the very same bus that hit Hank. I'll get stuck to something someday and either starve to death or have to chew my own arm off."

He got to Murphy, and his arm dropped. "And we all know that what you do is deadly. Don't you see? We will never wear capes that we rip off to save someone, because *we* are the ones who need the saving. We'll all be lucky to survive our childhood in one piece, and they are spending a fortune on us. And obviously, someone finally figured that out."

We sat in shocked silence for a second as Gary

leaned back with a scowl. His words hung heavy in the air until Hank sat forward, his face serious in the glow of the lamp.

"Gary, my friend," Hank finally said, "I suggest that you *not* take up motivational speaking as a career." Gary glared at him for a minute before snorting out a surprised laugh. The tension in the cave drained like the air out of a popped bike tire, and I joined in, the laughter loosening something wound tight inside me.

"So, Murphy," Hank said after we'd all calmed down. "You're the only time-travel expert we have. Do you think that by not telling the TTBI what those guys said, you fixed the future?"

Murphy shrugged. "I have no idea. It's possible that just by mentioning to the TTBI the RISK Reduction Act those guys talked about, a domino effect would be started that actually *made* it happen. It's also completely possible that we didn't change anything, just delayed it somehow. For all we know, we could have made it worse. That's what's screwy about the future. It's so touchy. It's why we aren't supposed to mess with it."

Everyone sat in silence for a moment, quietly processing everything Murphy had just said, and I wondered if thinking about the future made anyone else's brain hurt.

"But it *is* possible to change the future," Hank eventually said. "I mean, we changed your future, didn't we? Or at least Gary did. He saved your life, right? If it weren't for him pulling you out of the way of that bullet, you'd be a goner right now. So the future is already different from the one you visited where you were dead."

"Man, Gary," Anthony whistled. "You're a hero."

Gary just shrugged noncommittally and looked down. I eyed him suspiciously. That was not typical Gary behavior. With the exception of Hank, he was the most likely to boast and brag about his own accomplishments. I made a mental note to ask him what was up later.

Murphy bit his lip, still looking unconvinced. "You have a point," he finally said. "But—"

"No buts," Hank interrupted. "I'm going to consider the future changed until we know otherwise. Future you wouldn't have told Emerson what to do if it didn't fix something."

Murphy smiled wryly. "I'm really going to miss your positive outlook on things, Hank."

"What do you mean?" Anthony asked. "Aren't you going to come back next year?"

Murphy shifted uncomfortably and looked at the

dirt floor of the cave. "I can't make any promises, guys. This was my Make-A-Wish, remember? My parents could never afford this place otherwise." He paused as something dawned on him, and bit his lip worriedly. "In fact," he said, "I wasn't supposed to survive this summer. What if Make-A-Wish makes my parents pay them back or something?"

"They won't do that," I said, wishing I felt as convincing as I sounded.

"You have to come back," Zeke yelped, sitting forward so quickly that Hank's lantern toppled over. Mr. Stink jumped sideways, further upsetting the lantern. Zeke fumbled to right it as he looked to the rest of us for support. "We wouldn't be the Red Maple men without you."

Murphy's face flushed with pleasure at being not only accepted but wanted. And for the first time in my life, I knew how he felt. Camp O had given me that, given us all that.

"We'll find a way," Hank said confidently. "It can't be too hard to raise a little money."

"I get three hundred dollars for my birthday every year," I blurted. "It's yours, Murph." Everyone else caught on and quickly offered up their own birthday and lawn-mowing money. Murphy looked about to cry as he nodded his thanks.

"So it's settled," Hank said. "We all come back next year, and if something bad is going to happen in the future, we will face it together." He grinned at us. "We won capture the flag, after all. How much harder can fixing the future be?"

CHAPTER TWENTY-ONE

As we headed back toward camp, my heart felt lighter. When we got to the lake, I stopped, staring at the water.

"What's up, E-dawg?" Hank asked.

"I have to get my iron shoes out of the lake." I frowned. I'd forgotten about them until just that second. It seemed like a lifetime ago that Hank had sunk them on our first day at camp. The thought of putting them back on cast a shadow over my mood from moments before, but as a level five, I was required by law to have two forms of protection in place at all times. I'd been lucky to get away with just the vest for the entire summer.

"I'll go," Hank said, kicking off his flip-flops and wading in without a moment's hesitation.

"You don't have to do that," I protested.

"I tossed them in," he said. "Besides, you don't have your swimming weights here, and if you go in with that vest on you're liable to drown." I looked down and frowned. How had I forgotten about the vest? "Zeke! Anthony! Murphy!" Hank called. "Get down here and help me." The other boys waded in, and I stood on the bank next to Gary and watched as my friends dived for my iron shoes.

"So what's it feel like to be a hero?" I asked Gary after a few minutes of watching them splash around.

Gary scowled at the ground. "I'm no hero," he muttered.

I turned to him in surprise. "You saved Murphy," I pointed out. "That makes you a hero."

"I wasn't even thinking about Murphy when that first gunshot went off. I dived, and he just happened to be stuck to me." He snorted. "My dad would say that's typical Gary behavior, only thinking about myself."

"Gary," I said, surprised. "Do you really think that matters? It's human nature to react exactly like you did. But that doesn't change the fact that you saved Murphy's life."

"Still," Gary sniffed.

I eyed my glowering friend for a second and then decided to try a different approach. "Fine. If that doesn't make you feel like a hero, think about this. If it weren't for your sticky hands, we never would have been there in the first place. Murphy would have been a goner. You did that."

He sniffed. "It was your stupid idea to stick me to him in the first place."

"True." I nodded. "But I wouldn't be alive if *your* sticky hand hadn't saved my life on initiation night. You have a lot to be proud of."

"You think so?" he asked.

I nodded. "Definitely."

Before he could respond, Anthony found one of my shoes. It took two guys to swim it to shore. When they hefted it into my waiting hands, I almost stumbled. I'd forgotten just how heavy they actually were. I wrinkled my nose at the waterlogged leather, which smelled like rotten fish. It was going to be a real joy to strap this thing on tomorrow. Five minutes later Hank found the other one, with our Red Maple flag still tied to its algae-covered shoelaces. When he handed it to me, I discovered that this one also had a new occupant, a tiny turtle. I let the little guy go and sloshed out the water, one shoe in each hand. I wasn't going to put them on until I absolutely had to.

We were just passing Nurse Betsy's cabin when Hank came to a dead stop.

"What now?" Zeke asked.

Hank turned to us with a wild gleam in his eye. "I just got a brilliant idea."

"I already don't think I like this," Anthony said.

"Really?" Gary said. "Because I'm positive I don't like this."

"Haven't we broken enough rules for one night?" Murphy pleaded. "If we make it back to our cabin without getting caught, it's going to be a minor miracle."

"Come on," Hank cajoled. "One last adventure before we all head home tomorrow? I promise it doesn't involve fire."

"Does it involve girls?" I asked, cocking an eyebrow at my friend.

He snorted. "Of course." Sighing in resignation, we huddled around Hank to hear the plan. Five minutes later we were creeping up the hill toward the Monarch girls' cabin, and I couldn't keep the grin off my face. This was going to be good.

We didn't get done with Hank's prank until well after three in the morning, and I barely managed to secure my tethers before falling asleep. The sky was still dark, with just the faintest hint of the sun over the horizon, when someone shaking my ankle pried me awake. I sat bolt upright and cracked my head on the ceiling, muttered some choice words, and threw on my vest. I'd forgotten during our late-night adventures that we were waking up early for a polar bear plunge in the lake. Grabbing my pillow, I threw it across the room, hitting Hank square in the face. It was his fault, after all, that I'd only gotten about an hour's worth of sleep the night before. He sprang from his bed like he'd been shot and stood in the middle of the cabin with two invisible arms, his hair standing out in every direction, a befuddled expression on his face, as though he couldn't decide which way to run. He finally focused his blurry gaze, realized why he was up, and quickly began shaking everyone else awake.

There was a lot of grunting and groaning, but eventually we stumbled outside in our swim trunks, towels wrapped tightly around our shoulders against the chill of the morning. My teeth chattered, and I had pleasant thoughts about shooting whoever thought up the stupid tradition of jumping into a cold lake before dawn for your last day at camp. Halfway down the hill, the Redwood guys fell in next to us. Apparently a polar bear plunge was also a tradition for the last day of your last summer at camp.

Our flip-flopped feet slapped noisily in the predawn silence as we headed down the hill toward the lake.

The Redwood guys bantered back and forth, pulling us out of our sleep-deprived stupor one laugh at a time. Even Gary cracked a very reluctant smile when the guys revealed that we weren't the only ones to have scrubbed the bathrooms with a toothbrush. All of their smiles had a sad, melancholy edge to them, though, and I tried to imagine what it was like to know this was your last summer as a Camp O camper. Two of the Redwood guys planned on applying to be camp counselors when they turned eighteen, but I was sure it wouldn't feel quite the same.

When we reached the lake, I realized that there was another tradition involving the polar bear plunge. No sooner had I shucked off my vest and bent over to double-check the straps of my swimming weights than someone grabbed me bodily from behind and launched me skyward. Hank and Gary soared through the air next to me, their faces mirroring my own shock. My squawk of surprise was cut off as I hit the surface of the freezing-cold lake and the icy water closed over my head. I emerged spluttering just in time to dodge Anthony, Zeke, and Murphy as they plummeted into the water. A second later the Redwood guys cannonballed in with war whoops that echoed out through the still-sleeping forest. They came up laughing, their lips just as blue as the water, and together we swam for our towels.

I was so busy trying to prevent my chattering teeth from biting off my own tongue that I almost forgot about our prank from the night before. A loud-ringing shriek from the girls' hill brought it all rushing back to me, though, and I jumped guiltily. Eli and Redwood's counselor shot each other a worried look and took off up the girls' hill at a dead sprint. It took the rest of us only a moment to get our wits and towels around us before we were charging after them.

We made it to the Monarch cabin and stopped. The girls were standing on their front deck in their pajamas, a baffled look on their faces as they surveyed the surrounding trees. Every item of clothing they weren't wearing had been knotted together into long multicolored ropes and strung along the branches of the trees like deranged Christmas lights.

The prank had been almost too easy. Like us, they'd had to pack the day before, and all their bags had been piled by the cabin door. It'd been a simple matter to sneak them outside and tie everything together. I had done the honors of draping everything in the trees, with the help of a length of rope tied to my ankle. And, I thought proudly, I hadn't even puked when I did it. At the sight of the girls' bewildered faces, I burst out laughing. Hank was next, his throaty chuckle blending in with the deeper laughter of the Redwood guys. The girls smiled reluctantly after a few more moments of looking furious—although Kristy was looking at Hank with a calculating expression that made me uneasy. The only people not laughing were the counselors, but I could tell Eli was fighting back a grin.

Three of the Redwood guys, as well as Hank and Murphy, climbed the tree and quickly untangled the multicolored rope, dropping it down to the waiting girls, who gathered it up and headed back into their cabin to sort through their clothes. Eli turned to us, his arms crossed. "Anyone want to tell me anything?"

"Not a thing," Murphy said, rewrapping his towel around his shoulders. "It's pretty crazy that happened to their clothes, though. Don't you think?" Eli gave Murphy a hard look. Murphy looked back at him, all wide-eyed innocence. Maybe it was because Murphy had essentially just come back from the dead, but Eli let it go. "Hit the showers," he finally barked. "I want you down at the dining hall in ten."

"You know," Hank drawled, "the girls' showers are a whole lot closer. I bet they wouldn't mind . . ."

"Go," Eli bellowed, and we turned and took off down the girls' hill.

"I still say we should have left something that let them know it was us," Zeke whispered as we ran. "Maybe tie one of our T-shirts into the clothes chain or something? I don't even care if we got toothbrush-scrubbing duty again. It would have been worth it to get credit."

"Oh, I think they know it was us," I said, thinking of the way Kristy had been looking at Hank. I cranked the shower to scalding and sighed as I felt it heat up my frozen body. Ten minutes later we were back down the hill and sliding into our seats at the dining hall. The Monarch girls came in last, probably because we'd made sure our knots were extra tight. Their clothes were wrinkled, and they looked substantially less amused than they had earlier.

Without even glancing our way, they each grabbed a large pitcher of ice water off the trays and began making the rounds from table to table. I felt a pang of guilt that they'd gotten KP duty on the last day at camp, and I wondered if we should apologize. Suddenly, my Molly radar went off, and I turned in time to see her walking toward me. When I turned back, I discovered that all the Monarch girls were standing around our table, water pitchers in hand. Kristy smiled sweetly at Hank, who had just begun quoting lines from *Twilight*, and then she dumped her entire pitcher over his head. A moment later a gush of freezing water crashed over my head, turning my laugh into a gasp as ice went down my vest. I jumped to my feet, shaking myself like a wet dog in a desperate attempt to dislodge it. The entire dining hall was roaring and catcalling, and I looked back at Molly in astonishment.

Sweet, quiet Molly was grinning wickedly as she leaned in and whispered in my ear, her lips feather-light and warm against my skin. "Payback is never fun, is it Emerson?" She winked and whirled to join the rest of the Monarch girls as they sashayed back to their table. We sat back down, dripping, and tried to wring the water from our clothes. Anthony was steaming. Apparently it was harder to catch fire while soaked.

"Well, men," Eli said, sitting down at the only dry spot, "I think you probably deserved that one." None of us said anything, because we could see what Eli couldn't. A second later the Monarch girls' counselor dumped two whole pitchers of water over an astonished Eli's head. He jumped up in surprise and made a grab for her, but she spun neatly away and headed back to her own table, where the Monarch girls were whooping and cheering.

"What was that for?" he called.

"For not keeping your cabin under control!" she called back. Eli sat back down, and we all stared at him, waiting to see if he was angry. But he just grinned and dug his fork into his soggy plate of scrambled eggs. Hank burst out laughing, and the rest of us joined in. Mr. Stink chose that moment to lumber out from under our table, where he'd taken refuge. Zeke lifted him onto the bench beside him and slipped him a piece of bacon. I smiled. I was going to miss that skunk.

I was just helping Gary clear the last of the breakfast dishes when the dining room doors were flung open and a small herd of parents flooded inside. Murphy's parents were in the lead, crying again, but this time it was with happiness as they wrapped him up in a hug. Zeke and Anthony's parents were next, and finally my mom.

She stood silhouetted in the doorway, scanning the dining hall. Her eyes passed over me twice, as she disregarded the tan boy with the Mohawk and the black eye. As more and more campers were claimed by parents, she began to get nervous, shifting on her heels. Her head tipped back, and she did a quick check of the ceiling, probably to make sure I wasn't bobbing around in one of the corners. It wouldn't have been the first time she found me there. I took a deep breath and walked over to give my mom a hug. Her eyes widened in surprise as recognition slowly dawned on her face.

"Emerson? Boo-Boo? Is that you? What happened to your hair? And your face? My God, is that a black eye? Why are you wet?" she asked, her hand fluttering at her throat.

"It's me, Mom," I said, wrapping her in another hug. She felt small and birdlike in my arms, and I was surprised to find that I was now looking down at her instead of up. "I'm glad to see you," I said. "I missed you." And I realized it was true. She was too busy scanning my face to respond, as though if she stared hard enough she might find the pale, doughy boy she'd dropped off at the beginning of the summer. Realizing this, I guided her over to a table where Murphy and Hank's parents were sitting having doughnuts and coffee.

"Mom," I said, gesturing to the guys. "Meet Hank and Murphy, two of my friends." My mother's good manners won out over her shock, and she held out a shaky hand. To her credit, she didn't scream when Hank shook it with his invisible one.

"Friends?" she asked me incredulously. I nodded, trying not to look too proud of myself. "Wait a minute," she said, as she peered at Murphy again. "Haven't I met you before?"

Murphy glanced around, as though wondering who my mom was talking to.

"I doubt it, Mom," I cut in. "Murphy's from Ohio."

"No," my mom said stubbornly. "I'm sure of it." She studied Murphy for a moment longer before snapping her fingers. "That's it." She smiled. "You were that nice boy who came to the house with all the Camp Outlier information last December. Why, I already had Emerson enrolled at the local summer school, but you were so convincing that I changed my mind right there on the spot." She turned her too-bright smile on Murphy's parents, whose faces had gone whiter than the powdered-sugar doughnut his dad was holding suspended halfway to his mouth.

"Although," my mom went on, oblivious to everything but the story she was telling, "it couldn't have been you. The boy I talked to was older, maybe sixteen or so? Do you have an older brother?"

Murphy shook his head and shot me a pleading look as the cabin doors opened and Brawny and Burly, the two TTBI officers from the beginning of the summer, came in. They scanned the room, looking bored. Spotting our table, they started weaving through the crowd toward us, probably to escort Murphy home. I wondered if they'd had to give up a day off to come here, since Murphy was never supposed to survive long enough to *need* an escort home. And suddenly, the panicked look on Murphy and his parents' faces made sense, and I felt my stomach drop in realization. My mom had met Murphy, future Murphy, from the sound of it. He'd been the one to tell her about Camp O. He was the reason I'd been here to stick Gary to Murphy.

Murphy had broken the law to get me here, to save himself.

"Maybe a cousin?" my mom went on. "Either that or you have a doppelganger running around."

"Mom," I said, my eyes never leaving the TTBI officers, "drop it."

"Drop what?" she asked, looking down. "I didn't drop any . . ." Her words cut off as she uttered a surprised little scream. She was staring in horror at my feet. I looked down too and my heart sank. I'd forgotten to put on my stupid iron shoes.

"What? What?" she began, pointing at my feet with shaking fingers. Even as my mind scrambled for a convincing reason why I wasn't wearing my shoes, I felt a rush of relief that she was no longer trying to figure out how she knew Murphy. Before I could collect my thoughts enough to say anything, Hank jumped in.

"Oh, those? E-dawg doesn't need those. Didn't Nurse Betsy tell you? She evaluated him this summer and determined it was perfectly safe, and better, healthier even, for him to walk around without them. She got government approval and everything, see?" And to my utter amazement, Hank whipped an official-looking paper out of his back pocket. It was a bit damp, but my mother unfolded it and read quickly before glancing from it to me and back again.

332

"I don't like this," she said, already reaching into her purse for her faithful bottle of anxiety meds. "What if you lose your vest? Or it comes unstrapped? Without a second deterrent you'll float away."

"I won't, Mom," I assured her. "And there are worse things than dying."

"What could be worse than dying?" she gasped.

I shot Hank a look and grinned. "Not really living." Just then Mr. Blue approached my mother and offered her a cup of coffee and a reassuring smile. Hank took my arm and hauled me out of the dining hall as my mother accepted the coffee and gaped up at our big blue leader.

"Where did you get that form from?" I asked as we jogged up the hill. "I wasn't evaluated by Nurse Betsy."

Hank shrugged. "Are you sure? Because I have some pretty convincing paperwork that says otherwise."

"Thanks," I said.

He waved a hand dismissively. "No problem. I grabbed a stack of those forms at the beginning of the summer when I was in her office for that bloody nose I got from tetherball. Those kinds of things always come in handy and, well, when we got your shoes out of the lake last night, you seemed really bummed. So I thought I'd fix it."

I shook my head. "Not only for the shoes. For

everything." I stopped, not sure how to thank someone for being my first real friend.

Hank nodded and clapped me on the back. "That reminds me!" he said a second later, digging around in his pocket. He pulled out a dog-eared pile of envelopes and handed me one. Without any further explanation he whirled and ran back down the hill to hand Zeke, Murphy, Gary, and Anthony their own envelopes. I grinned when I saw what Hank had scrawled across the surface of the envelope in his slanted handwriting.

For E-Dawg.
Do not open until you are on your way
home on pain of death.
—H

Slipping it into my pocket, I jogged the rest of the way to the Red Maple cabin to collect my bags. As I was digging under my bunk, I spotted my shirt and tie from the first day, still crumpled up in the corner. I left them. To my surprise, I also discovered my dust-covered backpack. I'd completely forgotten about it. Sliding back the zipper, I peered in at the stash of electronics and chargers I'd brought along, thinking I'd be spending my summer holed up in the cabin playing video games. The thought was laughable now. I slung the heavy bag over my shoulder. The electronics would be worth a good chunk of change on eBay, and that money would bring us one step closer to making sure Murphy came back to camp next year.

My life list was still tacked to my bed, and I pulled it off gently. By life-listing rules I was officially twenty-five, which felt pretty good. My iron shoes sat glumly on the floor, the edges slightly rusted from their time spent at the bottom of the lake. Not quite sure what to do with them, I stood there a moment considering. I didn't really want to bring them home, but I couldn't exactly leave them under my bunk either. Grabbing one in each hand, I headed out the door, barely missing getting clobbered by the pillow Gary had chucked across the room at Zeke.

The woods were quiet as I jogged through them and down to the lake. Before I could think better of it, I launched the shoes in and watched them sink. Grinning, I ran back to the cabin just in time to join the rest of the guys as we marched back down the hill. I had to admit, the matching Mohawks were pretty awesome.

After a quick glance around to make sure that Brawny and Burly weren't lurking anywhere, I hurried to walk next to Murphy.

"So," I whispered, eyebrows raised, "your future self visited my mom?"

Murphy did the same quick look around I'd just done and shrugged. "Maybe? I have no idea. I guess I haven't done it yet?"

"Don't worry," I said. "My mom will never figure it out. I'll tell her your RISK factor is exploding warts or something."

"Gee." Murphy smiled. "Thanks."

All of a sudden Hank stopped, dropped his bags in the dirt, and took off down the hill. We turned to see the Monarch girls coming down their own hill, and without hesitation, we ran after our friend. By this point, it was a habit.

When he reached the girls, Hank threw himself on his knees in front of Kristy.

"My name is Humble Henry. You've slaughtered my heart. I am prepared to die if you don't give me your number. I can't bear the thought of going nine whole months without hearing your sweet voice."

"Is that from *Twilight*?" I whispered to Murphy. He shook his head.

"That was a very mutilated line from the movie *The Princess Bride*," he said. "Did you live under a rock until you came here?"

I shrugged. "Pretty much."

Kristy smirked, grabbed a marker from her backpack,

and crooked a finger at Hank, beckoning him forward. Hank fell over himself in his effort to get to her. She grabbed his chin with a glove-covered hand and carefully wrote her phone number across his forehead in thick black lines. She finished with a flourish, grinned, and gave Hank a kiss full on the lips. We all whooped as Hank pumped his fist in the air victoriously.

I felt someone sidle up next to me, looked over to see Molly, and did a double take. She was wearing a red hoodie. *My* Red Maple hoodie. The one I thought I'd lost on the night of the fireworks. When she saw me looking, her face went bright red and she turned into a cocker spaniel, still wearing my hoodie.

"Mystery of the missing sweatshirt solved," Murphy whispered in my ear.

"Hopefully she doesn't have fleas," Gary said. I punched him good-naturedly in the arm as I tried and failed to keep the goofy grin off my face. We trudged back to collect our scattered bags, and then walked back down the hill with the girls. Molly had turned back into herself, her face still a self-conscious pink. She looked pretty that way, but I didn't want her to be embarrassed about taking my sweatshirt. In fact, I wished that I had thought to give it to her. To be honest, I hadn't known that she would even want it.

"Red looks good on you," I whispered. She darted her eyes over to me. "You should keep it." For a half second, I worried that she hadn't known it was my hoodie. Maybe she'd thought it was Hank's or Anthony's. But then she smiled. I smiled back. And I hadn't been lying. She did look good in red. She leaned over and pressed her lips against my cheek.

"I'll see you next summer, Emerson," she murmured before turning and joining her parents. I stared after her until I noticed her father frowning at me. Before I could work up the nerve to go introduce myself, he turned into a gigantic Rottweiler with massive teeth, and I thought better of it.

"That doesn't count," Hank said, standing next to me, a grin plastered across his half-invisible face. "You have to get tongue for it to count." His lips had sprouted large blisters, but he apparently didn't care. I debated asking him if kissing Kristy was like kissing a frying pan like he'd thought, but decided against it.

"Yours didn't count either, then," I pointed out.

He shrugged. "There's always next summer." Mr. Stink chose that moment to waddle over to us, an expectant look on his face. Hank and I both crouched down to give the little animal one last scratch behind the ears before Zeke scooped him up and headed toward his waiting parents. Over his shoulder I saw Gary being hugged tightly by his mom and dad, and by the way, they were all smiling, I had a feeling that things might just be changing for him this year too.

My attention was torn away from the happy reunion by my mom walking out of the dining hall. She glanced around nervously, still clutching her Styrofoam cup of coffee like a life raft. She spotted Murphy's family and the TTBI officials and started wobbling toward them on her high heels, and I raced to intercept her.

"Ready, Mom?" I asked, grabbing her arm and turning her forcefully toward the parking lot.

She looked back one more time at Murphy, then nodded and started digging in her purse for her keys as she headed toward our van. I let out a sigh of relief, resettled my backpack on my shoulders, and followed her, remembering with a wry smile my original plan at the beginning of the summer to be a stowaway in one of these cars to avoid camp. As I slid in and buckled my seat belt, I felt a heavy weight of loss settle in the pit of my stomach. It was going to be a long nine months before I saw this place again. I waved out the window to Anthony and Zeke as the cabins of Camp O disappeared behind us.

It wasn't until I got home that I remembered Hank's envelope in my pocket. Inside was a slip of paper. I unfolded it to discover a list. I grinned at Hank's instructions.

Red Maple men, before next summer you MUST and I repeat MUST have completed the following items.

Write me an email. Here is my email address. LifeListsRule127@gmail.com. I will then send around everyone else's email addresses so we can stay in touch. Oh, and if you have a cell phone, send me the phone number too. I don't have one anymore after getting grounded for a prank-calling binge last year.

Be able to hold your breath underwater for at least two minutes. I have a capture-the-flag plan for next summer. Two words. Sneak attack. (Murphy, I know you crossed this one off your list already. Which is actually what gave me my brilliant plan. Thanks!)

Learn to juggle.

Murphy made me add this one. He wouldn't say why, but apparently it's important that we can all run a six-minute mile. So start running, men. Gary—this includes you.

Learn how to dance. Not like lame dancing either. Go to YouTube. The

Monarch girls won't know what hit them.

Age at least fifteen years by the time I see you again. I have my list of where you all left off, so no cheating.

Start lifting weights. No more string-bean arms for us. Chicks dig muscles, so I hear.

Learn how to quack and waddle like a duck. Kidding. Just wanted to see if you were still paying attention.

Start brainstorming an initiation night for when we're in Redwood, and we get to harass the new Red Maple boys. It's going to be hard to beat eighties prom dresses. Although you have to admit, I looked good in mine.

Check out the picture I stuck in your envelope. I pulled some strings and had Chad make enough copies for all of us, you know, just in case you forgot how fabulous we looked.

Sincerely,

Hank

PS After you've read and memorized this letter, either flush it or eat it. Whatever floats your boat.

Sliding the note aside, I found the picture he'd mentioned, and my face immediately spread into a wide grin. There, silhouetted in the headlights of a beat-up blue truck, were the Red Maple men in all our eighties-prom-dress glory. Confident I wouldn't forget anything in Hank's note, I shredded it into tiny pieces before watching it swirl down the drain of my toilet. His letter reminded me of my life list, and I pulled it out, smoothing the paper carefully before tacking it onto my wall next to the picture of us on initiation night. I stepped back to admire the effect and noticed for the first time just how filled to bursting my room was with video games, movies, and other pieces of technology. Before this summer, they had been my way of avoiding the rest of the world, allowing me to zone out and forget about what a nightmare school was, but now they were just things. With a sigh, I rolled up my sleeves. All this stuff was going to have to find a new home in the basement until I could get around to selling it. I wasn't going to have time for it if I was going to check off everything on Hank's list and check fifteen more things off my own life list before next summer. I felt lighter as I moved around my room shoving electronics into boxes, and I was pretty sure it had nothing to do with losing my iron shoes.

AUTHOR'S NOTE

Dear Reader,

My dad probably shouldn't have survived his childhood. This fact became clear to me very early on when he'd tell me stories about his summers spent on the shores of Lake Shafer. But, of course, that's why those stories were so good! We'd beg to hear about the time he and his brothers sneaked out in the middle of the night and accidentally lit the lake on fire, or how he'd tried to lasso a tiny pig he'd nicknamed Little-E and ended up lassoing a behemoth that dragged him from one end of the field to the other.

So when I sat down to write *Float*, I cheated. I borrowed my dad's childhood and gave it to a kid named

Emerson who happened to float. I even borrowed the depressing and stall-less line of pea-green toilets from my dad's own camp experience as a kid. (This horrifying detail stuck with me, even though the story that accompanied the toilet line has thankfully been lost to time.) As the youngest of four, my dad has three pictures of himself as a kid. And that's not an exaggeration—three. So in some ways, when I wrote this book, I was creating word pictures of his childhood for him. I wasn't there the day he flipped over a canoe to discover the nest of snakes underneath, or on the day he took that same canoe across the lake, convinced he could bail it out faster than it would sink, but I could bring those moments to life on a page and capture them forever.

I'm often asked where my ideas come from, and I think people expect me to tell them that authors have this magical well we can dip a bucket into and come up with an interesting story idea. Spoiler alert—we don't. (Although, gosh that would be nice!) What we have are life experiences. Times when we've been happy or hurt or laughed so hard that we couldn't breathe. Or, in my case, my dad's life experiences. And we take those experiences and we pour them into characters, and because we've felt those things, you get to feel them through our characters. This is the magic of writing. So my advice to young writers is simple—go live a great *big* life, and then write about it. And remember, some of the best things happen outside your comfort zone. It's a lesson that takes Emerson almost the entire book to figure out.

I'd love to tell you that I had a childhood as wild and crazy as my dad's, but this crazy thing happens to troublemakers when they grow up and have their own kids—they get turned into overprotective parents. Weird, right? Although, there was that one time my dad took my little brother and I parasailing . . . behind a pickup truck. But that might be a story that needs to wait for another book.

Signing off,
Laura Martin

Don't miss these books by
LAURA MARTIN!